TORN

BONDED DUET: BOOK ONE

BOND

ABIGAIL DAVIES

The Easton Family Saga

THE EASTON FAMILY SAGA CAN BE READ IN ANY ORDER. EACH DUET IS A STANDALONE DUET BUT CAN ALSO BE ENJOYED AS ONE BIG SERIES!

Fallen Duet

Book 1: Free Fall

Book 2: Down Fall

Fated Duet

Book 1: Defy Fate

Book 2: Obey Fate

Bonded Duet

Book 1: Torn Bond

Book 2: Tied Bond

Burned Duet

Book 1: Fast Burn

Book 2: Deep Burn

Torn Bond
Bonded Duet: Book One
Copyright © 2020 Abigail Davies.
All rights reserved.
Published: Abigail Davies 2020
www.abigaildaviesauthor.com

Editing: Jennifer Roberts-Hall
Proofreading: Judy's Proofreading
Photo Credit: © JW Photography
Cover Models: Bobbi Darting & Tyler Smith King
Cover Design: Pink Elephant Designs
Formatting: Pink Elephant Designs

Chapter One

BELLE

"How far away is this place?" Stella moaned for what felt like the thousandth time as she stared out the window. She huffed out a breath, causing the pane of glass to fog up, and I couldn't help but laugh.

Stella didn't have an ounce of patience. She wanted everything right then and there. It was something I'd quickly learned about her on our first day of freshman year at college. We'd been thrown together by random and assigned a shared dorm. The tiny room held two single beds as well as two desks, and we hadn't even made it to our third full week before we were talking about getting an apartment together as soon as the mandatory first year in dorms was over.

Now we were halfway through our junior year and living in an apartment, complete with a bedroom each. We'd become best friends in the two and a half years we'd known each other, but along the way, she'd picked up a long-term boyfriend.

I was all for being the third wheel because there was no way I was going to commit to any of these college guys whose lives revolved around parties and when their next lay would be. But fortunately, Stella's boyfriend also came equipped with a best friend and roommate, which made us the awesome foursome, at least that was what Stella liked to call us. I was sure she had visions of us being two couples who would go on double dates together, but it would never happen because I didn't look at Curtis in that way.

"Not much longer," Curtis told her, his tone fed up with her asking the same question over and over again. He knocked me with his elbow to get my attention, and I smiled up at him. Curtis was the definition of hot with his ink-black hair and the tattoos rolling over the skin of his arms. Too bad for Stella, he just didn't do it for me, which blasted her vision of double dates to pieces.

"C'mere, babe," Justin told Stella, holding his arms out to her, and she went willingly, shuffling across the seat toward him. Justin was the perfect guy for Stella. He put up with her mood swings and doted on her endlessly, but most importantly, he brought her ice cream when she was feeling down. A man who bought his girlfriend ice cream was perfection in my book.

Her sigh could be heard over the sound of the engine of the car, and I was starting to understand why she was making those noises. She wasn't wrong. We'd been in this cab for what felt like forever, and a quick look at the time on the dashboard said we were about to hit the thirty-minute mark. Thank god Curtis said he was paying the fare. After all, it was his idea to go to this club.

The cab took a turn, and I stared out of the window, spotting a line of people all dressed up in their party clothes. It kept going and going, and we just drove on past them until the cab stopped at the front of the line.

"Are you serious?" Stella asked, raising her brows at Curtis as he fished out his wallet. "Do we have to wait in that line?"

Curtis turned to look out of the window and shook his head. "Nah, Bennie is on shift."

"Bennie?" I asked, pushing out of the back of the cab with Stella and Justin on my heels. "As in, the doorman at your bar?" It wasn't technically *his* bar. Curtis worked in the only decent bar in our college town, which meant we drank for free and had access to the best sticky bar stools in town.

"Yep." Curtis flung his arm around my shoulders and moved toward the front of the line. He'd taken to doing that more and more often, but I didn't overthink it. We'd been on one date when we first met, and we both agreed there was nothing there, much to Stella's dismay.

"Stay here," he said and stepped forward to talk to Bennie.

Bennie looked over at the three of us, raised his brows, and then glanced back at Curtis. He crossed his arms over his chest, causing his beefed-up muscles to tense, and the grim look on his face told me we probably weren't going to get inside. He shook his head as his lips moved, and my stomach dropped. If we'd come this far just to get turned away at the door, not only would Stella be pissed, but so would I. And the both of us together would—

"Let's go!" Curtis shouted and waved his arm at us. Bennie moved to the side, and Curtis walked by him, waiting for us to catch up.

I smiled over at Bennie, then widened my eyes at Curtis. "For a second there, I didn't think we'd get in." His laugh echoed around us but dissipated as soon as the main doors opened. The music was so loud my eardrums screamed for relief, but once we were fully inside, they acclimated to the thumping beat and the packed club. "Holy shit," I whispered, but no one could hear me.

"We need to go to the bar!" Curtis shouted, but I could only just make out what he was saying. I grasped on to his arm as he stepped forward, and Stella's hand wrapped around my wrist so she didn't lose us.

Together, the four of us weaved in and out of people dancing as we pushed through the crowded club. Curtis lifted his hand and leaned over the shiny black surface to speak to the girl behind the bar. A couple of seconds later, shot glasses were lined up, and tequila was poured into them.

"Here!" Curtis shouted, handing each of us a shot. We made up our own little circle, and one look at Stella's face told me she thought this place was worth the long cab ride. Her gaze was flinging from one side of the room to the other, taking everything in, but all I could concentrate on were the three people surrounding me.

It wasn't that I'd never been to a club before, but nothing like this one. This was the kind of club you hear people talking about, but never actually go to. The DJ was on a raised podium and was talking over the mic while he played a mix of songs, effort-lessly streaming them together.

"Salut!" Curtis shouted, clinking his shot glass to ours, and we all downed them. The tangy flavor rolled over my tongue and burned its way down the back of my throat. I screwed up my face at the sensation and was thankful when Curtis handed me a slice of lime.

"Let's dance!" Stella said, and I didn't even

manage to get a word out in reply before she was grabbing my arm and pulling me through the crowds and toward the packed dance floor. She squealed as soon as we found our own little spot and dipped her head down to shout, "This is amazing!" in my ear.

"I know!" I held my arms in the air and swayed my hips left to right, losing myself in the rhythm of the music. The pounding of the bass felt like it was matching the beating of my pulse. Arms wrapped around Stella's waist, and she spun, coming face to face with Justin. Not two seconds later, Curtis appeared next to me and flashed me a grin.

"Told you it was cool!" His breath hit the sensitive skin of my neck, and I shivered from the contact. The packed bodies in this club made the temperature soar, and I knew I wouldn't last long with my jacket on.

"I'm hot!" I shouted back to Curtis, fanning my face.

"Take your jacket off and hand it over to coat check," he shouted next to my ear.

I frowned and looked around at the room, trying to see over the sheer amount of people, but with my five-foot-two height, it was nearly impossible. It didn't matter that the four-inch boots I'd paired with my black skinny jeans gave me a few extra inches, I still couldn't see if there was anywhere we could leave our jackets.

"Where is it?" I asked, and Curtis frowned at me and stepped even closer. Almost every part of his body was now touching mine, and my stomach dropped—but not in the good kind of way. "Where is it?" I asked again as I took a step back.

Curtis spun around and pointed toward the doors we'd come in, and I spotted the neon-lit sign next to a small hole in the wall. "I'll be back!" I told him, and he nodded to let me know he'd heard me. Pushing through the crowd on my own wasn't as easy as when you had the force that was Stella paving the way. It took me twice as long just to make it to the edge of the crowd, and I paused to catch my breath.

I turned to see if I could still see them on the dance floor, but they'd disappeared in the crowd too. My breathing started to pick up, and all the danger talks my mom and dad had given me came rushing back into my brain. I knew how to defend myself; they'd made sure of that. I could take down any guy who attacked me with my self-defense moves I'd been taught by my uncles. Well, they weren't really my uncles, but they were family.

The longer I stood on the edge of the crowd, the more I realized I shouldn't have left the group. There was safety in numbers, but what could really happen in a packed club? It wasn't like I was on my own in a dark alley. I was surrounded by people who would be witnesses if something happened to me.

My breathing started to slow the more I talked myself down, and I closed my eyes for a second to center myself completely. Once I felt back to my usual self, I spun around, not looking where I was going, and walked face-first into someone's chest.

"Shit, sorry!"

Hands wrapped around my biceps, righting me. "No worries," a deep voice replied. I could hear better now that I wasn't as close to the music, but even if I couldn't have, I would have known that voice anywhere. It was the voice I'd grown up with, the voice I craved every single day.

I tilted my head back and blinked several times as I looked up at him. He wasn't staring at me, though. He was too busy looking at whoever stood next to him. I took in every inch of his face, the scruff covering his jaw and his high cheekbones. I was getting my fill, because I hadn't seen him since before summer, and that was eight months ago.

Finally, he looked down at me, but the only part of his body that signaled he knew me was the slight widening of his eyes. I opened my mouth to say something, but the subtle shake of his head told me not to.

When I went home at Christmas, my dad had told me he was still undercover. Those uncles who taught me self-defense? They were also my dad's team members. As the head of his DEA office, my dad had put together the best team out there—

which included Ford, the man standing in front of me, silently trying to tell me not to break his cover.

I knew better than that, so I cleared my throat, stepped back, and headed right back to the dance floor. I didn't look over my shoulder to see if he was looking at me, I didn't do anything but pull my jacket off, tie it around my waist and disappear into the crowd.

––––––

FORD

I followed Eduardo Garza up the stairs and to the VIP area, gritting my teeth and using all of my energy not to look down at the dance floor. I had to keep my wits about me. I was here to do a job—I had been for the last eight months of my life, so I couldn't concentrate on the girl who had disappeared into the crowd. But fuck if I couldn't help it. What the hell was she doing here? In the most dangerous club in the state.

The VIP area was half full of people partying, but we walked right past them and to Garza's cordoned-off area. I hadn't been in this section often. Only people in his inner circle got to come up here to meet with him. But I'd been brought into his inner workings seven weeks ago. It had taken over six months to gain any kind of trust, and all that could be broken with a couple of words from the girl downstairs. *Shit.*

My job was to gather as much intel as I could, to collect all the evidence we needed to bring down the great Eduardo Garza, the cartel boss who had been running things for over thirty years. No one had been able to get remotely close to him, but I had. I was working in the dark—no outside contact. I was basically on my own, which meant if things went sideways, no one could help me.

And now all of that was at risk because a wrench in the shape of a girl who should not have stepped foot in this place had been thrown into the middle of my operation.

Garza sat down in his usual seat, and Rory and I took the seats opposite him. This was our regular setup, only we didn't normally come here on a Friday night. It was too busy for Garza's liking, but he'd been called here to handle some business, so we had to follow.

"Shipment gets here in three days," he said, his dark-brown eyes boring into me. "Is everything ready?"

"Yeah." I leaned back in my seat, trying to act unaffected, but it was proving harder than I thought. I could handle anything that was thrown at me. I'd done things in my life no sane person would even entertain, but I did it for survival. In the world I'd grown up in, if you didn't shoot first, you could be dead fuckin' certain your opponent would. It was your life or theirs, and I would always choose mine.

"I want them taken out," Garza growled. "No one crosses me. There are no second chances." The slight twang to his accent couldn't be mistaken for anything but Mexican, and the designer clothes on his back and the guards constantly surrounding him meant people moved out of his way when he was walking.

"You ain't gotta worry 'bout that," Rory told him, pouring himself a whiskey. "We got it handled." Rory had become my partner over the last few months. He wasn't as new to the cartel as I was, but he'd still had to gain Garza's trust. He may have gotten his trust, but he'd never have mine. There was only a handful of people I relied on, and even that had taken years to build up.

"Make sure you do, I don't want no gringos coming into my territory." Garza didn't stop fuming about the new gang who were trespassing into his territory and trying to sell their latest concoction of drugs. But I found my attention moving toward the dance floor, and I spotted her almost right away. She was on her own, her arms in the air, looking like she didn't have a care in the world.

She was in danger, more than she would ever know, simply by being here. How could she be so stupid to come to a place like this? And why the hell was she alone?

"See something you like?" Garza asked, his voice closer now, and I whipped my head around to face him. His gaze was on the dance floor too, and I had no doubt he'd have at least two girls in his office by the end of the night, but Belle would not be one of them.

"Maybe." I shrugged, acting indifferent. I was a master at putting on an act, and I knew he wouldn't doubt me for a second. I'd worked too long and too hard to take this motherfucker down. The first time I'd met him, I was a twenty-one-year-old who was second-in-command to the local drug dealer. Back then, I'd never thought I'd end up here, but now, twenty-one years later, I was in the inner circle, about to take him down once and for all.

Many people had tried to go undercover in his operation and failed, which was why Brody—my boss—hadn't sent me in until now. But the timing had worked, and the intel we had told us something big was going to go down. That something big would be our golden ticket, but in the meantime, I had to prove myself to Garza, which meant doing everything a lackey would do while making sure his territory was safe.

One of Garza's guards stepped closer and dipped down to whisper something in his ear. His brows knitted, his mouth moving into a straight line, and I knew he wasn't happy. Garza stood and wiped off the sleeves of his jacket even though there was nothing on them. "I have people to see. Make sure you both get the job done." He left without another word, and as soon as he was out of sight, Rory grabbed the bottle of whiskey and drank right out of it.

"I dunno about you, bro, but——"

"I gotta go," I said, not interested in listening to Rory and his life lessons. The dude was a liability and loved to drink himself into a stupor, but at least he didn't hesitate when it came to shooting his loaded weapon.

My gaze didn't move off Belle as I walked through the VIP area, but I got distracted when I made it to the top of the stairs. Two guys were starting a fight, and I managed to get around them unscathed, but I'd lost sight of Belle in the process. Fuck.

Even though every fiber of my being wanted to rush down the stairs and search for Belle, I managed to walk at a normal pace. Once I was on the edge of the dance floor, I scanned the room until I saw her hands in the air.

My breath stuttered with relief from finding her as I pushed my way through the crowd. I needed to get her out of here, but I had to do it so no one would be suspicious. She had to get out without garnering any attention from any of Garza's men.

I stared at her hips as she swayed them left to right, and even though I wanted to grab her arm and pull her out of here, I knew I couldn't. So instead, I moved closer to her and placed my hands on her waist gently.

"What the hell are you doing here, Baby Belle?"

Her back straightened and her muscles locked. She knew exactly who it was behind her, but she kept on dancing as she turned around to face me. Her gaze locked with mine, and my muscles loosened.

Belle had been part of my family since the moment she was born. Everyone else in my life had always wanted or needed something from me. I'd had to save my cousin's ass more times than I could count, and she was the reason I had gotten into the drug business in the first place. She'd crossed the top guy in our neighborhood—Hut—and the only way I knew she would get out alive was by making myself indispensable to him. That was how I met Belle's mom, Lola. She was Hut's stepsister, but she'd needed something from me too. She needed help to survive each day, and then along came Brody, who tricked me into becoming an informant.

I didn't regret any of it, though. Because without Brody and Lola, I probably wouldn't even be alive. Brody had given me a lifeline and let me create a life for myself, as well as welcoming me into his man-made family.

And then Belle came along. The sweet innocent girl who didn't want or need anything from me, but

I would give her everything she asked for. The last time I'd seen her had been just before I went undercover for this job, and I could have sworn she still looked like a kid. But right now, she looked like anything but.

Her makeup was minimal, and her wavy light-brown hair flowed down her back, but it was the tight clothes and the way she lost herself in the music that made her look older than she was. But then again, she was twenty. She was an adult, had been for several years, but it was hard for me to look at her as anything but the little girl who would run at me when I came back from being undercover and fling herself at me, knowing I would catch her, always.

She lifted up on her tiptoes, but even that wasn't enough to bring her lips to my ear. "I came with my friends." I gripped her waist tighter and glanced around us, making sure no one was watching.

"Come with me." I didn't wait for her to answer as I pulled her through the crowd, past the bar, and into the hallway the restrooms were in. No one knew there was a secret door at the end of the dimly lit hallway, which led to Garza's office and the security center, as well as the drug packing facility he'd set up. It wasn't his biggest facility, but it was the one that housed the block this club was on.

The music was a low hum now compared to the main area of the bar, which would mean I could talk to her properly. I pushed her against the wall and planted my hand above her head to cage her in. If anyone looked at us, they'd think we were just a couple of club-goers about to make out.

"You need to leave," I ground out, flicking my gaze to the right to make sure the coast was still clear.

"Why?" she asked, and even though this wasn't the time to argue, I could feel my lips quirking on one side. Belle was never afraid to ask what others wouldn't, and she never backed down. I didn't expect her to do that now, which would mean I'd have to at least tell her something. Her dad wouldn't like it, but I didn't have a choice.

"I'm on a job," I told her, moving my gaze back to her and staring into her dark-blue eyes. They held so many emotions, but the one most obvious was relief.

"I missed you," she murmured, and I stepped closer to her. All it would take was one sway of my body, and we'd be touching. "I was worried."

"I'm fine," I told her, swallowing against the lump in my throat. "You don't need to worry about me."

She rolled her eyes and puffed out a breath. "Whatever, you know I do." Her gaze flicked over my shoulder, and her eyes widened. "There's a couple about to have sex opposite us."

I whipped my head around and saw the sight

she'd witnessed. She wasn't wrong, they were about to have sex. I cursed and pulled her farther down the hallway, knowing I shouldn't have moved this close to the secret door, but also knowing if I didn't, she wouldn't leave, and I needed her to leave so she was safe—but also so she wouldn't blow my goddamn cover.

She pressed her back against the wall, and I leaned closer to her, my hand now on her waist. I squeezed it several times to try and silently communicate what I felt I couldn't say. "You need to leave. It's not safe here."

"Why is it not safe?"

"Jesus fuckin' Christ, Belle, can you just listen to me for once in your life?"

She raised a brow and tilted her head to the side. "You know I don't respond well to being told what to do, right?" She paused, and I opened my mouth, but she didn't give me the chance to speak. "I know you know that."

"Fuck." I slapped my hand against the wall, then leaned closer to her and whispered, "It's the cartel," in her ear. I felt her body tense, and a second later, her hand gripped the side of my T-shirt. Good, she was starting to understand why the hell she needed to leave. "You need to go—now."

She turned her head to the side and then slowly brought it back to face me. Her eyes swirled as she whispered, "Someone is watching us." I kept my body in the exact position and slowly moved my gaze to the right. I couldn't see Garza's face, but I recognized his shoes and the gold caps he had on every pair he owned.

"Fuck," I murmured. My nostrils flared, and my stomach dipped. I had to make this look like every other couple in this hallway, which would mean I'd have to cross a line. I'd have to overstep my bounds, something I didn't want to do but had no choice. "I'm gonna have to kiss you."

"What?" Her brows flew high on her forehead, and I could have sworn her cheeks pinked. "No—"

"I don't have a choice," I gritted out. "He's watching us, I need to make sure we look like every other couple in this hallway." Her throat bobbed as she swallowed, and her hand gripped my shirt harder. "I'll kiss you, then walk you out and put you in a cab. You get out of here and never come back. Got it?"

Her chest heaved on a breath, and her whispered, "Got it," was all I needed. I slammed my lips down onto hers and screwed my eyes closed, knowing this was what I had to do to make sure she was safe. But when her body pressed against mine, and her palm grazed over my chest and landed over my beating heart, I let myself relax into it.

This wasn't me overstepping my bounds. This was me trying to make it look believable, so I swiped my tongue over the seam of her lips, and she opened up without any hesitation. My body pressed closer to hers, and one of my hands gripped her waist while the other held on to the side of her neck.

Our tongues met slowly, and a shiver rolled down my back. I'd never felt anything like it before, but it was her moan that made me realize what we were doing. It was meant to be for show, but I'd forgotten that somewhere between our lips touching and our tongues tangling.

I pulled back, breaking the kiss, and shook my head. "Let's get out of here," I said, my voice deeper than usual. She didn't say anything as I grabbed her hand and walked her back out of the hallway. I wasn't sure if Garza was still watching, but part of me didn't care. There was no way he would have seen that and thought it was anything but me picking up a girl at his club.

My hand gripped Belle's harder as we pushed through the doors and out into the darkened night. The doormen greeted me, but I ignored them. I was on a singular mission: to get Belle out of here.

"What about my friends?" she asked.

"Call them. Message them. Tell them you've left." I held my hand in the air on the edge of the sidewalk to hail a cab. "Do whatever you have to, but you're not going back in there." I couldn't look at her as the cab pulled up.

"You're so bossy," she murmured, and my lips

quirked on one side. She was right. I was bossy, but only when it came to her safety.

"Get in," I told her, opening up the back door. I finally glanced at her and clenched my hands when my gaze immediately landed on her swollen lips. Fuck. I couldn't go there. I'd kissed her because it was the only option, but now all I could feel were her lips against mine.

"Don't tell your dad you came here."

Chapter Two

BELLE

I could hear the collection of barks ricocheting out of the building before I even opened the door. If I hadn't already known it was feeding time, I did now. Giving all the animals in the shelter their food was a two-person job, which meant I'd made it for my shift this morning just in time.

I'd had hardly any sleep because my mind was going around and around in circles, trying to piece everything together. All I could think about was every touch, every word, every single thing. I couldn't get the image of Ford out of my head.

He was undercover on a job, so the club we were at wasn't a safe space, and yet, I'd gone there without a second thought. My dad always told me it wasn't the weird, shifty people you had to watch out for, but the ones who looked normal. The ones who fit into a crowd and smiled at you to make you feel welcome. Those were the people you had to be wary of, but the longer I was away from home, the more I started to relax.

But last night...

Last night Ford had made me realize I'd become so lax in everything around me. I wasn't always aware of my surroundings, and I trusted people without fault. I'd grown up being taught to be cautious of everyone, while inside, I wanted to trust everyone until they'd proven otherwise.

"Belle!"

I jumped at the sound of Betty's voice and slapped my hand over my racing heart. I'd been so inside my own head, I didn't even notice the back door to the animal shelter opening and Betty appearing. "Sorry." She blinked and pushed her white-blond hair behind her ears. "I didn't mean to scare you."

I waved my hand in the air. "My fault. I was off somewhere in my head." I laughed and shook my head, trying to force my brain to concentrate on the here and now. Betty stepped back, and I followed her inside of the shelter and then made my way into the break room. It consisted of a sink, a couple of lockers, and a feeding station. We also stored things in here too. As a charity-run shelter, we had to make use of the little space we had, so each room was multifunctional.

I pulled my jacket off and stowed it away with my bag, then spun around. Betty had already gathered all the feeding bowls ready to be filled, so I put on my apron and gloves, and got to work. The dogs were first, their bowls being the biggest, and Betty flitted in and out of the room as she took the full bowls to their owners. The few cats we had were fed second, and then the birds and other random animals.

The rhythm of filling the bowls had my mind wandering. Seeing Ford last night had freaked me out, but what had me even more on edge was what he'd done. My hand started to drift to my lips, but I managed to stop myself halfway there. I couldn't think about it again, not after going over and over it in my mind last night. It was on a constant loop—the way his hand curved around my waist, the way his palm felt against the side of my neck, but it was nothing compared to the softness of his lips. *Damn.* I was thinking about it again.

Growing up with a family like mine wasn't easy. I was surrounded by men—men who protected what was theirs at any cost. My dad was a DEA agent who'd become the head of his department, and my "uncles" were all on his team. Uncle Jord was the guy I went to when I needed help with my computers. Uncle Ryan was the serious one, the one who I could talk about what I wanted to be when I grew up—spoiler alert, I still had no idea what that was. And Uncle Ky was… well, he was Uncle Ky, the womanizer of the group. All four of them had gone through the academy together and had known each other since they were my age.

But Ford…

Ford was different. Ford had had a rough life, and you didn't need to be aware of his entire history to know that. He had an edge to him, an edge which only ever seemed to soften when he talked to me. But the older I got, the more I realized I didn't look at him in the same way I looked at Jord, or Ryan, or Ky. My stomach fluttered when Ford showed up, and my smile would almost break my face when I saw him for the first time in weeks after he'd been away on a job.

It was different with Ford. So different. But I'd never acted on it. I'd known him all my life. He was part of the family, part of my dad's team, my mom's best friend. So I pushed it aside. And I'd managed to not think about it, not since I was a pre-teen with braces. But last night had brought it all bubbling back to the surface. One touch of his lips, and I was helpless to stop the flooding feelings consuming me.

"Feeding is done," Betty announced, once again making me jump. My fingers were wrapped around a scoop inside the dry biscuits tub, and I had no idea how long I'd been standing here. Betty pulled off her plastic disposable feeding apron. "I've got to head out to the library."

I nodded as I cleared my throat. "Sure. Who's taking over from me tonight?"

"I think it's Lou, but you'll have to check the schedule." Betty removed her apron and smiled wide at me. "I'll see you around campus?"

"Yep." I nodded. The shelter had around ten volunteers, seven who were college students. Some did it so they could add it as extra credit, but I did it simply because I liked to be able to cuddle the dogs and stroke the cats while they purred in my arms. It was such a simple reason, but no one ever believed me—not that I cared.

I washed my hands in the sink as I heard Betty exit through the back door, and pushed my shoulders back. It was time to go and show these animals some love, and I knew my first stop would be Lottie. She was gentle and loving; always tilting her head to the side as if she didn't understand what anyone was saying. Stroking her and making her feel safe was a universal language, so we managed just fine.

The smile on my face now was genuine, and the closer I got to the cage Lottie was kept in, the bigger it got.

"Hey there, beautiful lady."

I undid the lock on her door, and she sat in the middle of the cage, her tail wagging in excitement, but otherwise, she was deathly still. I opened the door and stepped inside, then closed it behind me. As soon as my knees hit the floor and I opened my arms, she came running at me. She was a Belgian Malinois; she was a big dog, but she managed to not knock me over.

I laughed, the sound echoing off the concrete walls. "I missed you too," I told her, pushing my fingers into her soft, short fur.

I liked to think I showed all the dogs the same attention as Lottie, but the truth of the matter was, I didn't. From the moment a stranger brought her in as a stray, and I'd looked into her eyes, I knew there was some kind of connection. It sounded insane, especially as my family wasn't big on pets, but there was just something about Lottie that had me wanting to protect her.

I'd taken her home a couple of times toward the beginning of her stay, but Justin—Stella's boyfriend —was allergic to dogs, so he wouldn't come around to see Stella. Which, in turn, meant I had to stop bringing her home.

I pushed my face into the fur of her neck as her paws rested on my shoulders and just breathed her in. It was only a matter of time before she'd have to leave, but I didn't want to think about that. I'd rather she left having been adopted than...

A lump formed in my throat. I couldn't bear to let the thought enter my mind. I'd do anything to make sure Lottie had a home to go to because the alternative wasn't an option.

After having a significant amount of snuggles, and giving her two extra treats I'd bought myself, I stood and wiped the fur off my dark-blue T-shirt. "I better get on with cleaning the cages out, Lottie." She stared up at me, her ears perking up at my words. "I'll come back before my shift is over," I told her, backing away toward the door. Her tail stopped wagging, and she watched me with rapt attention as I moved out of her cage and back into the pathway between the two lines of kennels.

I hated having to leave her little home, but I didn't have a choice. I had a certain amount of jobs I needed to get done before I could go, and one of them was checking the emails. We were also an adoption center, and we got to vet the people who would become their owners. I'd had hundreds of people walk through the kennels and choose their new pets, but each and every time, they'd look at Lottie and then walk on by.

Shaking my head, I opened up the emails and went through them one by one, setting up several visits. I was just replying to the last email when my cell rang on the desk next to me. Mom's face flashed on the screen, and my stomach dipped. Had Ford told Mom and Dad that he saw me last night? What if she was calling to tell me off? I mean, I could have destroyed his undercover operation, but...

My fingers drifted to my lips, and I could have sworn I felt Ford's gentle caress against them. As a kid, I'd imagined so many times what that would feel like, but nothing compared to when it actually happened. Butterflies fluttered in my stomach just thinking about it, and—

Crap. The cell.

"Hey, Mom."

"Belle." Her sigh rang out over the line. "I thought you were never going to answer."

I chuckled, the sound uneasy. "Sorry, I was…" I stared around the room and swallowed. Neither Mom nor Dad knew I volunteered at the shelter, and they certainly didn't know I worked a couple of shifts at the coffee house each week. I had a scholarship, and they were paying for my off-campus apartment, so they assumed that I was all set, but I wanted to have freedom. I wanted to be independent, explore everything I could, and that included working for actual money but also giving back to the community.

"Studying."

Mom made a sound in the back of her throat. "So, you can't talk?"

"I…I can talk a little. Why? What's up?"

"I just needed to ask your opinion."

I leaned back in the office chair and stared up at the ceiling. Mom and I had a close relationship. She was my best friend. The one person I knew I could go to about almost anything. *Almost.* There were some things I'd never tell her, like the job, the volunteering, and the kiss.

God, the kiss.

"Want to know how to punish Asher for leaving his training gear in your car again?" I chuckled, thinking about the last time he'd done that. Mom hadn't realized until she was blasted in the face with the smell a couple of days later as she got into her car.

"No, no." She groaned. "Although, speaking of your brother, Cade keeps trying to teach him lacrosse, but you know your little brother is all about his fighting."

I nodded, even though she couldn't see me. Asher had been training in different martial arts since I could remember.

"No, this is…I can't believe I'm about to ask this."

"What?" I sat up straighter, my attention on high alert. She sounded stressed, and I'd only ever heard Mom stressed a handful of times. "What's going on, Mom?"

"Do you think you kids are too old to go to the lake house with us?"

A breath whooshed out of me at the thought of the lake house. It was a safe haven of sorts, somewhere we could go and just be together without all the distractions. Not to mention the memories we'd made there.

"No. I love the lake house. Why?"

"Well, your dad wants us to go there for spring break—all of us—but Asher said we'd cramp his style and that he's too cool to be hanging around with old people. Am I old, Belle? I don't feel old, but I wonder if I'm becoming like one of those women who still think they're eighteen when they're actually forty-eight."

I chuckled and held a finger in the air. "First of all, you're not even forty until next year. And second, Asher is about to turn seventeen, so you'll always cramp his style."

"So…you're coming, then?"

I tapped my fingers on the desk. "Hell yeah, I am. The lake house is my most-favoritist place on earth."

"You know that's not a real word, right?" Mom huffed out a laugh. "Why are you attending college when you can't even use real words?"

A grin spread over my lips. "I go for the parties. Nothing else."

"The modern education," Mom sighed wistfully. "Talking about education, I have papers to grade."

I snorted. "You have fun with that, Mom. I'll message you later."

"Okay. Speak to you later. Love you, sweetie."

"Love you too, Mom." I ended the call and

stared at Jamie as she waltzed into the room. "Swapped with Lou again?" I asked her.

"Yeah." She smiled, but I could tell she wanted to roll her eyes. Lou rarely turned up for her shifts, and when she did, she half-assed them. "I didn't mind swapping."

I made a noncommittal sound and moved toward the feeding/break room, counting down the seconds until I would get more Lottie cuddles.

————

FORD

Rory stretched his arms above his head and groaned. "I hate fuckin' waiting."

I raised a brow as I continued to stare out of the windshield at the house we'd been watching for the last hour. It felt like any other undercover op, only I wasn't a person of the law sitting here and staring at the house on the block that dealt drugs. No. I was a member of the cartel about to go in there and take all of their product and issue them a final warning to get out of town. Whether they'd listen or not was yet to be seen, but my gut told me they wouldn't.

I remembered what Hut was like when I was his second-in-command. He ran his territory with a tight fist and didn't care who got hurt in the process as long as the job was done. Garza was more thoughtful with his moves. He waited and watched, seeing what his opponent would do, and then he'd strike. I wasn't sure which type of leader was more dangerous, but I knew people thought twice before crossing the Garza Cartel.

"How much longer we gotta wait?" Rory asked, his tone whiny. "We've been here for an hour now. What are we waiting for?"

"We're waiting for the house to be empty, or at least nearly empty."

"Why?" He twirled his gun in his hand and grinned at me. "We can just shoot the fuckers and get what we came here for."

I gritted my teeth and clenched my hands in my lap. It was people like Rory, who didn't think twice before he shot, that I couldn't stand. Once you had that weapon in your hand, you best be sure you were ready to take an answering bullet; otherwise, you shouldn't be pulling it in the first place.

"Because we don't need extra bodies. Extra bodies mean eyes on us from the law." I turned my head to look at him. "We go when I say we go, got it?"

Rory stared at me, his gaze flicking over my entire face, and I knew I'd pulled my mask on. The same mask I used to wear when I was a twenty-year-old who shot first and asked questions later. Those days had long since passed, but it didn't mean the memories weren't fresh in my mind. Rory looked away, his silence his answer.

Some people came filing out of the house, and I recognized one of them as the top dog of their little crew. He swerved to the left, and the woman under his arm righted him. First rule from Garza: never taste your own product. But it looked like this guy hadn't been able to stop himself, just like Hut hadn't.

Once they'd all piled into a car and left the street, I counted to ten and then pulled my gun out, making sure it was loaded. I didn't want to use it, but if my life was in danger, I would. Unlike Rory, who would shoot anyone in that house just because they were there.

"Let's go," I commanded, pushing my door open and slamming it closed. I wasn't quiet. I had no intention to sneak up on the house. I was coming in hot because I wanted them to see me. Garza had left it up to me how I handled this, and I knew I'd do it without a casualty, or at least, I hoped I would.

The front yard was littered with red Solo cups and empty baggies, and I shook my head. They weren't even trying to be inconspicuous about it. They just didn't care. I jogged up to the front door and knocked on it twice. I was going to try and be civilized, but I couldn't promise anything once that door was open. I had some pent-up energy I needed to release. Belle flashed through my mind, and I immediately pushed her away. I couldn't think about her or what had happened, not right now, not when the door was creaking open.

"Can I help you?" a squeaky voice asked. He sounded like his balls hadn't dropped, but he looked about forty with the scars on his face and the way his eyes sunk in. He was high, that much was obvious.

Instead of answering him, I pushed on the door, and he stumbled back. I hadn't even used much effort at all, and the sight of it had Rory laughing his head off. "Jesus! He's out for the count, and you didn't even touch him!"

I couldn't stop the quirk of my lips as I looked down at the guy and then back at Rory. He was out cold, but I had a feeling it was more to do with the drugs than it was me pushing the door into him. "Come on," I told Rory, walking through the main room the front door led us into. The walls were yellow, the furniture covered in stains, but it was the smell emanating from the house that was unmistakable. It was sweet and inviting, a lure these people couldn't deny. All you needed was one taste and you were hooked, and that one taste would never be enough for them.

We needed to make sure there wasn't anyone else in the house, so I took the upstairs while Rory checked down. Each room was empty—no drugs, no people. Had I not known the head guy was here ten minutes ago, I'd have thought it was just another crack house.

"Anything?" I asked Rory as my boots echoed on each stair.

He stood at the bottom of the stairs, his hands on his hips with his gun hanging off two of his fingers. "Nothing."

I frowned and narrowed my eyes on the walls. There were only so many places you could hide drugs and have easy access to them to sell to buyers. I thought back to Hut's house and all the hiding places we used to use. Lola had known about a couple of them, the main one being—

"What's behind that picture?" I pointed at the wall which held a picture, the only one I'd seen in this house. It was out of place, a beacon, which meant there had to be something behind it. Rory rushed over to the wall and stood on the sofa, yanking the painting off, and sure enough, there was the safe that I had no doubt held the drugs.

A groan rang out from the guy on the floor, and I stepped toward him. I may not have been here to take a life, but I had no problem knocking people out, especially those who were high as a kite. I slammed my fist down onto his temple, the one shot doing its job, and then sauntered over to Rory.

"Now, the question is, do we take the entire safe or just the contents?"

Rory's lips spread into a wide grin, and he

nodded like an eager puppy. "I say we take the whole thing." He turned and pushed his hands on the front of it to test how secure it was. "It's not even installed properly."

I shrugged. "Let's take the whole thing then." I hadn't even finished what I was saying before Rory had pulled the safe halfway out of the wall. Did these people not understand that a safe was meant to be a safe for a reason? This was just a glorified lockbox.

"Need a hand there?" I asked, wiping off my hands on my jeans and stowing my gun away.

"Nope." Rory clutched the safe in his arms and jumped down off the sofa. "I got it." His voice was strained, his face turning red, but he was used to lifting things this heavy. I was sure he spent every spare moment in the gym doing weights.

I stepped over the guy and pulled the front door open for Rory, but we couldn't leave without a parting message. I glanced around the room for something to write with and found a paper and notepad sitting on the table. It was full of numbers, probably their sales, but I didn't care about that. They were small fish in a big pond with a shark for company. I wanted the shark, not the bottom feeders.

I wrote a little note: *Courtesy of Eduardo Garza*, and placed it in the hole the safe used to be in. The guy was still knocked out cold, but it wouldn't be long until he woke up and found the safe gone, although I wasn't sure he'd even notice. Either way, my job here was done. Now all I had to do was go back and tell Garza, and then I could head to the apartment I was using.

The break I was waiting for was coming. I could feel it in my bones. Garza had me going to more meets and warehouses, and I knew of at least ten places that had copious amounts of drugs stored— enough to put him away for a long time—but we needed something else. We needed all of his businesses, not just one of his hustles. His clubs and bars laundered money. All I had to do was find the proof, and then we could take him down. Eight months. I'd been undercover for eight months, and I was at the stage where I wanted to go home. It was so easy to lose yourself on an undercover job, and I could feel myself on the edge of the cliff. I needed out and back to my normal life, if only for a little while.

I pulled open the car door and pushed inside, my gaze flicking over to Rory, who had the safe on his lap. "Why didn't you put it in the trunk?" I started up the engine.

"No point."

I supposed he was right. If he put it into the trunk, he'd only have to get it out again when we got to Garza's house, and it was only a twenty-minute drive until we were pulling up at the gates and being let inside by his security detail. That was another thing Garza didn't take for granted. He was constantly surrounded by people who would take a bullet for him without a second thought, which meant when we finally did take him down, we'd have a fight on our hands.

The car shuddered to a stop as I pulled up outside the front door, and I pushed out of the car, knowing Rory would be right behind me. The front doors to the mansion opened up, and one of his guards patted me down. He took my gun attached to my belt and the one on my ankle, but unlucky for him, I still had my knife taped to my side. I never went anywhere without a weapon I could conceal.

"Mr. Garza is waiting for you in his office," the guard said with his slight accent. He'd obviously been in this country long enough to lose most of it, but you could still detect the twang. I nodded and stepped into the main foyer. It was grand and full of marble and decadent lighting, precisely what you'd expect from a cartel boss. It was almost cliché.

Rory's heavy footsteps followed me down the right hallway and toward Garza's office. His door was half-open, but I still knocked on it and waited for him to say, "Come in." I pushed the door fully opened and let Rory go in first. He deposited the safe near the door.

"It's done," I told Garza, my gaze meeting his.

Garza sat behind his desk, a crystal glass in his hand filled halfway with light-brown liquid. "You took the entire safe?" he asked, standing slowly and then walking around his desk. His gaze was focused on the safe, a small quirk of his brows showing his surprise.

"Yeah." I pushed my hands into the front pockets of my dark-blue jeans and stared at him. "Figured it'd be easier." I waited a beat to see what he'd say, but when he was silent, I continued, "Left them a note in the hole in the wall too."

Garza chuckled. "Only you would think to do something like that." He pointed at me as he stepped toward his drinks cart and poured two thimbles of the light-brown liquid. "Here," he said, tilting his head at the glasses. I didn't move an inch as Rory eagerly moved across the room to gather them. He handed me mine, but I didn't take a sip. I wouldn't drink on the job, especially when it was Garza serving the drinks. I'd been at this long enough to know some of his men came into his office and never made it out alive.

"You both did good," Garza praised, walking back behind his desk. "Why don't you go celebrate? Drinks on me at the club." Garza's gaze locked with mine, but I didn't move an inch as he stared. "Maybe you'll see that girl again, huh, Ford?"

My shoulders tensed, my nostrils flared, and I knew he'd seen my reaction. Garza had never seen me with a girl before, which meant there was only one person he was talking about. *Belle.*

Fuck.

"What girl?" Rory asked, oblivious to the tension swirling around the room.

Garza tutted. "Did Ford not tell you about the girl he left the club with Saturday night?" I heaved in a breath, trying my hardest to keep my reactions under control. Why the hell were they so interested in what girls I hooked up with? I never cared who they kissed or fucked—not that I'd fucked Belle. I'd never do that. The only reason I'd kissed her was because I had to, but fuck, even I couldn't deny how it made me feel. I shouldn't have liked it. I shouldn't have wanted to do it again. She was Belle—Baby Belle. The girl I'd known since the moment she was born. It was wrong—on so many levels.

But then, why did it feel so right? Why was it, when my lips pressed against hers, I felt like I was home?

"No," Rory said, knocking his shoulder with mine. "He didn't tell me." I gritted my teeth and tried to push all my thoughts aside. I didn't have the luxury of being able to let my mind wander, not when Garza was staring at me with something unsaid in his eyes. "Who was it?" Rory asked.

"No one," I growled out. Rory wouldn't be able to detect the pitch in my voice, but I had no doubt Garza had. Fuck. I was fuckin' up beyond words. I'd always been able to keep my composure with anything, but when it came to Belle, I couldn't stop it. It was instinct to protect her. It always had been.

I placed my untouched drink on a side table next to one of the dark-brown sofas. "I'm heading out."

"I need a ride," Rory said, downing his drink.

I didn't look away from Garza, who leaned back in his seat with a small smile on his face. Had I just fucked up? Had I just put the whole undercover job at risk?

"I'll call when I need you next," Garza said.

I nodded, then spun around and headed out of the mansion with what felt like the weight of the world on my shoulders.

Chapter Three

BELLE

I wasn't the kind of student who sat at the front of the class, but I didn't want to sit at the back either. The do-gooders were at the front, and the students who didn't care and either messed around or slept the entire hour would be at the back, so I always aimed to get a middle seat. I was far enough from the front not to gain the attention of the lecturer, but not too far back where I'd be distracted.

Sometimes, on rare occasions, I felt the need to sit closer to the front. Like today. I'd hoped it would help me understand the subject more, but I had no idea the train the lecturer had taken with his teachings today. I simply was not on board. I was still on the platform, unsure which carriage to get on.

I made a copious amount of notes, so many that

my wrist was starting to cramp, but still, I didn't understand it. Philosophy wasn't a requirement, but an elective, and I was beginning to wonder if I'd made the wrong choice. Maybe if I knew what I wanted to do when I graduated next year, I'd have chosen better classes, but I was still in that "finding myself" phase—a phase I was afraid I'd never come out of.

"That's it for today," the lecturer finally said, closing his laptop. "I'll be uploading a piece of work onto the online system. Please make sure you read it before class next week."

I blinked several times at his words. Did he upload things for us to read before class often? Maybe I'd missed the online portion of today's class, and that was why I didn't understand it? That had to be the reason I had no idea what he was talking about in each class.

The students filed out, but the lecturer beat them all out of the door—it looked like he wanted to get this class over with too. I raised my brows and stared out the row of windows. His hair seemed to fly above his head in his haste to escape the college students milling around.

Shaking my head, I packed my notepad and pen away, and when I looked up, the room was almost empty, save for a few lingering students talking about a study group they were having. Part of me wondered if I should ask them if I could join.

Maybe then I'd understand the huge words the lecturer was using and not be lost in a sea of nothingness.

I stood, about to open my mouth and ask them, but they filed out of the room, just like everyone else, and my opportunity was gone. Maybe I needed to re-evaluate my class schedule.

Instead of dwelling on an hour of my life lost, I swung my backpack onto my shoulder and moved out of the class. My cell pinged when I was halfway down the hallway, and I pulled it out, reading the message from Stella and then shooting her off a reply.

Stella: We're at The Burger Bun Cafe. Meet us there?

Belle: Thank god. I'm starving. I'll be there in five.

My stomach grumbled on cue as if it'd just been woken from a deep sleep, and I clutched at it. There was nothing I loved more than food—burgers in particular.

The Burger Bun Cafe was across campus, so it would take me more than the five minutes I'd said to get there. As soon as I got out of the building, I started to speed walk. I weaved in and out of the students making their way to their classes, and was halfway across campus when the hairs on the back of my neck stood up. A prickly feeling washed over me, and I slowed down, scanning everyone around me, trying to find the source of the feeling.

People milled about, none of them looking at me, but that didn't mean the feeling dissipated. In fact, the closer I got to *The Burger Bun Cafe*, the more intense it became. I didn't want to spin around and look behind me, because I knew that would be too obvious, but I needed to check. My dad had always taught me to trust my gut, and right then, my gut was screaming at me.

A bench on the edge of the sidewalk gained my attention, and I stopped, placing my bag on it. I searched through my bag, pretending I was looking for something, but really, I was checking out the people behind me. Nothing looked out of place. In fact, it all looked super ordinary—students laughing, rushing to their classes, and a group of people gathered on one of the grassed areas. Maybe I was imagining it? I was still on edge after seeing Ford at the club last weekend, and maybe constant suspicion had seeped into my subconscious.

He was only thirty minutes away from me, so close, and I hadn't known this entire time. Maybe it was seeing him undercover and his warning to get out of the club that had me on edge. I hadn't told Stella the real reason why I'd left without finding them. I'd made up an excuse about being sick and needing to get home, and she'd taken me at my word, but part of me had wished she'd questioned more. At least then I may have had an excuse to tell her about the kiss. *The kiss…*

My heart beat like crazy in my chest, and I could feel my blood thumping in my ears as it rushed around my body. I wasn't sure if it was the memory of Ford holding me and his palms leaving their mark on my body, or the fact that I was still looking around, trying to find the source of my gut feeling.

"Hey."

I jumped out of my skin and spun around, my hand flying to my chest. "Jesus, Curtis!" I slapped my palm against his bicep and tried to slow my racing heart at the sight of his grinning face. "You scared the shit out of me."

He chuckled and pushed his hands into the front pockets of his jeans. "Sorry, Belle. I thought you saw me." I frowned, and he stepped closer. "You looked right at me." He tilted his head to the side and looked down at my bag on the bench. "What are you doing?"

"I…" I stood fully, bringing my bag with me, and scanned around us. There wasn't anything there. It was just my imagination. "I was heading to *The Burger Bar Cafe* to meet Stella and Justin."

"Same," Curtis said, stepping back from me. "Wanna walk over together?"

"Sure." I heaved out a breath, trying to loosen my tense muscles as we started to walk side by side. Ford had gotten into my head, and the next time I saw him, I was going to give him hell. I'd never felt unsafe here, not like I did when I was back home. At home, everyone knew who my dad was, they knew what he did and who he put away. But here, I was invisible. No one knew my dad was the head of a DEA team. They didn't know what he'd been doing for the majority of his life. They didn't know me as Belle Easton, daughter of Special Agent Easton. I was just Belle, the girl who couldn't understand philosophy and had a love of burgers.

"I was worried." Curtis' voice made its way through my thoughts, and I stared up at him. His dark-brown-eyed gaze met mine as he pushed his hand through his ink-black hair, and I realized he was waiting for my answer to a question I had no idea he'd asked.

"I'm sorry." I tried to laugh it off, but I had a feeling it wasn't working. "My brain is still in my philosophy class." I shook my head. "What did you say?"

Curtis pulled open the door to *The Burger Bun Cafe* and smiled down at me. "I was just asking why you left early on Saturday night. I was worried."

"Oh." I placed my hand on my stomach and glanced around the cafe, searching for Stella. I found her almost immediately with her lips attached to Justin's. "I wasn't feeling well and couldn't find you in the crowd, so I left." I didn't give Curtis the chance to answer as I slipped past him and toward the counter. I ordered my usual—double patty burger with extra onions, fries, and a Diet Coke—then took my table number and rushed over to Stella and Justin. "Hey!"

They kept sucking face until I banged the wooden block on the bottom of my table number onto the table.

"Oh, Belle, you're here." Stella's cheeks tinged pink, and I raised a brow. She was never embarrassed about kissing Justin in public. My gaze tracked over them both, and I spotted Justin's arm sliding back toward him. I screwed up my face, not even wanting to think about what they were doing under the table before I got here.

"Yep." I sat down, ignoring the way they were looking at each other. I waited for either of them to say something, but when they stayed silent, I finally said, "So, what were you two kids up to?"

Justin coughed as he took a drink of his soda, and I couldn't help the grin spreading over my face. I had to put up with all their kissing and moaning and groaning in the apartment, so I had no idea why they were so embarrassed. Unless they didn't know I could hear them? Oh man, what if they thought they were being quiet when all this time I could hear almost everything.

"Just…talking," Justin said, his usual deep voice high.

"What's that?" Curtis asked, sliding into the booth next to me.

"I was just asking what they were up to," I said, my voice sickly sweet. I turned to look at Curtis and quirked my lips. I knew he also heard them at *his* apartment because we'd spoken about it several times.

"Cool." Curtis pulled his cell out and looked back up at them. "So? What were you up to?"

"Nothing," Stella answered, right at the same time a tray of food was placed on the table. My food. "We going out this weekend?" Stella asked. "That club last weekend was awesome. Maybe we should go back there?" She was trying to push us into a new subject, and I would have normally called her on it if it wasn't for the fact she'd spoken about the club—the club I had seen Ford in. The club we'd kissed in.

I opened my mouth, about to make an excuse as to why I didn't want to go back—why I couldn't go back—but it was Curtis who said, "Nah. I think we should stay in town this time. Drinks are cheaper when you know the barman." He winked at Stella, and she rolled her eyes. "What do you think, Belle?"

I placed a fry in my mouth and picked up my burger. "Cheap drinks win every time." I took a huge bite of my burger, effectively cutting myself out of the conversation. I didn't care where we went this weekend, as long as it wasn't back to the club Ford had warned me to stay away from. But I couldn't deny the small part of me that wanted to rebel against his orders and turn up there, just to find him.

Would he be angry if I did? Or would he kiss me again? Maybe he'd leave with me, and I could ask him what was really going on. Why was he so close to the college I attended? Had Dad sent him this close because of me? Or was this where the undercover operation was taking place? Who was he undercover for? How much longer would he be undercover?

I was full of questions with no one around to answer them. It wasn't like I could ask my dad what was going on. If he found out I'd gone to the club, he'd probably come here and take me back home himself.

I'd always been inquisitive. I wanted to know what was going on around me, and I always wanted to be part of it, but I was rarely let inside the circle. I was always kept on the outside, not knowing what was really going on, and it was no different now. I was on the outs, not knowing why Ford was so close to my college but knowing I'd find out eventually, even if it took some undercover work of my own.

But first, I needed to figure out my philosophy class.

"Hey, guys?" I glanced around at the table. "Do any of you know what theoretical philosophy is?" The silence was deafening, and when they didn't answer, I groaned. "I didn't think so."

"Ask Google," Justin said, picking up his soda. "It's what I always do."

———

FORD

I pulled up outside the club, the same club Belle had turned up at over a week ago, only it wasn't nighttime now, and there wasn't a line of people queuing up to get into the jam-packed building. The sun was shining, its hot rays beating down on me as soon as I pushed out of my car, but there was something swirling in the air.

I'd always listened to my gut. I didn't fully understand what it was telling me half of the time, but I always paid attention to it. And today, it was telling me something wasn't right. It was the way Garza had called me down to the club and told me to be there within an hour. It was the way his voice was calm but also on edge.

It wasn't unusual for Garza to call me down to his office or to his mansion, but there was something about today that I couldn't quite put my finger on. I'd left an encrypted message for Brody before I left, but I was nearly five hours away from home, which meant I had to go in alone with no backup if something went down.

The way I worked meant I was often on my own when I was undercover, but I knew my limits. I could sense when something was about to go down, and I could call in the cavalry. But today, I didn't have any backup, so I had to keep my cool and get out of here without anything bad happening.

Learning the way Garza worked and conducted business felt like a full-time job, but at least I knew how to approach him and talk to him when he wasn't happy. Maybe the safe we'd brought to his house a couple of days ago didn't contain the drugs. Or maybe he wanted us to take care of the gang infringing on his territory.

Maybe I was overthinking? I'd been doing a lot of that since I'd seen Belle. I tried to deny thinking about her and what happened that night. I pushed it to the back of my mind because I needed to concentrate on finishing this job, but the memory of her lips against mine would sneak in just as I was falling asleep, and then the danger she was in while at the club would have me shooting upright in bed.

But I'd gotten her out of there. I'd managed to protect her, even if I had crossed a line while I did it. I'd done something I never should have. I just hoped she understood why.

"Ford," the guard at the door greeted. "He's waiting for you in his office."

I nodded, not bothering to reply as he opened the main doors for me. The club was so different during the day. Its darkness was replaced by light, and the music which usually drowned out everyone's voices was absent. The only thing you could hear were the machines whirring from the back of the building as they counted the laundered money.

I took a left and headed down the hallway toward the concealed door where another guard was waiting. This one was just as big as the one outside, but he didn't greet me. Instead, he pushed open the door and then resumed his position guarding it.

The machines were louder inside the back part of the club. Rows and rows of women stood with bags of cash as they put them into counting machines. But it was the back few rows bagging up cocaine and meth that caught my attention. That was new in the club, or had I missed it the last time I was here?

I didn't want to linger too long, so I walked past them all and toward Garza's office. His door was closed, so I rapped my knuckles on the heavy wooden surface three times and waited.

"Come in!" his rough voice said, and with a deep breath, I pushed open the door and stepped inside his office. Where his home office was luxurious and inviting, this one was cold and all about the business. It reflected him perfectly.

There wasn't an inch of sunlight in the room as all four walls were reinforced concrete, doubling as a safe room. A lone desk was in the middle, and Garza sat behind it, his gaze connected with mine.

"You called?" I asked. Usually, I would have waited for him to say something, and I knew by speaking those two words, I was showing how on edge I was. I cracked my neck to relieve some tension and tried to center myself.

"Yeah." He looked down and pulled a few papers off a stack of folders. "I need you to find someone." He rummaged through the papers and finally held one of them up. I stepped forward and took the photo from him. "I need you to find him and bring him to me."

It was on the tip of my tongue to ask why, but I knew better than that. I knew I had no right to know why he wanted someone, but it didn't mean I wouldn't try to find out through other means. "Okay," I said, pulling my cell out and taking a picture of the photo. I handed it back to him and waited again.

"I also need to—" A knock on the door cut him off and he growled out, "What?"

"Mr. Garza?" a soft, feminine voice asked. "We have trouble with drug, you help?"

"Jesus fuckin' Christ." Garza stood, causing his

57

chair to fly back and bang into one of the metal cabinets against his back wall. "Stay here, Ford. I'll be back."

I nodded and stepped to the side to let him past me, and as soon as he opened the door, he spoke in Spanish to the woman, his words flinging at her a mile a minute. The door banged shut behind him, the wood against metal scraping throughout the room. And then I was alone. Alone in his office. Alone in the only place in this club that didn't have cameras. He was too afraid of being caught on camera and it being used against him, but he hadn't factored me into the equation.

My instincts kicked in, and I lunged forward to look at the papers he'd pulled out. Maybe there would be something on there about the guy I had to basically kidnap to bring to him. I shuffled through the lone papers on his desk, and when I didn't find anything, I paused, making sure I could still hear Garza. His voice was distant, but unmistakable as he got angrier and angrier about the machine being broken.

I pulled off a couple of folders and started to rifle through them, and saw nothing about the man, and just a whole lot of lists of numbers. My cell was still in my hand, so I quickly snapped a few pictures and put them back. As I was stacking them, the word east on the side tab of a file toward the middle caught my attention.

My stomach swirled, something telling me to open up the manila folder and see what was inside it. The voices from outside the office were no longer raised, which meant he could walk back in any second. But the draw to open it up was too much, so I did just that. I didn't even take in the information on the page as I snapped as many pictures as I could of the first five sheets and then closed it back up. The handle of the door started to turn as I stacked the folders back on top of it, and I made it back to the other side of the desk just in time for Garza to open up his office door and re-enter.

He mumbled something under his breath and looked up at me, his eyes widening. "Fuck. I forgot you were still in here." He paused and glanced around the room, almost as if he was trying to remember what he was saying before he left. "Yes," he said to himself. "I need you to find this man, bring him to me, and make sure no one knows where he's going. I shouldn't have to tell you to be discreet, Ford. That's why I'm sending a gringo, you understand?"

"I understand," I ground out. "How soon do you want him?"

"Three days." He moved around his office and sat back in his chair. "I don't want to see you until then. Alejandro has a folder of information ready for you." He pulled his cell out and spun his chair around, effectively dismissing me.

I gripped my cell in my hand, turned, and exited the office, needing to get out of there as soon as I could. All the women were working twice as hard as they had been when I first entered, and I had no doubt it was because Garza had been out here shouting. The guard from outside the door was now placed inside, and he handed me a folder and then pulled the door open for me without speaking.

My feet wanted to carry me faster out of the club, but I managed to keep a normal pace. I didn't want to throw off any kind of energy to make anyone suspicious, so I walked outside, the sunlight almost blinding me with how bright it was, and then pushed into my car. My car was a fortress, made for any kind of impact and bulletproof. Whenever I was undercover, I made sure to use my own car because it was the only safe and secure place I had. The one thing I could trust when I was neck-deep in a dangerous world.

I started the engine and pulled away from the curb, staring in my rearview mirror at the guards outside the club. One of them was looking my way, and one was staring ahead. I took a right, turning at the end of the road and drove for about twenty minutes, making sure no one was following me.

A small diner gained my attention, so I pulled into its lot toward the back. I wouldn't go in, but it'd be a good cover while I checked out the folder I'd been given. The engine idled as I opened the folder and looked through it. The man was a manager for a bank in the city, a forty-something guy who had gotten himself into some serious debt, and I was guessing Garza had bailed him out and loaned him the money in exchange for his services.

I took a photo on my cell, intent on sending it over to Jord, the computer guy on our team. Switching to the photo album app, I clicked on the first one I'd taken and zoomed in to read it. I hadn't even gotten to the second line written on the first piece of paper when I knew this was why I'd had that gut feeling.

My heart beat rapidly in my chest, and I could hear the whooshing in my ears from my racing pulse. This couldn't be right. Surely he wouldn't have…fuck. He had. He'd investigated Belle, and it was all my fault. I'd played my hand the moment he mentioned her in front of Rory, and now he'd gotten a file on her, and I'd only managed to look at the first few pages.

I scrolled through the other photos I'd taken, but all they had was her information, where she went to college, the courses she was taking, and the jobs she was working. I don't know why it was the latter that had my brows rising, but I couldn't picture her working, not when her dad was paying for everything, and—

Fuck. If they knew who she was and who her

dad was, did that mean he knew who I was too? Shit. Fuck. Shit.

I didn't hesitate as I dialed the one number you only called when shit hit the fan and there was no way out but through.

"Please enter your code," a woman's computerized voice said.

I clicked in the eight-digit code, which would connect me to the right person, and a couple of seconds later, another voice said, "Easton."

"Brody?" I croaked out.

"Ford?" His tone pitched higher, and I could imagine him standing up at his desk. "What's—"

"We have a problem." I closed my eyes and clenched my hand on my lap. "A really big fuckin' problem."

Chapter Four

FORD

Waiting had never been my strong suit, but the five hours it took for the team to get here nearly broke me. I was on edge, more so than ever, but I wasn't sure if it was because the operation had just gone to shit, or because I was about to tell Brody what had happened at the club...with his daughter.

I winced as I thought about his reaction, but it wasn't like I could lie to him—fuck, I had to lie to him, at least a little. I didn't have a choice, not if I wanted to make it out of here alive.

The guys had found a safe house an hour away from Garza's club, and now I was pacing the length of the living room complete with seventies furniture, waiting for them to pull up outside. I should have been looking for the banker Garza wanted, and scoping him out. Instead, I was about to blow up eight months of undercover work. I just hoped we had enough intel to take him down, because if we didn't, those eight months had been for nothing.

An engine roared closer to the house. I stood next to the window and peeked out of the dirty pane of glass. Sure enough, another car followed, and then all of the guys piled out of the vehicles. My stomach churned with nerves, and I tried to calm myself. I kept my gaze fixated to them as they walked closer to the house, and seconds later, the door was opening, and I was seeing their faces for the first time in months.

Brody looked a little older, his hair graying, but Jord still looked like the thirty-something guy I'd met twenty years ago. No one said anything as they all piled in the house, and Jord started to set up a station for his laptop. Kyle and Ryan scoped out the house, something I'd done when I first got here, and then after what felt like hours but was actually minutes, Brody said, "Fill us in."

I stepped away from the window and toward the back wall of the living room, my breaths sawing in and out of my body. "I…" My nostrils flared, and my hands clenched. I was never like this. I was always straight to the point, but this was different. "I don't even know where to start."

"Maybe with why it's all gone to shit?" Brody said, his face carefully expressionless.

"I was meeting with Garza last weekend at his club." I pushed my hands into the front pockets of my jeans and leaned against the wall, trying to act calm when I was anything but that. "When I got to the club, someone...ran into me." I swallowed, looking at each of the guys in turn. Brody was watching me carefully, while Kyle and Ryan flicked their attention between me and the files full of information on Garza that I'd brought with me as Jord logged in to his laptop.

"So, your cover was blown last weekend?" Brody asked, a muscle in his jaw ticking. I knew what he was thinking—that I should have contacted him then, but I thought I had a handle on it. I'd thought... Fuck. I shouldn't have thought, not when it came to someone else's safety. Dammit.

"No. Not exactly." I closed my eyes briefly, and when I opened them back up, I blurted out, "It was Belle."

Brody blinked. "Belle?" He paused, almost as if he was playing the conversation back out in his head. "As in my Belle?"

My stomach dropped, and I managed to get out, "Yeah," then pushed up off the wall and pulled my hands out of my pockets.

It was so quiet you could have heard a pin drop, and then Brody exploded, "What the fuck was she doing there?" He threw his hands up in the air and started to pace back and forth. "I fuckin' knew she shouldn't have gone to college here. I should have forbidden her."

Jord laughed. "You know there ain't no tellin' that girl what to do."

Jord was right. "I got her out of there, and I told her not to come back, but"—all of their attention was on me now—"Garza must have noticed and mentioned her to me a couple days later after I'd done a job for him." I took a couple of steps across the room and pulled out the papers of the photos I'd printed off. "He called me into his club today to give me another job, and while he was out of his office, I had a look around." I handed the papers to Brody. "I found these."

Brody frowned down at them, his mouth pinched as he read what was on them, and then he slowly lifted his head. If looks could kill, I'd have been dead right now. "He's done a background check on her." Brody handed the papers to Jord, who read them with Kyle and Ryan looking over his shoulders. "Which means he knows who I am. And if he knows who I am—"

"Then he knows who *I* am," I finished for him. It wasn't confirmed that my cover was blown, but you only had to put a couple of pieces together to get to that conclusion.

"We need to make sure we have enough to bring him down," Brody demanded. "No one leaves this room until we have a solid case and evidence. The faster we move, the better."

————

FORD

It had been thirty-seven hours since Brody and the team had come through the door of the safe house, and now we were walking back out of it. Only this time, we were geared up and ready for a takedown.

More members of the DEA had come down to assist us. We weren't stupid. Garza had the kind of manpower the president had, only these guys would kill you without a second thought because there were no consequences.

None of us talked as we piled into a reinforced black van. We checked our coms, made sure we could hear each other, and went over the plan one last time. We knew Garza would be at his house and in bed. It was the only time we knew he wouldn't see us coming.

It only took us just over an hour to make it to his mansion, and the driver pulled up a couple of hundred feet away so Jord could jump out. I couldn't make him out as he stealthily moved toward the gates, and only seconds later, they were opening up slowly. The driver sped through them, pulling up outside the main doors, and we all shot out of the sliding side doors.

Jord caught up to us, and I could hear shouts and warnings from Garza's men, but I didn't take in what they were saying. My focus was one hundred percent on getting into his mansion and arresting him. I hadn't told Brody everything that had happened at the club. I hadn't mentioned that I'd kissed Belle, so he didn't realize how close Garza thought we were. Brody's main concern was that Garza knew who I was and that Belle shouldn't have been there, but I knew there was a reason behind Garza looking her up. You didn't just do a background check for no reason.

And it was all my fault.

I'd shown my hand when he'd mentioned her in front of Rory. I'd played my cards, and now he was ripping them out of my palms and laying them all on the table for everyone to see.

The front man held the battering ram to breach the house, and with one swing, the doors flung open. Several guards were in the main foyer, but they were taken down in a matter of seconds, and then I was leading the way with Brody and Kyle behind me. I'd gone over this route in my head hundreds of times in the last day, so I didn't hesitate as I ran up the stairs and right toward Garza's bedroom.

There was no way he hadn't heard the shouts

and gunshots, so I knew he wouldn't be so surprised, but I also knew his safe room was on the other side of the house, and he would most likely be making his way there through a secret tunnel. Unlucky for him, he had to come out of that tunnel to open up the door, and that was exactly where we were standing, waiting for him.

Not thirty seconds later, he appeared with two women at his back, all of them looking frantic, and as soon as Garza spotted us, he froze. We were all geared up head to toe, so there was no way he could make out who I was, and I had no intention of showing him my face, not until he was safely in the back of the van.

Brody stepped forward with Kyle while I kept my rifle trained on him. One wrong move, and I wouldn't hesitate to shoot him, and I think he realized that because his throat bobbed as he swallowed, and then he raised his hands in surrender.

Cuffs were slapped on his wrists, and Kyle led him down the hallway as the two women followed while Brody and I brought up the rear. It was almost too easy to get him out of the house, and although I wanted to tell Brody that, I kept my mouth shut. He still wasn't happy about Belle turning up at the club, and I could understand why, but he was acting like she was a fifteen-year-old girl trying to fight for her freedom when, in reality, she was twenty. She'd be twenty-one this summer.

All the lights were on outside, making it feel like the middle of the day instead of two in the morning. Officers were still apprehending the guards on the grassed areas, but we bypassed them and piled back into the van, this time with Garza in tow. Once we were safely out of the grounds of his mansion and on the way to a black site where he could be detained until we could move him again, I pulled my mask down off my face, revealing myself to him. There was no point in pretending it wasn't me. He already knew if the way his gaze stayed on me had anything to do with it.

Garza laughed, the sound echoing throughout the inside of the van. "I knew it." He shook his head and waved his finger in my direction. "I knew it."

I smirked. I could play that game too. I was a master at it, and even though I'd doubted myself several times over the last day and a half, I didn't doubt I could rile him up. "Yeah?" I leaned forward. "How long did it take you to figure it out, huh?" I waited for his answer, but all I got in return was his nostrils flaring. He was a man who could shut down his emotions at a moment's notice, same as me. But just as I had shown my hand with a couple of movements of my body in his office, he also had tells.

"The way I see it"—I leaned back—"I was undercover for so long, I know almost every single place you hide your drugs." I smirked and tilted my head to the side. "Not to mention the money you like to filter into all of your forty-five businesses." His eyes flared at that, and I knew then that I had gained access to the right amount of businesses.

I expected him to come back at me, to say something now that he knew all of his businesses were being taken down and his warehouses raided, but he stayed silent, something which was making me want to talk more and more. But I realized that was his tactic. He was trying to get all the information out of me as possible, and I wasn't willing to give anything more away. I'd already said too much.

The warehouse was empty when we arrived, but we weren't staying here. A secret passage ran from the back of the warehouse underground and to a black site. We had countless of them scattered all over the country, and only those who needed to know about them knew. They were the safest place you could bring someone like Garza, because not only did people not know about them, but they were almost impossible to get into unless someone from the inside let you in.

The steel-forced walls of the underground site would keep him safe, but also meant we could be sure in the knowledge he couldn't escape until we charged him. Because we would charge him. There wasn't a doubt in my mind he'd be put away for a long time.

Teams had been trying to take Garza down for

over thirty years, and Brody had been itching to do it for at least twenty, but no one could ever get in until I was assigned the case. Garza had remembered me from my time with Hut, and with some well-placed documents and a fake prison record, I'd gotten in with barely any trouble.

Brody and I each held one of Garza's arms as we led him through the central headquarters and toward the back hallway of cells. Only five rooms were available, but each of them was a steel square complete with a toilet and one window which looked out into the hallway at a whole lot of emptiness.

Brody unlocked the door, and I walked Garza in, intent on not saying another word to him, but then he said, "I never would have found out if it wasn't for your little puta."

Anger burst through me like lava exploding out of the top of a volcano. I couldn't stop it, no matter how much I tried, and I slammed him into the steel wall, the bang reverberating around us. "The fuck did you just say?"

"Ford," Brody ground out, but I didn't care about his warning.

"Where is she now?" Garza asked, his voice sounding bored. "You think she's sleeping in her sweet little apartment that she shares with her best friend? Or maybe she's getting ready for a shift at the coffee shop?" His lips lifted into a smirk, and I wanted nothing more than to wipe it off his face. "Or do you think she's in someone's bed fuckin' them nice and slow?"

I wound my fist back, ready to smash it into his face, but Brody stepped inside and stopped me. "Don't," Brody's deep, commanding voice said. "That's what he wants."

"He's fuckin' pushin' it, Brody," I growled out, not moving my gaze off Garza's eyes.

"Ahhh." Garza flicked his gaze to Brody. "And you must be the girl's father. Agent Easton. I seem to remember you from many years ago. The Emerson Hutton case if my mind remembers correctly."

"Did you just threaten me?" Brody asked, his voice deadly calm, but I knew he was raging inside.

"Me? Make a threat?" Garza raised his brows. "I'd never do such a thing."

My blood was boiling to the point I couldn't control it, and I knew the only thing I could do was walk away from him. One wrong move while he was under arrest and he'd get off on a technicality. We had to play this safe. I let him go, not caring that he nearly didn't land on his feet, and backed away a step. "I hope you enjoy looking at four walls because that's all you're going to see for a very long fuckin' time."

I spun around, feeling Brody behind me, and together we locked up the cell and then walked away. Neither of us said anything as we moved through the den and up to one of the conference rooms on the upper level. I could see Jord standing in the doorway, his attention on us, and when we finally made it into the room and closed the door behind us, Brody gritted out, "He was threatening her."

I nodded. "He was."

"Who did he threaten?" Jord asked.

Brody glanced at me, something unsaid shining in his eyes, and I knew what would have to happen. I knew I wouldn't be coming home, not yet anyway. If there was one thing more important than taking a criminal off the streets, it was keeping my family safe.

"Belle," I croaked out. "He threatened Belle."

BELLE

Perks of working in a coffee shop were being able to drink as much stuff as I wanted, but that was a real problem when I didn't actually like it. I loved the smell of the fresh beans, but the taste...that was something to be desired, unless it had the lowest amount of coffee and was full of caramel syrup.

My shifts never changed, thanks to my class schedule, and today was my last shift of the week, which also meant it was Friday. I worked three hours on Mondays and Wednesdays between classes, and then six hours after my only class on a Friday.

I had less than an hour left on today's shift, and even though Stella had messaged me saying she wanted to go out tonight, I was in the mood to order takeout and veg in front of the TV. A new series on Netflix had been added three days ago, and I was dying to watch it.

The store was getting busier the closer to the end of day classes got, and the soundtrack was a mix of groans from tired students and keys tapping from those who were trying to whizz through the assignments they'd put off until the last minute. It was either try and get it done today or attempt it when you had a monster hangover on Sunday.

"Hey, Belle, I'm gonna top up the napkins," Trisha said as her gaze locked on a table near the cart we kept the napkins and sugar packets in. Trisha had worked here as long as I had, but I was sure she only kept the job to pick up guys.

"Sure," I replied, but she didn't hear me because she was already halfway there and making a beeline for the table of guys. I wouldn't have thought you could pick up guys at a coffee shop, but even the hot college boys needed somewhere to buy their caffeine on campus.

I wiped down the counter and started to sort the

display case out. We'd sold out of most of our muffins and pastries, and we didn't have another delivery due until early tomorrow morning.

The bell above the door dinged, but I didn't look up and carried on rearranging the display. Footsteps neared, and I could feel someone standing at the counter, but I only had one section left to—

"What's a guy gotta do to get some service around here?"

My eyes widened, and my breath caught in my throat. I whipped my head up and smacked it off the underside of the display unit. "Fuck."

His chuckle sounded out. "Language, Belle."

I closed my eyes and counted to three as I tried to get my thoughts in order. What the hell was he doing here? The last time I'd seen him was moments after he'd kissed me. A kiss that I hadn't been able to stop thinking about. A kiss which continued to drive me insane.

Rubbing the sore spot on the top of my head, I moved back and out of the display case, finally looking up at him. "What are you doing here?" I asked, not knowing what else to say. I was stumped, words escaping me, which was unusual because I was always saying or doing something, but I had no idea how I was meant to act with him standing in front of me.

"I'll have a coffee, black." I raised my brow and planted my hand on my hip. There was no way he'd come all the way here just for a coffee, and he was avoiding my question. It may have worked when I was a little kid, but I was a grown-ass woman now. I wanted nothing more than to ask him again and demand an answer but now wasn't the time and place. Instead of grilling him, I spun around and made him a coffee.

I placed the to-go cup on the counter and stared up at him as he asked, "What time do you finish?"

My nostrils flared, and my stomach sank. Why did he want to know what time I got off work? And more than that, how did he even know I'd be here? "I get off in"—I flicked my gaze up to the giant clock on the wall—"ten minutes."

"Good." He nodded and wrapped his long fingers around the cup at the same time he threw ten dollars on the counter. "I'll wait for you."

I frowned, not sure what was going on, but I'd find out either way. I just needed to finish my shift first. He turned around, found the last empty table, and sat down, his gaze swinging around the store as he took everything in. I'd missed being around people who were so observant.

"Who's the hottie?" Trisha asked as she sauntered back behind the counter.

I wiped down the machine and shrugged. "No one important." It was a lie, but I couldn't tell her the truth. I couldn't tell her the man I'd had a crush on for what felt like my entire life was sitting only a few feet away from me. The same man who had kissed the life out of me and stamped the feel of his lips into my brain never able to be erased. Was that why he was here? Because of the kiss? Would he really stray from his undercover operation because of that?

As soon as the minute hand on the clock hit 12, I threw the cloth down and pulled my apron off. I walked into the back to grab my jacket and bag, then headed to the front of the store with a wave at Trisha.

"I'm finished," I told him, trying not to look directly into his eyes. I was scared of what I'd see, or more importantly, what I wouldn't see. I moved toward the door, weaving in and out of the students milling around.

The bell rang overhead as I exited, and I could feel Ford directly behind me. I'd always been able to sense when he was close, but it was different now, more heightened. As soon as we were both outside, I spun around and stared up at him. His hazel eyes were mesmerizing, as always, but there was a darkness behind them that hadn't been there the last time I'd seen him.

"What's going on, Ford?"

"We need to go to my car." He tilted his head to signal where he'd parked, but I didn't look away from him.

"Not until you tell me why you're here." I

planted both hands on my hips and didn't move my eye contact. I wasn't the same little kid who needed protecting. I wasn't the one person in the family who couldn't be told what was really going on. I'd spent too much time being sheltered from the world around me, and I refused to let that happen anymore.

"Nothing is—"

"Don't lie to me," I fumed as I pointed at him. I knew I looked ridiculous, reprimanding a man who was at least a foot taller than my five-foot-two height, but I didn't care. This was my home for nine months of the year, and him turning up out of the blue didn't mean anything good. Not after what had happened at the club. He'd warned me not to go back, told me it was dangerous, and now he was here, standing a couple of feet in front of me.

"In. The. Car."

"No." I shook my head, refusing to move.

Ford glanced around us, and I frowned up at him. Why was he so on edge? Why was he moving closer to me as if to shield me from something?

"We need to get into my car, Belle. I can tell you what's going on then," he ground out, and it was the first time Ford had spoken to me like that. He was demanding, and there was no room for argument, so I huffed out a breath and stomped toward his car.

I knew full well that I was acting like a child, but I had no doubt he'd make up a story to try and protect me. It was what he, my dad, and my uncles always did. They thought I was a delicate little flower, and one puff of wind would knock me over, but what they failed to comprehend was I was half my dad and half my mom, and they were the two strongest people I knew.

Ford pulled open the door for me, and I slid inside. The smell of leather and vanilla filled my nostrils, and my muscles relaxed. It was the smell of home. A scent I only ever put together with Ford and his car.

He opened up the driver's door and pushed inside, but kept his gaze trained out of the windshield. "Your dad said he was calling you." He pushed his hand through his short blond hair. Hair that was turning gray at the temples but somehow made him look even better than he ever had. Why was that? Why was it the older a man got, the sexier they were?

I pulled my cell out of my bag and saw several missed calls from my dad and my mom, plus a few messages. Instead of reading any of them, I clicked the return call button and lifted my cell to my ear, all the while keeping my gaze trained on Ford.

The dial tone only rang once before my dad's deep voice answered, "Belle."

"Dad?" Ford's hands grasped the steering wheel harder, and I knew he could hear Dad's voice too. "Why is Ford here?"

"I think the question should be, why the hell are you going to a club owned by the goddamn cartel?"

My breath stalled in my chest, and my hand reached out to Ford, grasping his arm. Shit. Fuck. "I—"

"Ford told me you were there." There was a pause, and Ford turned his head to face me. His hazel eyes swirled with something I couldn't place, and then he glanced down at my hand and back at my face. "He told me he got you out of there." I was waiting for him to mention what Ford had done before he put me in a cab and demanded I went home, but he didn't. The silence rang louder than anything, and I wondered if Ford hadn't told him everything that happened. And why had he told him in the first place? What the hell was going on around me?

"I...I didn't know what the place was, Dad."

Dad sighed, and Ford's arm dropped off the steering wheel and moved to the center console, but I still didn't let go. Ford didn't stop staring at me, and I ate it up because I didn't want him to look anywhere else. I wanted to have his attention only on me.

"There's been a development in the case, and a threat has been made." There was some shuffling over the line, and then he said, "Ford is there to protect you."

"A threat?" Ford tensed under my palm.

"Against me?" My voice was small, and I knew I sounded exactly how they thought I was—delicate —but I was in shock. Why would a threat be made against me? What had I done to anyone?

"Yes." Dad cleared his throat. "Ford will be staying at your apartment until further notice. He'll be following you and—"

"So, he's basically my bodyguard?" I inter-rupted. "You sent Ford to be my bodyguard?" I was getting angrier the more I spoke. Could he not trust that I could protect myself? He'd taught me how to defend myself. He'd taught me how to shoot a gun, and more importantly, actually hit my target. I'd been prepared my entire life, and now he was sending someone else to watch over me because of a measly threat?

"Yes, Belle. You have no idea the kind of people they are. You need someone looking out for you."

I gritted my teeth. "But—"

"I've gotta go, Belle. Tell Ford I'll be in touch." The line went dead, and I pulled my cell from my ear and stared down at it. Dad had done what he always did—given me just enough information to tell himself he'd tried but still kept the majority back.

"I…I don't understand," I whispered, my anger quickly turning into frustration.

The silence in the car was stifling. Was Ford about to do the same thing Dad had? Would he fill me with elaborate lies, or would he not tell me anything? I blinked at Ford, hopeful that he'd trust me to know what was happening.

"I was undercover, trying to take down the cartel. The guy who was standing at the door when I…" He glanced away, and I knew what he meant —when we kissed. He looked back at me and cleared his throat. "That was Garza. The boss." I gripped his arm harder, but I wasn't sure whether it was because I'd been so close to a cartel boss, or because Ford was actually telling me information. "He saw you, Belle."

My brows knitted as I replayed his words in my head. "He saw me?"

Ford nodded, and his hand covered mine on his arm. My breath caught in my throat as his long fingers wrapped around my small hand, and I was fascinated with how his tan skin looked against my pale skin.

"He asked me about you and I…I fucked up, Belle. I tensed, and he saw it, and then…fuck." He let his head drop back on the headrest of his chair and gripped my hand harder. "He had a file on you. So we took him down, but he threatened you. He knew everything about your life, the coffee shop, your apartment, your class schedule."

"But you arrested him, right?"

Ford rolled his head to face me. "Yeah, but this isn't the kind of guy you let your guard down with,

Belle. And I'm not taking any chances, and neither is your dad." I bit down on my bottom lip, and it was on the tip of my tongue to ask him if he'd told my dad about the kiss, but I knew I couldn't ask that, not yet anyway. "You okay, Baby Belle?" Ford asked, and the way he used the nickname he'd given me when I was little had butterflies swarming in my stomach.

"I...I think so," I said, my voice small. I looked around, seeing people walking around outside, but I was on edge. Maybe I hadn't imaged that prickly feeling the other day on campus. Maybe someone had been watching me. I knew I should have told Ford about it, but he looked tired if the bags under his eyes were anything to go by. "I'll be fine," I told him, removing my hand from under his. "Let's head to my apartment." I paused. "You'll be okay sleeping on the sofa, right?"

He laughed as he sat upright and switched the engine on. "I've slept in worse places, Baby Belle."

"I have no doubt about that," I responded, and for the first time since he'd turned up, I smiled at him, a genuine smile.

Chapter Five

FORD

I didn't need to ask Belle directions to her apartment.

I'd taken the intelligence Garza had on her—a whole file full of all her movements from the last week—and I also had a folder provided by Brody. You'd think after knowing Belle for all her life, I wouldn't have needed it, but apparently, I did.

My gaze slid to Belle, and I stared down at her clutched hands in her lap. She was nervous, and if her shuffling feet were anything to go by, she felt the need to run away. I didn't blame her. Brody hadn't wanted me to be honest with her. In fact, he'd specifically told me to not tell her anything, but it didn't feel right leaving her in the dark. It wasn't like I was going to go into every little detail and tell her exactly what Garza did to the people who betrayed him, but that didn't mean I wasn't going to make her aware of what was going on.

She was twenty, an adult. I mean, Jesus, Lola had given birth to Belle when she was her age. Even though we all saw her as the little girl we needed to protect, I always knew she was so much more than that. Even before we kissed—

I shook my head and gripped on to the steering wheel tighter as I pulled into her apartment parking lot. I couldn't let my mind wander to what had happened in the club. It wasn't a choice. I'd needed to do something to keep her safe, and that was the only thing I could think of at the time. There was nothing else to it. There couldn't be anything else to it.

"Not parking in the back?" Belle asked, and when I glanced at her, she had a small smile on her face. She remembered where I liked to park, with a view to see everything, but this time was different. The distance between the back of the lot and the stairs to her apartment was too far. Anything could happen in that time, so I opted to pull into a space near the stairs.

"Nope. I'm parking here from now on." I expected Belle to comment about it, but all she did was nod and unclip her belt. I turned the engine off and grabbed my bag off the back seat, making sure

I had my extra gun in there, then I scanned the area. "Let's go."

Her door flung open at the same time as mine, and I darted around to her side to make sure she was covered—just in case. She didn't mention the fact I was so close as she walked up the outside stairs in silence. But Belle and silence didn't really go hand in hand, so I knew it was because she was thinking. She needed to process everything that was happening and the fact I was here for an unknown time. Her life was about to change, but I'd do all I could to make sure it looked and felt as normal as possible.

I followed Belle as she turned at the top of the stairs and onto the walkway, which was exposed to the outside. I didn't like how open it was, but there was nothing I could do about it. She halted in front of a door in the middle of the row, and I turned to look out onto the lot. I could see the entire lot and even part of the college campus from here, and I didn't like it one bit.

My nostrils flared as I watched Belle insert her one key and push the flimsy door open, and my instincts to tell her we wouldn't be safe here kicked in. "Is that all you have on this door?" I asked, stepping inside and right into the living room. It had a small kitchen attached to it, and only a waist-high wall separating the two rooms.

She closed the door behind me and shrugged.

"Yeah. This block is mainly students, so we don't need anything more than one lock."

"You need more than one lock, Belle." I scrubbed my hand down my face and glanced around the small apartment. "Jesus fuckin' Christ, you can't stay here. It's not safe."

Belle huffed out a laugh and planted her hands on her hips. "Are you serious?" She paused, waiting for my answer, but when I just stared her down, she threw her hands up in the air. "I can't believe you. This is my home, Ford. I'm safe here, I've been safe here since I moved in at the start of my sophomore year. There's never been trouble here, and—"

"And you've never been threatened by a cartel boss, Belle." I took a step closer to her and lowered my voice, trying to drive my point home. "This isn't fuckin' playground antics. We ain't playin' house here. It's fuckin' serious."

"You think I don't know that?" she whispered, and her throat bobbed. "You're here because I came to that club. You're here because I apparently can't protect myself." Her eyes welled with tears, and my shoulders tensed. If there was one thing I couldn't stand, it was Belle upset, but I couldn't cave. It wasn't safe for her here. "I know you'd rather be at home—anywhere but here." She glanced down. "I'm sorry."

Fuck. Jesus. I was too harsh. I...

"Look..." I pushed my hand through my hair

and gripped on to it. "I'll check the apartment over and see if I can make it safe, okay?" She didn't answer me. Instead, she moved aside and stepped past me. "Belle." I reached out and wrapped my hand around her forearm, the exposed soft skin sliding against my palm. The touch gained her attention, and she finally looked up at me. "I wouldn't wanna be anywhere but making sure you're safe. Got it?"

Her blue eyes looked lighter than they ever had before, like a clear, calm ocean. "Okay," she murmured. "I really am sorry, though. If I hadn't come to the club, then..." She trailed off, and even though I knew she meant I wouldn't be here, I couldn't help but finish the sentence off in my head: we wouldn't have kissed.

I wondered if she thought about the kiss. Did she think I went too far? Maybe touching her now was crossing a boundary? I had to keep my mind focused on the job at hand: keeping Belle safe.

"It's fine." I pulled my hand off her arm and clenched it by my side. "I'm gonna check the apartment." My gaze flicked around what I could see. A central room, which was the living room and kitchen, and a hallway leading off either side. "Is your roommate here?"

"She won't be home until later, although I'm not sure how she'll feel about you staying over." It was on the tip of my tongue to tell her that we may not be staying here if I didn't think I could make it safe enough, but instead, I remained silent. "Do you need to check her bedroom too?"

"I need to check every room and every entry point." I placed my bag on the arm of the sofa, then pulled out a couple of pieces of equipment. The first was to check if there were any bugs in here, and the second was to see how easily I could gain access to the apartment.

"I'll let you get on with it," Belle said, but I didn't turn to acknowledge her. The only thing on my mind was checking the apartment. Her footsteps echoed as she walked down one of the hallways, and I let out a breath. Maybe it wasn't such a good idea sending me here to make sure she was safe. There was a tension between us that had never been there. Maybe I was imagining it?

Instead of overthinking it, I got to checking the entire apartment. There were three entry points, four if you counted the front door. One window in the living room, one in her roommate's bedroom, and one in her bedroom. All three needed to be replaced with safety glass and then fitted with sensors. The flimsy wooden door also needed to go, and an entire alarm system had to be installed. The list was getting longer and longer, but I knew I could make it safe for her.

I pulled out my cell, about to call Brody, when Belle stomped out of her bedroom, her face red and her lips pinched. "No, Dad, I can't just stop my studies! I only have five months left of this year." She halted in front of me, her blue eyes no longer calm but instead fiery. "Ford's here, he'll make sure I'm okay—no, Dad." Her shoulders slumped. "That's not fair. You can't just demand...I'm a grown-ass woman." My nostrils flared as I tried to hold in the chuckle, which was desperate to escape. She didn't sound like a grown-ass woman right now. She sounded like a teenager arguing with her dad. "Here, talk to Ford. I'm done letting you boss me around."

Belle handed me the cell with a raised brow, and I glanced down at it. "What?" I asked.

"You talk to him. He won't listen to me." She shook her cell between us. "He wants me to come home. He said I'm not safe here with only you."

My back straightened at her words, and I took the cell out of her hands. It was one thing for me to be worried about keeping her safe, but for Brody to second-guess what I was best at didn't sit well with me. I'd never let anyone hurt Belle, and he should have known that. I was all for taking chances, but only when the time called for it. And when I was protecting someone who was family to me, I didn't take chances.

"Brody," I growled down the line, and Belle's brows shot up on her forehead. Yeah, she wasn't used to the way I was talking. I always spoke so gently with her, but she was going to have to learn the different sides of me, sides I'd kept her sheltered from.

"You need to bring her home," he demanded.

I widened my stance, almost as if I was standing face to face with him, but Belle didn't move an inch. Her eyes were focused on me, her lips parted, and her head tilted to the side. She was fascinated by the way I was acting and talking, and I shouldn't have liked seeing that look on her face.

"Why?"

"He got bail."

My carefully constructed control on my emotions evaporated, and anger replaced it at lightning speed. "What the fuck?" I backed away from Belle and started to pace the apartment. "How the fuck did he get bail?"

"They said he wasn't a flight risk, but we all know it was the fuckin' judge. He's on his payroll," Brody boomed over the line, and I could imagine him pacing just like I was.

"But I thought he had Judge Weston?"

"He got replaced thirty minutes before he was due in court."

I slapped my hand on the wall next to the front door, the vibrations shooting up my arm. "Motherfucker."

"Which is why I need you to bring my daughter home. Now. She's not safe there, Ford. She's not—"

Brody's voice faded away as I turned to look at Belle. Underneath the anger at being told to go home, I could see her hope. She wanted to stay here because both she and I knew, if she went home, it could be months until she'd come back, and then she'd be a year behind. But I also knew, if she went home, there wasn't anything there for her. Her mom and dad had no idea what she'd dealt with at school, but I did. Belle had confided in me so many times over the years, and I hated the thought of her going back to the way she was before she left for college.

Making friends wasn't easy for Belle. She talked…a lot. She wasn't afraid to say what she was thinking. She was outspoken and had an opinion on everything. She was exactly who she was meant to be, but that hadn't sat well with the kids at her school. Belle had made out like she didn't care, but I knew what it was like to feel like an outsider at school. I'd been that person. I'd been the one you could pick out in a crowd because they were different.

"I can keep her safe," I heard myself croaking down the line. "I need some things to be installed into her apartment, but I can keep her safe."

"I'm not asking for your opinion, Ford. I'm giving you a goddamn order," Brody growled.

"Yeah?" I tilted my head to the side even though he couldn't see me. "And I'm telling you, as the agent on the ground, that I can keep her safe."

ABIGAIL DAVIES

The silence stretched for so long, I was afraid of what Brody would do. There was no one in this world he'd protect more than his kids, we both knew that, but sometimes you had to trust other people to do what you couldn't. And in this case, that other person was me.

"I don't fuckin' like this," Brody started. "Tell me what you need. I'll have it there within two hours." I blew out the breath I'd been holding. "But, Ford?"

"Yeah?"

"She gets hurt, I'll fuckin' kill you with my bare hands. I don't care about the shit we've been through or how long we've known each other. You understand me?"

"Understood." I nodded. "I'll email you the list." I ended the call and sauntered over to Belle. "You can stay, but there's gonna be a hell of a lot of changes to the apartment." Belle took her cell from my grasp. "You might want to tell your roommate to stay somewhere else tonight because your dad is sending everything we need, which includes a new front door and windows."

Belle's eyes widened. "New door? Maybe I should have just gone home."

I shrugged. "If that's what you want, we can leave right now."

She was silent for a beat and then shook her head. "No. I can't go home like this. I want to stay."

94

"Okay." I pulled my cell out. "I'll email this list to your dad, and then we can get started."

Belle raised her hands in the air with a bored look on her face. "Yippee."

The chuckle I'd held in earlier came bubbling up to the surface, and I let it out, staring at her back as she walked down the hallway to her bedroom. I wasn't sure how long I'd have to stay here with Belle, but I knew it wouldn't be uneventful.

———

BELLE

The inside of the car was silent, the only sound the roaring engine of Ford's car. He hadn't said a word since I'd won the argument on whether we would stay in or go out tonight. Ford obviously wanted to stay inside to keep safe, but after the last couple of days I'd had, there was no way I was going to stay in.

I needed a drink. An alcoholic one. And STAT.

The apartment had been a flurry of activity for the entirety of Friday night. Thank god Stella agreed to stay at Justin's place, although I knew I'd have to explain to her what was going on. But Ford's orders were that she was the only one to know, and I couldn't tell her everything. I was sure Justin would wonder why the old wooden door was now replaced with a different one complete with five locks. I doubted he'd notice the windows and alarm system, but the red door turning white was a definite change you couldn't miss.

My brows rose as I spotted the flexing of Ford's jaw and the tenseness of his shoulders. If he was going to be like this all night, then maybe we should have stayed in. But what was the point of me staying at college if I wasn't going to do what I normally did? Wouldn't it have been more suspicious if I completely changed my schedule? That was the final line that had caused Ford to give in not ten minutes ago.

And now we were pulling up outside the bar, and Ford was double-parking, not having a care in the world that there was a clear *no parking* sign on the sidewalk.

"You can't park here."

Ford turned the engine off and unclipped his belt. "The rules don't apply to me." He pushed his door open and exited the car, so I did the same, only my door opened out into the road, and a car whizzed by.

"Asshole!" I shouted at the retreating car and then sauntered onto the sidewalk where Ford was staring at me with a small quirk of his lips. "What?"

"You're trouble, you know that? Trouble with a big fat capital T."

My head flung back, and a brash laugh burst

out of me. I jabbed my finger into his chest, feeling his muscles against my fingertip in the same kind of sensation as if I'd poked a brick wall. "And don't you forget it." He murmured something behind me, but I couldn't hear what he said as I walked toward the main doors of the bar. There was only one man standing at the door tonight, and I didn't recognize him.

I felt a hand against the base of my back, and I turned my head just enough to see Ford directly behind me. My mouth went dry at the contact, and even though he didn't look down at me, I wondered if he could feel the way I'd tensed and then relaxed at his touch?

He pushed forward and through the doors with me in front of him, and as soon as we were inside the bar, I scanned it, looking for Stella and Justin. Usually, they'd be standing at the bar talking to Curtis, but I couldn't see any of them there.

"I can't see them," I said, but Ford shook his head as if he couldn't hear me, so I lifted up onto my tiptoes and shouted, "I can't see them," in his ear. He pulled back a fraction, his face so close to mine I could see every speck of honey and green in his hazel eyes. His lashes framed his almond-shaped eyes perfectly and led down to what I was assuming was once a straight nose, but now had a crook in the middle.

Ford's gaze batted behind me, but I didn't flatten

my feet to the floor. I liked being this close to him, more than I ever had. I'd always wanted to be near Ford, but something had changed in the last week. I craved being near him. Craved it so much I wasn't sure I could breathe if he wasn't close by.

"Someone's waving at you," his gruff voice said.

I spun around, trying to spot who he was talking about, and then saw the top of Stella's head and her frantically waving arm. Lifting my arm, I waved back and then proceeded to move through the crowd around the bar and toward the booth she was sitting in near the dance floor.

"What are you guys doing in a booth?" I asked, wrapping my arms around Stella in a greeting and then nodding at Justin.

"Curtis isn't working tonight, so we didn't want to stand at the…" Stella's eyes widened, her mouth opening as her jaw dropped. "Who is this?"

I pulled in a breath, spotting Justin staring at Ford with the same kind of awe, and realized they were seeing what everyone else saw. Something I never fully understood. To me, Ford wasn't scary, but as I turned and faced him, I could see why he'd come off like that. He'd perfected his broody, don't-mess-with-me look. His defined muscles couldn't be mistaken, and the tattoos on his arms didn't scream rainbows and unicorns. To the outside world, he was a threat, but to me, he was just Ford, the same guy who had let me paint his nails bright pink and played tea parties with me until I fell asleep on the floor in my bedroom.

"Stella, Justin, this is Ford." I waved my hand at him. "Ford, this is my roommate, Stella, and her boyfriend, Justin."

"Nice to meet you," Ford greeted, his deep baritone able to be heard over the music. He held his hand out to both of them, the veins in his arms popping under the surface from the movement. They were in a daze as they greeted him, and I couldn't help but laugh. "Drink?" Ford asked, raising his brows at me.

"Tequila," I said, pushing into the booth opposite Stella and Justin.

"You do realize that's illegal, right?" Ford commented, but I just shrugged. I'd been drinking tequila since my first party on my first night here, and I was only a few months away from turning twenty-one.

"I'll...erm, I'll come to the bar with you," Justin stammered, his face paling, but from the jab Stella gave him in the ribs, I didn't think he had a choice in whether he would accompany Ford or not.

They both maneuvered away from the table and through the crowd, and I stared at the back of Ford's head, surprised by how well he fit in with all of the college students. But then I shouldn't have been really, because it was his job to go unnoticed, to fit in with the crowd, to blend in seamlessly.

"So…" Stella started. I could feel the burn of her stare on the side of my face. "Are you going to tell me what's going on?"

Ford had pushed his way to the bar and was ordering drinks, but his gaze veered back over to me. I wasn't stupid enough to think it was because he wanted to look at me. He was making sure I was okay. Making sure I was safe.

"I…" I turned to face Stella, my gaze finally meeting hers. "You can't tell anyone what's going on, okay?" She raised her brow as if to say she would never, but I had to make sure I said it. "There's been a threat."

Her eyes nearly popped out of their sockets, and she practically lunged across the sticky table at me. "What?"

"It's nothing serious." I wasn't sure whether I was trying to get her to believe my lie, or to convince myself. "But Dad has sent Ford to make sure I'm safe."

"So Ford is"—Stella glanced around us, and I did the same, spotting Ford weaving back toward us with Justin following him—"DEA?"

I nodded, not wanting to say anything else because if I opened that can of worms, I wasn't sure what would pop out of it. "He'll be staying with us for…a while—on the sofa. Is that okay?"

Stella's gaze slid to my right as Ford pushed into the booth. "Yeah, I'm good with that."

"Good with what?" Justin asked, glancing at all of us in turn. His expression looked like a weird mix of scared, excited, and apprehensive. It was not a good look on him—at all.

"Nothing." Stella pushed closer to him and smiled. "Belle was just asking if it was okay if Ford stayed on the sofa for a while."

"You need a place to crash?" Justin asked, leaning his elbows on the table. I cringed, thinking about the last time it was probably wiped down, and then reached for the glass Ford placed in front of me. I took a sip, knowing full well this definitely wasn't the tequila I'd ordered. "You can crash with us if you want."

"Who's 'us'?" Ford asked, and I turned to face him, wondering why he wasn't shutting him down right away. And why the hell would Justin say that anyway? He'd met Ford a few minutes ago and was already offering up his place.

"Me and Curtis," Justin said, his gaze not veering off Ford's. "He's my roommate, works here too."

"Where is Curtis?" I asked, interrupting the conversation. Whenever we were here, so was Curtis, especially on a Saturday night because tips were his life.

Justin leaned back in his seat, his eyes meeting Stella's briefly. "He had to go home a couple days ago. Said there was a family emergency." He paused and cleared his throat. "His mom is in the hospital."

"Oh…" I'd never met any of Curtis' family, but when I really thought about it, he hadn't really spoken about them either. We'd had conversations about seemingly everything, but when it came to all our families, we seemed to stop sharing. "Well, I hope it's nothing too serious."

The conversation lulled, and I shuffled in my seat, taking another drink of…*what the hell was this anyway?* It definitely wasn't alcohol.

"I'm good staying with Belle," Ford finally said, and for a second, I wondered what he was saying, and then remembered what Justin had suggested.

Justin nodded, and then Stella whispered something in his ear, and I knew what was about to happen. This was the exact reason why neither Curtis nor I liked to be a third wheel. They'd go off into a world of their own, and within seconds—yep, there it was. Now they were practically swallowing each other's faces.

I felt Ford lean closer to me, his shoulder brushing against mine, and then his breath brushed the side of my neck. "Do they do this often?" his deep voice whispered.

"All. The. Time," I replied, not turning my head to face him. I knew if I did, we'd only be inches apart, but the temptation was almost too much to resist. I lifted my drink again, then slammed it back down onto the table. "I'm going to get a real drink." I didn't wait for Ford to reply and pushed on his arm so he would move out of the booth. He raised his brows at me, and I raised mine right back. "I need to get past," I told him. He shrugged and didn't make to move, so I climbed over him and made a beeline for the bar, ordering a shot of tequila.

I'd wanted to try and forget all about what had happened over the last couple of days, but being here, the music pumping throughout the bar and Ford's watchful gaze focused on me, made me think about it all the more. I needed a break, something to lull my thoughts into a false sense of security. So, as the girl behind the bar handed me my shot, I ordered another one and downed them both.

I turned, looking right at Ford, and then sauntered onto the dance floor, intent on losing myself to the music, and giving my mind a break.

Chapter Six

FORD

College had never interested me. I didn't see the point in going to school for an extra four years just so I could party and then leave with a degree I probably would never use. So being here in this college town wasn't the highlight of my life.

I'd expected Belle to not know her limits, to get so drunk I'd have to carry her home, which was why when she'd ordered a tequila last night, I'd gotten her some froufrou non-alcoholic cocktail—a cocktail was what the bartender had called it. I should have known she'd have gotten herself tequila anyway, but I hadn't expected her to only do two shots and then spend three hours dancing away.

Stella and Justin had left sometime during her

dance-a-thon, and I hadn't been able to take my eyes off Belle the entire time. Several guys had tried to dance with her, but she'd brushed them off without a second thought. And that was when I realized I wasn't the only one who had been watching her. I hated to admit the jealousy than ran through me, but the longer she was out on the dance floor, the bigger it grew, until I was ready to grab her and throw her over my shoulder so we could leave.

But then she turned to face me, her gaze meeting mine, and she drifted closer. Her hips swayed, her arms moving gently by her sides, and I was entranced. Her skin was soaked in sweat, but the giant smile on her face was worth me not stepping in and going caveman on her. She was a grown-ass woman, and I had no right to tell her who she could and couldn't dance with, but that didn't mean I liked it.

She didn't talk much on the way back to her apartment, and as soon as I opened up her new door with all the security measures, she pushed inside and went right to her bedroom.

And now I was here, at five in the morning, wide awake after having three hours of sleep. My brain was on overdrive, my mind going over and over every piece of evidence we had on Garza. He shouldn't have gotten bail. He should have been locked up and never let out again. But he was out.

He was on the streets, and we had no idea what his next move was. An unpredictable man was a dangerous man.

I unlocked my cell and opened up my email to send an encrypted message to Brody, asking for an update. The secretiveness we had when I was undercover was no longer needed, but the security of our conversations was.

Rolling on the sofa, I gritted my teeth at the lumps pushing into my back. I'd told Belle I'd slept in worse places, but goddamn, this was one of the worst. I'd have been better making a pallet on the floor. In the end, I decided I wouldn't be getting any more sleep, so I sat up to type out the rest of the message. I wanted an update on Garza's last known location and details of any units which were following him. I needed a heads-up if he was nearby because I needed the time to be able to get Belle to safety if necessary.

I locked my cell, threw it down next to me, and leaned my head on the back of the sofa. The ceiling was an off-white, but I was sure it wasn't meant to be that color on purpose. It hadn't been updated in years, much like the door which had been replaced. The super of this building didn't give two craps about the safety of the people living here, most of whom were college students.

Why the hell did Brody give the okay for Belle to live here in the first place? She could have stayed on campus and in the dorms where it was safer, but if she had been there, I wouldn't have been able to stay with her.

My eyes drooped the longer I stared at the ceiling, and I could feel sleep overtake me just as a door closed and footsteps neared. I shot up off the sofa, knowing it was still dark outside because of how early it was. My hand was reaching for my gun, ready to confront whoever it was.

I widened my stance, waiting for the person to come into the living room, and then… "Belle?" I blinked and frowned, letting my hand drop beside me. "What are you doing up?" She wasn't just awake, but she was fully dressed in a pair of dark jeans and a hoody.

"My shift at the shelter starts in thirty," she answered, not looking at me as she moved into the kitchen. I stared at her, wondering how the hell she managed to get up after only a few hours' sleep and look like she'd just slept a full eight hours. She turned to face me, her brow raised. "Well, are you going to get ready?"

"I…" I scraped my hand over my face and through my hair, trying to wake myself up. "Yeah." I took two steps back and then shook my head. I'd known she volunteered at the shelter thanks to all the intel which had been gathered by other people, but I hadn't realized she did shifts this early. This would be prime time for Garza to make his move—still dark, and early enough to go unnoticed.

I gathered my bag and stomped toward Belle's bedroom. I'd been using her bathroom while I was here, but I didn't take any of her room in as I walked through it and then into the bathroom. All I was thinking about was the need to switch up her usual schedule. If someone was watching her, then we needed to make them second-guess where she was and what she was doing. We had to keep them on their toes so we would be one step ahead of them and not on the back foot.

By the time I was changed into black jeans and a black T-shirt with my belt attached around my waist to hold my guns and a knife, Belle was waiting by the front door, her fingers flying over the screen of her cell. I didn't say anything as I dropped my bag next to her sofa and grabbed my keys, wallet, and cell, then walked by her and opened the door. I kept my arm outstretched in a silent command to stay back while I checked the walkway and looked down into the lot. It was quiet, so quiet you could hear a pin drop.

"Clear," I told her, moving my arm and then closing the door behind me. The alarm would go into effect as soon as we were out of the apartment, and the door would be impossible to get past, so at least we knew no one would be coming in there who didn't belong.

Belle's footsteps followed behind me as we made it to the stairs, and once we were at the top, I glanced down, and then back at her. Her ears were bunched up to her shoulders, her gaze shifting left to right, but those two things were the only tell that she was nervous. An outsider wouldn't have been able to spot those things, but I could. I'd trained to identify each and every movement of the body, to read its language so I didn't need words to figure someone out. It was a natural thing for me to do, something I'd learned when I was a teenager on the streets.

I swallowed, my instincts kicking in and demanding I comfort her, but I couldn't. I had to stay focused and make sure there wasn't anyone out there wanting to take a cheap shot at us. Keeping on high alert, I maneuvered down the stairs and then to the car without a problem. Maybe I was being overly cautious, but I'd rather be too prepared than not prepared enough.

Once we were both in the car and I was pulling out of the lot, Belle seemed to relax. I had a feeling it was because she knew how safe this car was. It was a safe house on wheels, and I made sure to use it whenever I was away on an assignment. It wasn't only bulletproof, but I'd also had Jord install equipment to block out any signal so my calls couldn't be traced or listened to from inside it.

"Do you need the address?" Belle asked, and I turned to face her. My brow rose in silent response and she shook her head. "Of course you don't. I don't know why I asked." The straight line of her lips told me she wasn't happy about me knowing the ins and outs of her schedule, but neither was I. The only reason I knew was because Garza had gathered the intel on her. The one man who should have never even known about her.

"So…" I cleared my throat and relaxed my hand on the steering wheel, wanting to get my mind off the situation at hand. Being constantly reminded of the danger around you wasn't good for anyone, especially when they weren't used to high-pressure situations. It was starting to wear me down, so I had no doubt it was doing the same to Belle. "How long have you been volunteering at the shelter?"

I felt Belle's arm on the center console, so close to mine but not actually touching. Was she aware of how one little movement would make our skin touch? Did she do it on purpose?

"Since freshman year," she said, her voice small. "No one knows…well, no one *did* know, but I'm guessing Mom and Dad are aware now, huh?"

I cringed, not knowing what to say. "Yeah, they know." I shifted in my seat and pulled to a stop at a red light. "Why did you keep it secret anyway? You have this whole life none of us knew about and—"

"I didn't want you to know," she interrupted, her gaze meeting mine. Her blue eyes swirled with an emotion I'd seen often in her mom's eyes twenty years ago. She wanted to run, escape from the situation she was in, but I had no idea why Belle felt the need to do that too. She had a good life. She had two parents who loved and protected her. So why? Why did she create an entire life none of us knew about?

The light turned green, and I took a left turn, almost immediately coming into the lot of the shelter. Belle directed me toward the back of the building, and I pulled up directly outside the metal door.

Neither of us moved as I turned the engine off. The clock on the dash told me we were ten minutes early for her shift. Silence stretched between us, but I couldn't hold my tongue. I couldn't keep my question inside. "Why?" I asked, turning in my seat to face her. I leaned my arm over the top of the steering wheel, intent on giving her all of my attention.

"Why what?" Belle kept her gaze fixated out the windshield.

"Why didn't you want us to know?"

The silence swirled around us, but I didn't make a move to fill it. Over the years, I'd learned you had to give Belle time to think about what she wanted to say. Everyone assumed because she talked so much that she was always ready to say anything, but it wasn't the truth. It was when she stopped to think that you knew she cared.

"Because..." She huffed out a breath and

turned to look at me. Her gaze flicked over my entire face before she finally met my eyes. "You all see me as Belle, the little girl who needs protecting. Baby Belle, Princess Belle. I'm the one you all need to make sure is okay, I'm the one you like to keep close, but it's suffocating, Ford. I felt like I couldn't breathe." Her throat bobbed as she swallowed. "I'm twenty years old, and I had to fight tooth and nail to be able to attend this college, and it's only five hours away. Do you have any idea the kind of offers I had?"

I shook my head because I didn't. I'd been away more and more on undercover jobs these last few years. It seemed the older Belle got, the more assignments I was on. "No."

"I had an offer from Stanford, Ford. Freakin' Stanford. And you know what Dad said when I told him?" She laughed, but I could tell it wasn't funny. It was the kind of laugh to mask the hurt you were feeling, and hearing it come out of Belle's mouth sent goose bumps over my entire body. "He told me it was too far away and that the community college would do just fine." She threw her hands up in the air. "The community college, for real?" Her nostrils flared. "But if Asher gets offers all over the country, I can guarantee Dad won't say a word to him. And why is that? Because I'm a girl? Seriously?"

"He's just tryin' to look out for you, Belle. You're his little girl, and it's—"

"I'm not a little fuckin' girl, Ford." Her cheeks reddened, a blush spreading through her that once upon a time I found cute, but right then, sitting so close to her, I found it sexy.

Fuck.

I couldn't find it sexy. I couldn't think about her like that.

"I haven't been a little girl since I lost my virginity to the captain of the football team when I was sixteen years old. I haven't been a little girl since my dad taught me how to shoot a gun and hit my target."

I swallowed, feeling my skin get hotter the longer she talked. I couldn't think straight. I couldn't comprehend all of her words, because all I could think about was that goddamn football player touching her. Feeling her soft skin against his palm and taking what she was willing to give him.

"I'm not a little girl, Ford. I'm a woman. A woman who knows her own mind, one who needs space from the people who treat her like she's only ten years old." She pulled in another deep breath. "That's why I didn't tell anyone. I didn't tell them because they would have told me I didn't need a job at the coffee shop, that I needed to focus on my studies and not volunteer at the local shelter. But I do need to do these things. I need to be independent. I need to be myself. I need to separate my life from the one I grew up in."

I stared at her, really stared at her, and for the first time, I saw the woman she was talking about. I saw the fierceness in her eyes, the determination on her face, and I couldn't stop myself from reaching forward and placing my palm on her cheek.

"I get it," I whispered, rubbing my thumb back and forth. "I get it more than you'll ever know." I pushed my long fingers into her hair. "I'll always protect you, Belle. That goes without saying, but I'll try to stop treating you like the little girl you used to be." My gaze flicked down to her lips. I hadn't looked at her like she was a little girl since I'd pressed my lips against hers. I'd stopped thinking of her as Belle, Brody's daughter, since my tongue intertwined with hers. At that moment in the club, she'd become so much more than just Baby Belle, but it didn't matter, because that was all it would ever be. One moment in time that would never be repeated.

"Thank you," she whispered as she glanced at the back door to the shelter and then back at me. "We need to go inside now."

"Okay," I responded, my voice low. I was afraid to speak too loudly, afraid I'd say something I couldn't take back.

"I want to introduce you to someone special," Belle said, her face lighting up so much a grin spread on my face.

"Yeah?" I asked, rubbing the pad of my thumb

on her cheek one final time and then pulling away. I couldn't keep touching her like that, not when I was meant to be putting more distance between us.

"Yep." She opened the door and sprung out of the car like a bouncy ball. I followed after her, glancing around the outside and then moving toward the door she was holding open.

The barks echoed off the concrete walls, but I noticed Belle's shoulders drooping from the sound. She looked at home—like she belonged here—and as I followed her and she greeted first the cats and then a bird, I realized this was what she loved. Even if her dad told her to stop, she wouldn't. She'd found her passion, but I wasn't sure she was aware of it.

"This is her," Belle announced, stopping in front of one of the crates. This dog was different from the rest, though. She waited patiently, her gaze never leaving Belle's as she opened up the door and stepped inside. I didn't follow her because I had a feeling I knew what this dog was, and me being inside this kennel with her right away wouldn't go down well.

Belle got down onto her knees and opened her arms, and only then did the dog lunge forward and lick her entire face. Belle's laugh echoed around us, and I couldn't help but smile at the sound. It was something I'd missed so much over the years because it was less and less frequent.

"This is Lottie," Belle said, turning her and the dog so they were now both facing me. "I shouldn't have favorites, but she's my favorite." She shrugged and then turned to stare at Lottie. "Although, sometimes, she looks at me like she has no idea what I'm saying and——"

"Sitz," I commanded, my voice deep, and the dog immediately sat. Belle gasped, but I didn't move my gaze from the dog who was waiting for my next order. "Platz." Lottie stretched out on her front legs, getting as low down as she could.

"What the——"

"Hier." I didn't move from just outside the kennel as Lottie trotted toward me and halted at my feet. "Sitz. Braver hund."

"Ford!" Belle rushed forward and stared at Lottie, then me in awe. "What the heck was that?"

"I had a feeling when I first saw her." I knelt down and patted Lottie on the head. "But when you said it was like she didn't understand you——"

"So I was talking the wrong language? What even was that?"

I chuckled and dipped my head back to look at Belle. "It was German." I pushed my hand through Lottie's short fur, then stood. "She's a trained dog. Maybe army?"

Belle's head swung from Lottie to me and then to Lottie again. "She's...oh my god."

"How did she end up here?" I frowned. I had a

feeling Lottie was highly trained if her immediate response to my commands were anything to go by. She wasn't out of shape, and her eyes looked clear as day. So how had she ended up in the shelter?

"She was wandering the streets about ten months ago. Her chip had been removed, and the blood was matted in her fur. It was like whoever had her didn't want us to know."

"Wow." I grimaced as Belle's eyes misted over. "I'm sure someone will take her, though. She'll get a good home, right?"

"Right." Belle stroked Lottie once more. "She has two months until the year is up and then…well, let's just keep our fingers crossed."

"Two months until what?" Belle stepped out of the kennel and closed it behind her but kept silent. She'd gone into her own little world, so as she wandered off between the rows of kennels, I stayed back a few steps behind her.

All of a sudden, she spun around, her lips spread into a wide grin. "You ready for feeding time?"

"Feeding time?" I asked.

"Feeding time," she repeated, and just like that, the sadness that had been on her face disappeared, and the Belle I knew was present again. Whatever she was feeling had been pushed down. I'd let it go for now, but not forever because I knew what pushing things down did to a person.

I knew better than most.

BELLE

Having a six-foot-four, broody man following you around campus wasn't exactly inconspicuous, but the students barely seemed to notice Ford as he walked me to each of my classes and then stood in the back with his hands behind his back. I wasn't sure if he was aware we could see a glimpse of his gun attached to his belt, but no one said anything to him. The professors and lecturers didn't bat an eyelash at the sight of him, and part of me wondered if he'd already spoken to them—or maybe my dad had. Either way, Ford knew how intimidating he was being, and I couldn't help but want to make his straight face crack a little.

If Ford was bored of standing and listening to my classes all day, he didn't show it. I expected him to show at least a little relief when I told him litera-ture was my last class of the day, but all he did was nod, walk me to my seat, and then head toward the back. One thing that helped having Ford with me was that I had been early to every class. I wasn't sure if that was his plan, or just because students seemed to part ways so he could maneuver through.

I sat in my seat and then pulled out my notepad

as several students got out their laptops. I'd tried to take notes on my laptop when I'd first started college two and a half years ago, but I'd failed miserably. You could never go wrong with a pen and piece of paper.

My skin buzzed, aware of Ford behind me, but I didn't turn back. I was sure people were wondering who this guy was watching us all, but I didn't want the attention. With attention came questions, and I refused to answer any. Here, I was just Belle. I didn't need to be Belle, daughter of DEA agent. That had followed me throughout my entire school life, and I'd come here to get away from it, not to be haunted by it.

"You okay?" a voice asked, and I turned to the left, blinking at the girl sitting next to me. Her name was on the tip of my tongue, but I couldn't for the life of me remember it.

"I…yeah, are you?" I whispered back.

"I am. But I'm not the one trying to snap a pen with my bare hand."

I flicked my gaze down to my hand and spotted my white knuckles, then slowly let my pen roll out of my palm and onto the desk. I laughed, trying to play it off as nothing, but I knew better than that.

My entire life was being uprooted, and as much as it was nice to have Ford here—especially after not seeing him for so long—this wasn't the way I wanted it to be. I didn't want to have him be my shadow. I didn't want to feel on edge all the time. I just wanted to hang out with my friends at the bar or get a burger between classes, but even that had become almost impossible. Ford had to scope out each place we went to when we weren't in my apartment, and he had to be with me at all times.

I turned a little in my seat to stare at Ford and wondered if he was frustrated too. He was at the height of his career, and yet he'd been lumped with babysitting me. Maybe he hated it just as much as I did?

"Miss Easton? I hate to draw your attention away from the handsome man standing at the back of my lecture hall, but I'm going to have to insist you stop drooling over him and look to the front of the class," Professor Heartland said.

My face burned so hot I swore you could have fried an egg on it. Ford's lips quirked on one side, and I narrowed my eyes on him, then spun in my seat to give the seventy-year-old professor my attention. Her gaze was fixed on Ford, and her brows rose as she got to his face.

"Now." Professor Heartland clapped her hands. "If I could have all of your attention." She looked at me again, but this time she winked and took a quick glance back at Ford. I had no idea what that wink meant. "I know it's hard to concentrate when we have an Adonis standing at the back of the room." I snorted, the sound echoing around the now quiet room. "But we must talk about the importance of this piece of literature. The way men talked about women in their works of art in the sixteenth century needs to be assessed. I want your opinions, your facts, how you think this would have made women at the time feel."

I shuffled in my seat and tried to write down what she was saying, not really understanding what it was I had to do.

"Miss Easton." I snapped my head up, my wide-eyed gaze meeting Professor Heartland. "What differences do you think there are between a man and a woman in the modern day compared to back in the sixteenth century?"

I shrugged. "As in romantically?" Professor Heartland nodded, waiting for me to say more. It was just my luck she picked me out of all of the students when Ford was listening to every word I was saying. Could I not catch a break? "I…erm, I don't really know." I bit down on my bottom lip. "Women are more forward than they were back then." I paused, waiting to see what she'd say, but when she was silent, I continued, "A woman would never have been able to tell a man her true feelings. Women have more choice now. They can marry for love and not because their father said so."

"So, if your father told you that you had to marry a certain man, would you?"

It felt like the entire student body's eyes were on

me, and I could feel the burn of a blush making its way over my face. "It'd depend."

"On…"

"If I loved him." I tilted my head to the side. "The thing is, my dad is protective—too protective —so if he had it his way, I'd stay unmarried for the rest of my life." A round of chuckles sounded out, but I wasn't joking in the slightest. If only they really knew. "But he knows better than anyone that love knows no bounds. He followed his heart with my mom, and if they had met back in the sixteenth century, it would never have been allowed to happen."

"I see…" Professor Heartland stared at me. "And although your father and mother followed their heart, do you feel like you can too?"

I looked down at my hands on the desk and could feel my pulse racing. It didn't really matter what my heart felt because I didn't have a choice. For way too many years I'd been obsessed with Ford, determined to marry him when I was older, but as soon as I'd turned into a teenager, my hormones took over, and I realized how stupid the notion of being with someone twice my age was. But right then, sitting in a classroom full of college students who were waiting for my answer, I knew it wasn't stupid.

"I think I can," I croaked out. "In America, we have rights, we have free speech, but there are still places in the modern world where women don't have the choices we have. They have to marry who they're told to. They don't get to follow their hearts. So…yes, I think I owe it to everyone who doesn't get a choice to follow my heart."

"Are we actually going to talk about the work we're meant to be doing, or just listen to Tinker Bell's feelings all day long?" a guy toward the back shouted. The heat from my blush increased tenfold, and I realized what I'd just said. I'd spilled my guts to a room full of people who I didn't really know, and Ford. Fuck. Ford had heard all of that.

"Well, Mr. Reed, aren't you the perfect male subject to talk about. What was it about Miss East-on's words that made you uncomfortable?"

"I'm not uncomfortable," he growled out. "I just don't want to hear all this froufrou bullshit. I'm here to pass this class, not be part of a fuckin' girl cult where we're talking about hearts and flowers. Jesus Christ."

Every bone in my body wanted to snap back, tell him it was men like him who were the problem, but I didn't. I kept my mouth shut, and my gaze focused on Professor Heartland.

"I see," she said, tilting her head to the side. "And in your opinion, Mr. Reed, what do you think I should be teaching in my literature class?"

"I don't know," I heard him answer. "Books? Anything but Tinker Bell's feelings."

"How about we talk about the respect men had for women in the sixteenth century?" Professor Heartland took a couple of steps forward. "Do you think men would have spoken about women the way you just spoke about Miss Easton?" I turned in my seat to look at the guy and realized several students were watching him. As soon as I glanced at Ford, I could see he was fuming.

His eyes were narrowed on the guy, his hands clenched by his sides. Part of me wanted Ford to step forward and teach the guy a lesson. Mr. Reed—otherwise known as Elijah—had been a thorn in my side since he'd asked me on a date freshman year. Apparently, he didn't like the word no, and he'd made me aware of that almost every day since.

"I don't know, Mrs. Heartland—"

"Professor. My name is Professor Heartland, Mr. Reed." She paused and took another step toward him. "In the sixteenth century, things were vastly different, and women felt like they didn't have a voice. Do you think women have a voice now?"

"I guess?" Elijah answered, but he was squirming in his seat now, and watching how uncomfortable he was made a smile spread on my face.

Professor Heartland made a noise in the back of her throat and spun around. "Maybe we should get a woman's opinion on this?" My eyes widened, and I hoped she didn't— "Rose? What do you think? Do you think women are represented in literature the same way they were when in the sixteenth century?"

"I think it's different," the girl next to me said. Rose. Her name was Rose. I should have remembered that because I was obsessed with the movie Titanic.

"In what way?"

"I think prejudice is still rife in America. Whether it be gender, skin color, sexuality. There will always be someone who doesn't like something, but the difference is freedom. We now have the freedom to reply back and tell them it's not right. We have the freedom to speak out grievances, whereas in the sixteenth century, it was white men who controlled what was said in the media and what wasn't said."

"Well said, Rose. Well said."

"Thank you, Professor," she replied with a huge smile on her face.

"Your assignment this week is to research a sixteenth-century piece of literature and rewrite it in a modern-day language. Change it around, have fun with it. Speak from the heart." Professor Heartland clapped her hands. "That's today's class over. See you all next week." She didn't wait as she grabbed her bag and then sauntered out of the class, not another word spoken, and I kind of lived for it.

I packed my things away, and shuffled out of the

row of seats, only to be met with Elijah's scowling face. "Thanks, Tinker Bell."

"Move along," a deep voice said from beside us. "Now."

Elijah turned his head and chuckled. "This your bodyguard, Tinker Bell?" He stepped closer to me, but I just stared up at him with a raised brow. Elijah loved to provoke me, but I never bit, and I think he hated that about me. "He know you like to fuck frat boys on the daily?"

I shrugged. "It's a shame you're not one of those frat boys, huh?"

A muscle ticked in Elijah's jaw, and I smiled sweetly up at him. He knew for a fact I hadn't slept with any frat boys, but he enjoyed making out that I did. It wasn't the first time I'd heard it, and I was sure it wouldn't be the last.

"I'm gonna tell you once more, move the fuck along," Ford growled. He stepped between us, completely blocking my view of Elijah.

Elijah grumbled something and then moved back, but his gaze met mine, and I knew it wouldn't be the last time I heard from him. Not that I cared one bit. He was just a sore loser who held a grudge.

"You know you didn't have to do that," I told Ford, slipping past him and moving down the steps toward the lecture hall door.

"I know," he grunted. "It was either that or lay

him out. Fuck, Belle, why'd you let him talk to you like that?"

I halted at the door, my hand on the knob, and turned my head to look at him. I could see the anger and frustration on his face, but he needed to understand I wasn't the same person I was when I left for college all that time ago. I didn't feel the need to fight fire with fire.

"I'm used to it," I told him. "When people aren't scared what your dad will do to them, they tend to not give a shit what they say to you."

"That don't mean you gotta put up with that shit, Baby Belle." My skin buzzed at his nickname, but goose bumps spread everywhere when he stepped closer to me. He towered over me, just like he always had, and made me feel safe in the cocoon of his body. "You hear me?"

I let out a breath, feeling my shoulders sag. "Yeah, Ford, I hear you. But he's just bitter because I refused to fuck him."

A beat of silence stretched between us, and Ford's eyes swirled with something I couldn't quite understand. I'd never seen that look in his eyes before. "And the other frat boys?"

I knew what he was asking, but there was no way I was going to tell him I'd only slept with one guy since I'd been away at college, and that one guy had been the nerdy TA in my freshman year. So instead of telling him my entire history, I just shrugged and opened the door, leaving him wondering. Maybe he'd stop seeing me as Brody's daughter if he believed it, or maybe he'd just think I was a skank.

I was kind of okay with either one.

Chapter Seven

FORD

You didn't realize how important your privacy was until it was taken away from you. Sleeping on someone's sofa meant your bed was constantly in use during the day, and the small open-plan room was the hub of the apartment when both Belle and Stella were home.

Part of me wanted to tell Stella it was late and to turn off the goddamn TV so I could get some sleep. Belle had a packed day of classes and a shift at the coffee shop tomorrow, so in turn I had a jam-packed day too. But apparently, Stella was unaware that she was overstaying her welcome on my bed, otherwise known as her sofa.

My cell rang, and Brody's name came up—a video call, something Brody only did when the team needed to talk, which meant there was no way I could take this outside, or in front of Stella. Belle had told her just enough so she wouldn't keep asking questions, but not too much that she'd be in danger herself.

I stood, answering the call. "Two seconds." I glanced back at Stella, but her gaze was fixated on the TV, and having noticed I'd stood, she stretched out on the sofa, getting comfortable. I was never going to get any sleep tonight.

My feet carried me to Belle's room, and I knocked twice, but when there was no answer, I pushed the door open. I could hear her shower running from her bathroom, so I stepped inside and closed the door behind me and then sat on the edge of her bed.

"Brody," I greeted, holding the cell in front of my face. The grim line of his lips was the first thing I noticed, and then Jord in the background, typing away on a laptop.

"Ford." Brody huffed out a breath. "We've lost eyes on him."

My stomach sank, but it was something I'd been expecting. I knew Garza would have gone underground, and I'd been waiting for this call to tell me. A man like him didn't give you any excuses to create more of a case against him. He was going to make it difficult, or damn near impossible. But we already had everything we needed, at this stage, we had eyes on him so we could track his movements and keep Belle safe. "Thought he would." I leaned my hand on the bed behind me. "When was the last time someone had eyes?"

"Two hours ago," Jord said, not looking up in my direction. "He's probably fleeing the country—"

"Nah." I shook my head. "He won't go back to Mexico, not when his business is still alive here. He'll try to rebuild low-key." My stomach dropped as I thought about what else he would do. He didn't like to leave loose ends, and right now, I was a loose end, just like Belle was. And Belle was a tool he could use to tie up his loose end, one he wouldn't hesitate to utilize. "You got eyes in his clubs?"

"Yeah." Jord finally looked up. "But it's on a loop." I nodded. This wasn't the first time Garza had been arrested and raided. He knew the score and knew how to rebuild without leaving a trail behind. But now that he was rebuilding, and we didn't have anyone on the inside, we had no idea what was really going on. We could guess and estimate based on experience, but none of us truly knew.

"I'm posting extra men around you and Belle," Brody's gruff voice said. "I'm not taking the chance with either of you." I couldn't argue with him. Extras bodies meant there would be more protection, and I wasn't willing to let Belle get hurt.

"Okay." I heard the water from the shower turn off. "I gotta go. Ears."

Both Brody and Jord tilted their heads in acknowledgment, understanding what I was saying. "Look after her," Brody warned, although he didn't need to. He didn't need to tell me to look after the one person in this world who I would die to protect more than anyone else.

The line went dead, so I let my arms drop between my legs and hung my head. I was tired, and my brain was overloaded with so many things. I imagined what I would do and the steps I would take if someone managed to get past the apartment door. I played out the scenarios in my head time and time again, going over and over each route to the closest safe house.

A door clicked open, but I didn't move from my position. I could still hear the sound of the TV playing some reality show in the living room, and the thought of going back out there wasn't one I wanted to entertain.

Footsteps padded closer to me, and I made the mistake of looking up. I shouldn't have. I should have kept my gaze focused on the light carpet between my booted feet, but instead, I stared up at Belle. Belle, who was freshly showered, her light-brown hair hanging loosely around her shoulders and only a towel covering her body.

She looked so much smaller standing there like

that with a light blush on her cheeks. A blush I could have watched all day long. What was it about the redness on her face that drew me in? Was it the thought she was thinking something she couldn't be?

"Ford?" she whispered. Her throat bobbed as she swallowed, and I didn't move a muscle. She was my prey, and I was afraid any movement would have my instincts kicking in, and I wouldn't be able to stop myself. But I had to. The kiss in the club was just to get her out of there safely. It was nothing more and nothing less. So why was I staring at her and taking in every contour of her exposed skin that I could see? Why was the thought of her lips pressed against mine making me rock hard?

"I need—" My voice broke, the deepness even surprising me. "I need you to walk back into your bathroom and not come out until I've left this room."

"What?" Her eyes widened, and her hands clutched at the front of her towel. It would have been so fuckin' easy for me to push up off this bed and yank it off her in one fail swoop. Then I'd have been able to see every single part of her body. "What's happening?"

I shook my head, trying to get the image of her body out of it, but it was no use when she was standing there with that wide-eyed innocent look. An innocence that drew me in more and more with each day that passed. Belle was so much more than she let everyone see, and just following her for two weeks had taught me that. I'd put her in a box, a box I'd opened when our lips had first touch, and now I was tempted to peek inside and see what else was there.

My muscles screamed at me to stand, and I couldn't deny them any longer. I moved slowly and with purpose as I stepped toward her. I was giving her the opportunity to do as I'd asked and remove herself from the situation, but she just stood there, her blue eyes getting darker the closer I got to her.

"Ford?" her breathy whisper asked, but I wasn't sure even she knew what she was asking. Her chest rose on a breath, and I looked down at it and watched her hands let go of the towel. She was opening herself up to me, making sure there weren't any barriers between us, and this was the one time I was so glad I could read people's body language. She wasn't offering herself to me because the towel still covered her, but she was being open. She was welcoming me closer, and damn if I wasn't gonna take that chance.

In the back of my mind, I knew—*I fuckin' knew* —I shouldn't have been stepping closer to her and stopping only inches away. I knew I shouldn't have lifted my hand and placed my palm on the side of her neck. I knew trailing my thumb into the dip of her collarbone and feeling her soft skin wasn't a thought I should have entertained. And yet, I was here, my skin connected with hers, and my gaze focused on the lips she trailed her tongue over as she stared up at me.

She wanted it just as much as I did, and part of me wondered if she'd been thinking about the kiss in the club. Maybe I was imagining the signs. Maybe I was overthinking the way her body was talking to me. Fuck. I'd known Belle her entire life, and now I was practically drooling over her like she was my next meal.

What the fuck was I thinking?

I yanked myself away from her, putting three giant steps between us and feeling her bed at the back of my knees. My hands clenched by my sides as I tried to gain control of myself and not think about the way her smooth skin felt against my palms.

"What..." She paused, and I kept my gaze fixed to a spot on the wall behind her. "What the hell was that?"

"I need you to move, Belle," I growled out. I couldn't overstep the mark with her. I refused to destroy an entire lifetime of memories to the one girl in this world I cared about most. Girlfriends came and went, but Belle was always there with a smile on her face and an attitude to rival anyone who got in her way.

"Why?" I glanced at her as she slammed her

hands down onto her hips. "Why, Ford? Why do you need me to move? You want to leave this room, then walk around me." She heaved in a breath. "I'm not your goddamn toy to do with what you please. You can't boss me around all the time and think it's okay."

"That's not—"

"Yeah, it is." She threw her hands up in the air. "Jesus Christ, Ford. You're here to make sure I'm safe, but I'm not sure I'm safe with you." My stomach dropped at her words, and I felt like my entire life was crumbling in front of me. Was that how she saw me? Did she really think she was in danger because of me? "You're driving me freakin' insane!"

I frowned at her, not sure what she was talking about, but fuck, I couldn't keep looking at her when she was barely wearing anything. "I don't understand—"

She laughed, the kind of laugh that was conde-scending. "As if you don't fuckin' know. You may be oblivious, but I see the way you look at me."

My nostrils flared. "I don't know what you're—"

"Jesus, Ford." She raised her brow. "I haven't been able to stop thinking about the way you touched me at the club. I've gone over and over it in my head so many times, imagining you getting into that cab with me." Her cheeks blushed.

Had she been anyone else, I would have gotten

into that cab with her, but she was Belle. Belle Easton.

"But then you go so cold," she continued. "And I think to myself, 'did he not like it?' And then I realize it's because I'm just Baby Belle to you. I'm still that little girl you can tell what to do and she'll follow your rules without much of a fight."

"Belle——"

She shook her head. "It's fine. I get it. Just——"

"Will you let me talk?"

"——leave, and we can pretend you weren't in here and we'll forget about everything I've said. We can start fresh tomorrow, and put the stupid kiss behind us and——"

I couldn't listen to her go on any longer, not when she had that sad look in her eyes. She was so much more than she realized. So much more.

I lunged forward, letting my primal instincts take over, and wrapped my arms around her waist. I didn't hesitate. I didn't let my brain kick in. I didn't let my body take over. I listened to my heart and pulled her flush to my body.

"What the…"

I bent my knees, not needing to say anything else. Time for talking was gone, and it didn't matter what I said to her. She was right. I was blowing hot and cold. My body was saying one thing, and my words were saying another. So I pushed them both aside, and did what my heart and soul demanded me to.

"I'm going to kiss you now," I told her, my words gruff but low. I wasn't asking for her permission. I was telling her what was going to happen, and for once in her life, she was speechless. This wasn't like the kiss in the club. This wasn't out of desperation. This was because the thought of our lips never touching again broke something inside me.

I held her as tight as I could. Our gazes met, and there was so much said with one single look. I felt the world tilt, and it only righted itself when I pressed my lips to hers in a whisper-soft kiss. It was gentle, loving, and so much more than I ever thought I was capable of. My body screamed at me to go harder and faster, but I knew I couldn't. I had to show Belle that she wasn't the only one still thinking about that night at the club. I had to show her she wasn't going insane, because if she was, then so was I.

I pulled my lips away and then pressed them lightly again. Several times I repeated the action, and each time they connected, I felt part of my heart crack and then mend again. It was Belle's name being stamped into it, and I wasn't sure there would be a way for me to erase it, but right then, I didn't care.

All that mattered was Belle and me, and this moment no one could ever take away from us.

BELLE

I'd woken up this morning with a smile on my face and my lips tingling at the memory of Ford. My mood was the best it had been since the last time he'd kissed me in the club, and I couldn't help wondering if this was the start of something.

A part of me expected him to kiss me as soon as I walked into the living room, but he was silent. It wasn't unusual for Ford to be so focused on the task at hand that he didn't talk much, so I didn't pay much attention to it.

I went to each of my classes, Ford standing at the back, and got on with my work, all with a grin plastered on my face. My shift at the coffee shop flew by, and I was sure it was because I knew as soon as this day was over, Ford would turn back into the person who had pressed my back against my bedroom door and told me he was going to kiss me.

His gruff voice from last night kept repeating in my brain. But it was as we were walking back to his car to go home that I finally realized he'd not said more than a couple of words to me today, and even those had been only to tell me which way to walk and when I'd asked him what time it was.

I hadn't imagined last night, but maybe I was creating a fantasy in my head that wasn't reality.

Maybe it was because of what I'd said in my literature class? Maybe it was because I hadn't given him an answer about the frat boys. But...

No. Ford wasn't like that, was he?

The fact of the matter was, I knew only one side of Ford. I knew the side that had acted like an uncle to me, and not the Ford everyone else saw. Maybe I was being stupid and immature?

"Ford?"

He grunted in response and unlocked his car, but I halted on the sidewalk. There was no way I was going to get into his car while he was acting like this. "Ford," I repeated, and he finally turned to look at me. His face was a careful mask, and I knew right then that I'd lost the Ford from last night. He'd pushed him down and replaced him with this version, the version I was starting to hate. "What's going on?"

"Nothing," he replied, but it was way too fast. He was ready for my questions because he knew I'd have them.

"Last night, Ford——"

"Was a mistake," he interrupted. "You're my boss's daughter. It was a mistake that won't be repeated." His voice was so sure, but also dismissive as if he was telling me he didn't like the color pink.

I stood there, my stomach dropping and my heart beating wildly in my chest, and although part of me wanted to scream and shout and tell him he was an asshole, I just didn't have the energy. I couldn't argue with him, not when he was this closed off. I knew better than to try to talk to him when he'd put on his mask. There was no getting through to him, no making him see sense.

Not only that, but I refused to beg him to open up to me. It didn't matter how safe he made me feel. It didn't matter that he was the one man in this world who made me feel whole. Because if he didn't want it, then I wouldn't push it. We were on the edge of something, and I'd never been good at knowing my limits, but what I did know about myself was that I wasn't going to chase. I wasn't going to try and persuade him to touch me, to kiss me. No matter how much I wanted it.

If he thought it was a mistake, then that was his viewpoint, whether I believed him or not. I opened my mouth, not sure what was going to come out, and he pushed his shoulders back, almost as if he was bracing himself for a fight. Did he think that was what he was going to get from me? I'd fought almost everything growing up, but I was different now. And this situation wasn't me being told I couldn't have cookies before dinner. This was Ford telling me that him touching me was a mistake, and I couldn't help but feel part of my heart crack. I'd imagined this for so long, and now I was just tired. Tired of being the person people could push aside. Tired of being the little girl in everyone's eyes.

No more. I wasn't going to let people put me into their own little boxes. "Right." I nodded and pushed my shoulders back, determined not to let it look like he'd affected me. He wasn't the only one who could school his expression. "If that's how you feel…" I trailed off, giving him the chance to tell me otherwise, but all he did was stare at me with his uncrackable hazel-eyed gaze. "Okay." I swallowed, then repeated, "Okay."

I didn't know how to react to his steely stare because I'd never been confronted with anything like it before. Maybe I was too close? Or maybe I was afraid if I pushed too much that I'd lose him altogether, and the thought of losing him wasn't one I could entertain. So I did what I always did. I accepted what he had to say and moved to the passenger side of the car, then slipped inside.

He didn't get in for several seconds, but when he did, I looked out of my window, intent on not giving him my stare. I couldn't let him see how much his couple of words had shattered me. I hated how much I felt for him while he didn't feel a thing. I was off-balance, sure to be the only loser here, and I needed to do something to put me back on track.

Which was the reason I messaged Curtis, telling him to bring a bottle of tequila to my apartment.

If Ford was only going to be here to make sure I was safe, then I may as well let loose. I'd never let myself go fully, so I was going to take advantage.

Plus, trying to forget about the last twenty-four hours by drinking it away was alluring.

It only took us a couple of minutes to get to my apartment block, and as soon as we were inside, I headed for my bedroom to get changed into my pj's. Tequila, pj's, and a shitty movie on TV would fix the mood I was now in, or at least help a little.

Knocking sounded throughout the apartment about fifteen minutes later, and I stepped out of my bedroom just in time to see Ford answer it.

"Who are you?" I heard Curtis ask.

I danced down the hallway and pushed up onto my tiptoes so my face could be seen over Ford's shoulder and grinned at him. "He's a family friend staying with us. Did you bring it?"

Curtis flicked his gaze to Ford and then back to me. "Hell yeah, I did." He held the tequila in the air. "You gonna invite me in or what?"

"No," Ford growled. He crossed his arms over his chest and stared Curtis down, but I was so over him right now. I didn't have the patience for his demands. He didn't get a say in what I did or how I acted, especially after what he'd said.

"Come in, Curtis." I pushed past Ford and grabbed the bottle of tequila.

"Belle," Ford grunted, wrapping his hand around my wrist to stop me. I raised a brow at it and then stared up at him, silently warning him to let me go. "What are you doing?"

"Being a college girl and letting loose." I waited for a beat, knowing that secretly I was baiting him, but he didn't bite. He just let me go, huffed out a breath, and then took a step back to allow Curtis to come in.

"I got limes too," Curtis said.

"I'll get the salt!" I sauntered into the kitchen and grabbed shot glasses and salt with Ford on my tail. I could tell he wanted to say something, but he was keeping his mouth shut. Maybe it was because he regretted crossing the line by kissing me in my room, or maybe it was because he knew it didn't matter what he said to me right then. Nothing would change my mind and my decision to forget in the only way I knew how.

I moved back into the living room and sat next to Curtis on the sofa, but Ford had stayed in the kitchen. I could feel his eyes burning a path over my skin, but I wasn't going to look at him. So many things had happened in the three weeks since I'd seen Ford at the club, and I just needed a night where I could drink tequila and not think about why there was now an alarm system in my apartment, or why I was being followed everywhere.

Curtis poured us each a shot, and I downed it without a second thought. But it was as I was about to take my second shot that Ford's cell rang. I turned my head to look at him and spotted him staring down at it. He glanced at me, his hazel eyes no longer protected by the way that he felt. I could see in his swirling eyes that he wasn't happy with what I was doing, but I couldn't bring myself to care.

I licked the salt off my hand, downed my shot, and pushed the lime between my teeth, all the while staring at him. He shook his head and lifted his cell to his ear, but I didn't hear what he said as he walked down the hallway and toward my bedroom.

"So," Curtis said. "You gonna tell me what's going on?"

I shrugged. "Nothing really. Just needed some tequila and some Curtis time." I grinned up at him. "I haven't seen you for a couple of weeks, so how about you tell me what's going on."

Curtis scraped his hand over the scruff of his jaw. "Just been dealing with family shit. You know how it goes." I nodded because I did know how it went. I *really* knew how it went. "It's all sorted now though, so I'm back." He poured us each another shot and handed me my glass. "Cheers to that?"

"Cheers." I clicked my glass against his and downed the shot. "Let's watch a movie." I grabbed the remote and turned on the TV, heading straight for Netflix and pressing on the first movie I could find. I wasn't even sure what it was about, but it was just background noise to drown out my thoughts at this stage. I poured myself another shot and leaned back on the sofa, drinking it up and wincing at the burn.

"Jeez, Belle. You're going hard tonight." I chuckled at Curtis' words but didn't look over at him as he stretched his arm behind me on the back of the sofa. "You sure everything is okay?"

"Yep." I heard footsteps but didn't turn to look. "I'm good. Better than I've ever been." I kept my gaze focused on the TV, knowing that I was lying through my teeth. I wasn't good. I was so far from good it wasn't even funny, but it wasn't like I could talk about it. It wasn't like I could spill my guts to Curtis and tell him that the man I'd had a crush on since before I could even remember had kissed me and then told me it was a mistake.

In the grand scheme of things, it wasn't anything life-altering, but right then, my heart denied that truth. I was licking my wounds, and alcohol always made them heal faster.

Chapter Eight

FORD

I growled and pounded my fist on her bedroom door for the sixth time, wondering if she was ignoring me on purpose, or was still asleep after her session with Curtis last night. I'd sat and watched Belle drink herself into a stupor with Curtis next to her and got angrier and angrier the more time went by. Had I not been here, I had no idea how Curtis would have behaved with her.

It wasn't the first time I'd heard his name, but it was the first time I'd met him. And the fact that he was supplying Belle with the alcohol she wanted meant he had a black mark against his name in my book. Who the hell supplied an underage girl with alcohol? And okay, I was aware she was only underage by six months, but the law was the law for a reason, and this fucker had broken it. But I hadn't been able to do anything about it, not after what I'd said to her.

"Belle?" I called again. I huffed out a breath and looked down at the time on my watch. "You're gonna be late for your shift at the shelter."

I heard a bang come from inside her room and then a groan. "I'm awake," her rough voice said, and I couldn't help the quirk of my lips. Yesterday was a day that I wanted to forget. I didn't want to remember the way her eyes dimmed as I told her it was a mistake when we'd kissed. I didn't want to think about the sagging of her shoulders, and I really didn't want to think about the way she'd shut down her emotions in the blink of an eye and got into my car.

She didn't understand I was saving her from me. She didn't need someone like me in her life in that way. I may have been on the right side of the law now, but that didn't mean I didn't do bad things. Even the law crossed boundaries and made it okay to hurt other people. I wasn't the kind of man she should latch on to. I wasn't the kind of man who deserved someone so good in his life—at least, not in that way.

She was better off without me. All I'd do was bring her pain, and I wasn't willing to let that happen. I'd given her some bullshit excuse about it being because she was my boss's daughter, but in reality, I didn't give a fuck about that. I was doing it for her. I was denying what I wanted to protect her. Because I'd always protect Belle, at any cost.

Her bedroom door swung open, and her face appeared, covered in the largest sunglasses I'd ever seen. "Let's go," she croaked out as she pushed past me. I stared at her as she walked down the hallway and toward the front door but didn't move as she halted next to it. Even in her hungover state, she knew not to go outside without me checking first. I expected her to give me a snarky comment when I hadn't moved, but all she did was stare at me. I couldn't see her eyes behind her sunglasses, and I hated it. I hated that I couldn't tell what she was thinking.

It was on the tip of my tongue to tell her I didn't mean what I'd said yesterday. That I despised seeing Curtis next to her with his arm behind her on the back of the sofa. But I didn't. Instead, I walked toward her, pulled the door open, checked it was okay, and then gave her the nod for her to follow me.

My stomach churned the closer we got to my car, knowing we'd have to be in an enclosed space, and I wondered if she felt the same. Belle was never one to hold back on what she thought. She always made sure people around her knew exactly what she was thinking. But right then, I had no idea what was going on inside her head. Maybe that was a good thing, though. I needed to distance myself as much as I could because the closer we got, the harder it would be when I'd have to leave.

Because that was what would happen. It was inevitable that at some stage, I wouldn't be here anymore and would be undercover on another case. I'd be gone for months at a time, and that was no way for her to live. I refused to let her settle for something like that. She deserved a guy who doted on her, and more importantly, was around when she needed him, and not in the middle of nowhere trying to take down drug dealers and gangs.

And with those thoughts in mind, I knew I was doing the right thing. This was for her. I was making sure she was the happiest she could be.

The silence stretched between us as we got into the car and made our way to the shelter, and by the time we got there, she'd pulled her sunglasses off. But she didn't look at me. She just walked into the shelter and got on with her shift while I tried to fade into the background. I watched her feed all the animals and do some admin work, but it was when she opened Lottie's kennel that I nearly cracked.

She pushed her face into the fur of Lottie's neck and held on to her tightly. I knew I should have stayed toward the back of the kennels where I'd been standing for the last two hours, but I couldn't help moving closer. My feet carried me before I even realized, and by then, it was too late because Lottie had seen me.

Belle whipped her head around, her blue eyes staring up at me. "Hey," she croaked out. "My shift finishes in fifteen." She paused, her hand still stroking Lottie's back. "Is it okay if we take Lottie for a walk after my shift?"

"Yeah," I said, my voice cracking.

She nodded. "Would you get her harness and leash? It's in the office."

I spun on my heels and headed to the office without a word, needing to get away. The Belle I'd known as she grew up never held things inside, but the one around me now only seemed to do that. It was almost as if she was too scared to say what she really thought, and I didn't like that one bit. I wanted her to speak her mind, to tell me how she was feeling, but I didn't know how to get her to do that.

I grabbed the harness and leash, which had Lottie's name on, and then made my way back to them. Lottie was waiting patiently, her side pressed against Belle's thigh, and I knew the black jeans she had on would be covered in dog hair in no time.

"Thanks," Belle said as she took the leash and harness from me. It only took seconds for her to get it on Lottie, and then she locked the kennel behind her. "I'm going to tell Jamie that I'm leaving." She handed me the leash, and Lottie sat next to me, her gaze fixated on Belle as she walked away. I moved my palm between Lottie's ears and didn't move from the spot I was in until Belle reappeared.

It was awkward between us as we exited the shelter, but I didn't know what to say to break the tension. There wasn't anything I could say, not unless I was going to tell her the truth, but I wasn't sure I even wanted to admit that to myself, never mind saying it out loud. My head was a mash of thoughts, but I knew one thing—when Belle looked at me, I never wanted her to turn away.

I was here to do a job, but that didn't mean spending time with her almost twenty-four hours a day didn't enlighten me on the woman she'd become. Everyone always saw her as a little girl, someone who needed to be protected from everything. And I wasn't saying she didn't need protecting, but there was so much more to her, and I was only now seeing that.

Her caring nature, and the way she was with the animals in the shelter, spoke volumes. Not many people volunteered their time to causes like these, but she didn't even think about it like that. She loved each and every animal in this shelter, maybe a little too much. But that was the beauty of Belle. She cared more than most people.

I was witnessing a side to her I never even knew was there, and that was part of the problem. The more time I spent with her, the more time I wanted.

It was a vicious circle, one I needed to get out of as soon as I could because I was afraid that if I didn't, I'd be stuck here forever.

And I didn't hate the idea.

———

BELLE

I wasn't sure what had my eyes springing open and my ears perking up, but something had woken me up. There was no sunlight streaming through my room, just darkness surrounding me, so I knew it was the middle of the night.

My body was still as I tried to hear what had woken me up, but after several seconds of nothing, I rolled over and closed my eyes. I'd been on high alert since Ford had moved in with me, so it wasn't unusual for me to wake up thinking I'd heard something when, in reality, it was just my brain working on overdrive.

I sighed as I thought about the last few days. It had been five days since Ford had kissed me. Four since he told me it was a mistake, and things hadn't been the same between us since. He was distant, but so was I. I wasn't willing to expose myself, not when he'd shut me down so epically. I told myself over and over again that I was living in a fantasy world. I'd made the entire thing up in my head. I'd imagined the way he looked at me, and the way he touched me.

It was the only way I could get past what he'd said.

I inhaled a deep breath and told myself to stop thinking about it, but as soon as I was starting to fall back asleep, I heard the noise again. I stilled. I hadn't imagined it that time. I knew I hadn't. A scraping sound, but I couldn't place where it was from. It sounded close, but also far away, but maybe that was because my blood was pumping through my body so fast that I could hear it in my ears.

A small thud echoed and then scraping again, and I realized it was coming from my bedroom window. I lifted my head a little, trying to see what it was, and a small light flashed. I gasped and then slammed my hand over my mouth. How the hell had someone gotten that high up? And how did they know this was my window?

My heart beat wildly in my chest, and even though I knew they couldn't get in through the new safety windows Ford had installed, I was panicking. I had to get out of my room.

I slowly slid to the other side of my bed and kept my gaze latched on to the window. My blind was three-quarters of the way down, so I could only see a sliver, but I could tell someone was out there because of the shadows.

My body slipped off the side of my bed, and I

crawled toward my door, then slowly reached up. The door handle squeaked, and I winced, wondering if whoever was out there could hear me. But when the scraping rang out again, I knew they hadn't.

I opened the door, just enough for me to squeeze through, and once I was out in the hallway, I stood. For a second, I stood there, wondering for the thousandth time if I'd imagined it, but metal banging against metal had my feet sprinting down the hallway and to Ford in the living room.

A small lamp near the kitchen was on, giving just enough light to illuminate his sleeping face. His hand was behind his head, his blanket covering half of his bare chest, but I didn't have time to take in the tattoos that I'd only ever seen part of. I didn't have the chance to see if they continued down his back. Not when a click rang out in the apartment.

My head swung to the door, and my heart pounded. Would they try and get in that way too?

"Ford," I whispered, and when he didn't answer me, I crouched down and pressed my palm against his bicep, pushing on it. "Ford." His eyes opened, and his hand whipped out, grabbing my wrist in a vise-tight grip. "Ford," I repeated again, and at the sound of my voice, the pressure on my wrist lowered, but he didn't let go. "Someone is trying to get into my bedroom window."

I thought it'd take a second for what I'd said to

sink in, but it didn't. He sprang up off the sofa, revealing his bare chest and abs, and reached for something underneath the pillow his head had been resting on. I spotted the blink of metal and knew it was a gun.

He hadn't let go of my wrist, and he continued to hold it as he pulled me down the hallway and toward my bedroom. "Stay here," he whispered, and I stared at his back as he flung open my bedroom door and slammed the lights on. He lunged over my bed and yanked on my blind string, causing it to fly up my window, and then he was face to face with someone dressed entirely in black. All I could see were two dark eyes, and then he was gone.

Ford leaped through my bedroom and grabbed ahold of me again as he rushed into the living room and grabbed his cell. "Open my laptop," he demanded, and I reached for it on the coffee table and did as I was told. He pressed his cell against his ear. "Agent Easton." He looked over at me, his swirling eyes meeting mine. "Password BB-seven-two-nine." I wasn't sure if he was talking to me or the person on the line, but when he pointed at me and then the laptop, I realized it was possible he was telling us both.

I typed in the password, and the computer came to life. I didn't take in what was on his home screen as I turned it around. He crouched down in front of me, still talking on his cell and clicked the keys. My hands started to shake, my body going into shock. Someone had tried to break into my apartment. And it was then I realized just how real the threat was.

What would they have done if they would have gotten inside? Would they have taken me? Would they have killed me? Was I really that important?

"Belle." Ford's voice sounded far away, but his hands gripping my face pulled me into the here and now. "Belle." I swallowed and blinked, causing a lone tear to slip from the corner of my eye. "Sweetheart," he croaked out. "It's okay. You're safe."

"Why?" I asked, my voice sounding nothing like my own. "Why am I so important that they want to break in?"

Ford moved closer and gripped my face harder. "Because he knows that the way to get to me is through the people I care about most. He's been running searches on all of us. Your dad called yesterday to tell me. You're the only way he can get to us—get to me."

"I..." I pulled in a stuttering breath. "I'm scared, Ford."

"I know, sweetheart." He pressed his forehead to mine. "But I won't let him get you. I promise. I'd die before he got his hands on you." The way he said it had no doubt in my mind that Ford would do everything in his power to keep me safe, but that didn't mean I was safe. They'd tried to get into my bedroom window, and the alarm that Ford had installed hadn't even gone off. If I hadn't woken up…

I couldn't even think about what would have happened.

Loud banging on the door had me jumping in my seat, and I grabbed Ford's arm, my eyes wide. "It's okay," Ford said, turning the laptop to face me. "It's just backup."

I stared down at the screen and saw four frames. Each was black and white, but one looked out from the front door and toward two guys, waiting on the other side of it. "What…what's that?"

"Surveillance," Ford grunted. He lifted my hand off his arm as they knocked on the door again. "Take my laptop to keep watch and go into Stella's room. Don't come out until I get you."

I couldn't stop looking at his laptop as I tried to make sense of it. There were three other cameras, all pointing on the outside of the building, and then in the corner, there was a little box with four more frames, and when I looked closer, I saw it was inside the apartment. How did I not even know he had cameras in here?

"Belle."

I blinked and shook my head. "Yeah?"

"Did you hear me? Go into Stella's room and don't come out until I come and get you."

I swallowed and nodded, then stood on shaky

legs. My body was taking a minute to realize what was going on. I halted in front of Stella's door and knocked on it twice, then opened it up. She'd said Justin was staying at his place tonight, but I wasn't sure if she'd be with him or not.

The darkness of her room had my heart racing, so I switched on the light and jumped out of my skin when Stella shot up in bed, her hair a matted mess around her face.

"What the fuck?" Stella rubbed at her eyes, but it took her a few seconds to open them, and in that time, I closed the door behind me and then started to hear voices coming from the living room. Half of me wanted to be out there with Ford, but the other half wanted to hide in a closet until Ford told me the monsters were all gone.

"I…I need to stay in here."

"Huh?" Stella finally looked at me, her brows furrowed. "What's going on?"

I clutched Ford's laptop to my chest and tried to find the right words. I didn't want to scare her, but I needed her to know that Ford being here was for something very real and not just in case something would happen. "Someone tried to break in through my bedroom window."

"What the…" Stella slipped out of her bed and lunged at me. Her arms wrapped around me, but I just stood there, as still as a statue. "What happened?" She pulled back but kept her hands planted on my shoulders.

"I…I don't know. I woke up and…" I huffed out a breath, and my body sagged against her. "Someone was trying to get in, so I got Ford, and now there's police here and—" I tried to swallow back the lump building in my throat. "Ford told me to come in here until he comes and gets me."

"Okay." Stella maneuvered me toward her bed. "Come sit."

I did as she said, then placed the laptop on my legs. The warmth of it hit my thighs, and it was then I realized all I was wearing was a tank top and my boy shorts.

"What's that?" Stella asked, and I turned to look at her, but all her attention was on the screen.

"It's the cameras Ford has set up." I spotted him standing in the doorway of the apartment. I wondered why he wasn't checking the outside, leaving it to the backup that had turned up really quickly, but I had a feeling it was because he didn't want to leave the apartment with me inside.

"Jesus, Belle. This is some serious shit. I didn't think anything would actually happen, but fuck."

"I know," I whispered. "I didn't either." And I didn't. I'd lived my entire life knowing that there were threats out there because of what my dad did, but they'd never touched me. I'd never been close to anything like this, and now I was firmly in the middle, and all I wanted to do was escape.

Stella and I sat on the edge of her bed for twenty-seven minutes until I heard the front door close and then the beeping of the alarm. I watched on the screen as Ford came toward Stella's room, and I stood, opening the door before he could lift his hand to knock.

His swirling hazel eyes met mine, but then they focused on Stella. "The alarm wasn't on."

Stella gasped, and I turned to see her eyes wide and hand covering her mouth. "Justin left just after midnight, and I forgot to turn it on."

Ford made a noise in the back of his throat. "If the alarm would have been on, as soon as someone tried to get in, it would have gone off and sent a signal straight to the local station and to Belle's dad. It's important that it gets put on."

"I…I didn't realize."

I expected Ford to say more than that, but when I turned to face him again, he just nodded and then took hold of my wrist. "Get some sleep," he told Stella, pulling me out of the room. "We'll talk about it tomorrow."

I followed Ford back into the living room, still holding on to his laptop. I didn't know why I expected him to stop, but he didn't. He led me back to my bedroom and then took the laptop off me.

"You too, Baby Belle." I wrapped my arms around myself as he stared down at me. "Get some sleep."

"I…" I pulled in a breath and tried to be strong. I couldn't show him any weakness, not when he was used to strong people around him at all times. I felt like a whiny girl next to everyone else he knew, so instead of telling him I was scared, I pushed my shoulders back and stepped into my room.

His face was a carefully placed mask as he closed the door, leaving me standing there in my room, terrified of turning around and looking at the window. Having his laptop with me had been the security I'd needed not to think about what had just happened, but now I was alone, back in my room, scared to death to be in here.

I turned around slowly, my gaze hitting every-thing but my window. My palms became clammy, my stomach bottomed out, and every bone in my body screamed at me to get out of this room.

"Belle?"

I squealed, my heart racing even more than it already was. Ford's voice was close, almost as if he hadn't moved since he closed the door. "You okay?"

"I…yeah, I'm fine," I croaked out.

I heard a huff, and then the squeak of my door handle, and I felt him step into my room. "No, you're not." His voice had my heart rate slowing, and I hated how much I needed him at that moment, but I wouldn't lie to myself.

"I'm just…" I turned to face him, hoping he could tell what I was thinking so I didn't have to voice it, and from the way he stared down at me, I knew he could see it.

"Want me to sleep on the floor in here?"

I clutched my hands in front of me and whispered, "Yes, please."

He nodded, almost as if he was telling himself something. "Okay." He placed his laptop and cell on my bedside table and then walked out of the room, but he was back seconds later with his pillow and blanket.

"I'm being stupid," I whispered, wishing I could be the strong woman my mom had brought me up to be. "The alarm is on and—"

"No." Ford placed his hands on my shoulders, and I shivered from the contact. "You're not being stupid. It's normal to feel what you're feeling right now. Don't try and push it down and pretend it's not there. The Belle I knew—the Belle I've gotten to know over the last month—wouldn't do that. She'd feel every single emotion and not give two shits about it." His lips quirked. "Now, get into bed. We have a day full of classes tomorrow."

I pulled in a breath and tried to center myself. "Okay."

His hands slid off my shoulders, and I wished he didn't have to stop touching me. At least when his skin was connected with mine, I was grounded. But now I just felt like I was floating on the wind like a lone balloon.

Ford made his pallet on the floor near the door as I slid back into my bed and pulled the covers up to my chin. There was nothing between me and the window, and I couldn't stop staring at it, not even when Ford turned out the lights. My gaze refused to move off the window, just in case someone was still out there. What if they came back? What if they were just waiting for me to be asleep again, and then they'd try a second time.

A tear fell from my eye, and it was closely followed by another one. I didn't know what had caused it, maybe my body needed relief from what had happened, but I couldn't hold them in, and the lump in my throat became so big, I couldn't swallow past it.

I was so inside my own head that I didn't hear Ford moving around the room until he was crouched beside me between the bed and the window. "Sweetheart," he whispered, and that one word said so much more than just its syllables. "No one can get to you now."

"I know," I choked out, not looking away from the window. "But...I just..." I ripped my gaze away from the pane of glass and stared right into Ford's eyes. He was so close I could feel each of his breaths on my face. "I'm just...I can't stop looking."

Ford was silent for several seconds, his attention

not moving off me, and then he said, "Move over." I didn't hesitate to do as he said, and as soon as I was on the other side of my bed, he moved in next to me. He lay on his back and turned his head to face me. "Better?"

I couldn't bring myself to say anything, so instead, I just nodded and closed my eyes. Even if I couldn't fall asleep, I'd at least try to. I counted his breaths and kept as still as I could with the space separating us.

Chapter Nine

FORD

It didn't matter how many times I told myself to pull away from Belle, I always found myself getting closer and closer. The bond we had was unbreakable. And after last night, all I wanted was to hold her as tight as I could and protect her from the evil that was trying to get her.

Belle was pure. As pure as they came. At least, she was in my eyes. She didn't deserve to be part of this fucked-up world, but she was. She was born into it the day Lola had given birth. It was only now it was finally finding her, and I knew it was partly my fault. If I hadn't had a reaction when Garza had mentioned Belle, we wouldn't be in this position. She'd be safe here, and I'd probably still be undercover.

The dark sky started to lighten, and I looked at the time on my cell. 3:45 a.m. My movement caused Belle to shuffle closer, and I swallowed as her hand landed on my bare chest. I hadn't thought about the fact that I was in bed with her, not until that very moment. All I'd been concerned about was making her feel safe, but now...now I was only too aware of how close we were, and the fact she was asleep, and I couldn't stop staring at her.

Her small button nose led down to her parted lips, and each of her exhales made a small noise that I was becoming slowly obsessed with. But it was the way her lashes rested against her cheeks that had me enthralled. Her light-brown hair fanned around her and rested on her shoulder, where the strap of her tank top had fallen down.

I didn't know what possessed me to reach out and right the strap, but as soon as my fingertips touched her soft skin, her eyes slowly opened. The blue of her irises was so much brighter as she stared at me, and there was a life behind them that I craved to be part of. There may have been twenty-two years between us, but at that moment, all that separated us was the space in the bed that I craved to evaporate.

Neither of us said a word as I righted her strap and then trailed my finger across her collarbone and up her neck, landing on her lips. I hadn't been able to stop thinking about them since I'd first touched them, and it was time I was honest.

"I lied," I croaked out, trying to keep my voice low. I stared at her lips for a beat and then flicked my gaze up to her eyes. I could see the question showcased in them, but I didn't give her the chance to ask it as I said, "It wasn't a mistake."

Her tongue swiped over her lips, and then she whispered, "What wasn't a mistake?"

My palm flattened on the side of her face, and the tips of my long fingers pushed into her hair. "The kiss." I turned my body so I was closer to her, and she answered me by shuffling toward me.

"But you said——"

"I don't care what I said." I pressed my body flush with hers, needing to feel her against every part of me. "I fuckin' lied to you, sweetheart. You think I give a fuck if you're my boss's daughter?" I gritted my teeth, trying to tell myself to slow down, to take my time, but it was impossible when it came to Belle. "I didn't want you involved in this fucked-up life. People think just because we're on the right side of the law, everything is fine, but it's not, Baby Belle." I took a breath, about to reveal things to her that I'd never told anyone, but her hand pushing through my hair had me speechless.

"So what I hear you saying is that you did want to kiss me?" The small quirk of her lips had me drifting even closer to her.

"No." I shook my head. "I didn't want to kiss you." I wrapped my arm around her waist and yanked her against me. "I fuckin' needed too." Our breaths mingled, and something snapped inside me. The carefully placed control I'd held on to for my entire life evaporated, and I knew I was about to take exactly what I wanted. "Just like now."

She opened her mouth, about to answer me, but I wasn't willing to give her the chance to say anything else. Words could be spoken all day long, but it was my actions that mattered most. She should have known I was lying because there was no way I kissed someone just because it took my fancy. When I opened myself up, I meant it, and I'd never opened myself up like this. I'd never wanted to. But as Belle's eyes focused on me, I knew if I was to do it with anyone, it would be with her.

I slammed my lips onto hers, taking everything I needed, but I hadn't expected her to be just as fierce back. She didn't let me take over and dominate. No, she was fighting for control just as much as I was, and I couldn't do anything but relent to it. She wanted this as much as I did, and I wasn't going to put a stop to it. For the first time in my life, I was putting myself first and not worrying about everyone else around me.

I rocked my hips against her, my body taking over, and Belle's answer was to roll on top of me and place her legs either side of mine. We were going hard and fast, and I wasn't thinking about what would happen after this. I wasn't thinking about tomorrow or next week. All I was thinking about was the way her body felt against mine and how I hated the clothes which separated us.

Pulling back a little, our lips parted, and I stared at her as I sat up. Her face was the same level as mine, and I slowly reached for the bottom of her tank top. My rough fingers trailed over her stomach as I pulled it up, and as soon as it was over her head, and her chest was bared to me, I dived for her nipples.

The moan she let loose was the best sound I'd ever heard, so I sucked on the pink bud harder and lapped my tongue against it, loving the way her fingers gripped my hair.

"Ford," she groaned, and I swore, every hair on my body stood on end at the sound of her breathy voice. "Please, Ford."

I wasn't sure she really knew what she was asking, but I'd bow down to her demands just to hear her say my name like that again. My palms wrapped around her waist, and I drifted my fingers lower, pushing them underneath the boy shorts she had on. I pulled back from her nipple and stared into her eyes, so bright they looked like two blue diamonds, twinkling against the lights.

"Belle," I ground out. All I wanted was to go hard and fast, but she deserved more than that. She deserved slow and sensual, but I wasn't sure I could give her that, not at that moment. Not when she was half-naked, pressed against my cock. "I need to—"

"No." She cut me off and placed her finger against my lips. "Don't think about it," she whispered, her hips jutting forward and causing my eyes to close. She was tearing me apart and gluing me back together again, all in one movement. How the hell did she do that? How the fuck did she know exactly what to do to drive me crazy and make me lose my mind?

"Just feel it, Ford." Her hand drifted over my shoulder and down my pecs, and I knew she was following the trail of my tattoos. I opened my eyes as she leaned closer and pressed her lips to my neck, then whispered, "Feel me."

I wanted to tell her that I could feel every inch of her pressed against me, but I couldn't get my words out. She was a vixen, and I had nothing in my arsenal to stop her attack. I trailed my hand up her back and wrapped my palm around the back of her neck, then pulled her back so she could stare into my eyes. I needed her to see how serious I was, and the only way she could do that was by looking into my eyes.

"I'm only gonna say this once, Baby Belle. You want to forget this happened, then you need to get off of me right now." I paused, waiting to see what she would do. But when she didn't move, I continued, "Because right now, you're seeing me holding back, but if you rub yourself against my cock once more, I ain't gonna be able to—" I groaned as she moved her hips against me, and that was all the answer I needed to slam my lips back down onto hers.

I spun us around and laid her on the bed, throwing the covers off so they didn't get in my way. Nothing could separate us, not now that she'd given me her silent answer. Actions spoke louder than words, and her actions had screamed in my face.

My lips traveled down her body, between her breasts, down to her hips, until I was centimeters away from her pussy. I inhaled a deep breath and flicked my gaze up at her. She was watching me in a daze, her hands gripping on to the sheet below us, and I grinned up at her.

I latched on to one side of her boy shorts and held them tight. I twisted them, and the tearing of material was the only sound in the room right before she gasped. I didn't give a fuck if they were her favorite because they had to go. And fuck…I didn't know what I expected once they were off her body, but it wasn't what I saw. Part of me wanted to take my time and stare at her pussy, but that side of me wasn't in control, so I dived right in and licked her. My tongue flattened so I could touch as much as I could, and her answering moan and hands gripping my hair were exactly what I wanted.

"Ford," she groaned out and pushed her hips closer to my face.

I moved my hands beneath her, my fingers biting into the soft skin of her ass as I held her to me and feasted like I hadn't eaten for months. And that was exactly what it felt like. I'd never tasted something so goddamn divine. Maybe it was because she was forbidden fruit, or maybe it was because I'd been holding myself back for so long. Or maybe it was just because she was Belle, and impossible to resist.

"I don't know how much more I can take," Belle gasped, her fingers tightening so much in my hair that my scalp burned. But I could feel how wet she was as I licked her harder and faster. She was close, and I wasn't willing to let up.

I pulled away so I could look up at her and licked my lips, tasting her all over me. Her head was thrown back, her chest pushed up in the air, and it was the sweetest sight I'd ever seen. "Hold tight, sweetheart." Her gaze met mine, and I winked at her before I dove back in, going even faster this time and needing to feel her pulsating clit as she let herself go for me.

It was mere seconds until she was shouting my name, and then I latched on to her clit. She went off like a rocket, fast, impactful, and fuckin' beautiful. I could have felt, tasted, and listened to her orgasm all day long.

"Fuck, Ford," she groaned out, and I finally let go of her pussy and climbed over her. I swiped my arm over my lips.

"You like that, sweetheart?"

Her hands cupped each side of my face, and I expected her to shy away from me, but she just planted her lips against mine and pushed her tongue inside my mouth. Wrapping my arms around her, I pressed the length of my body against hers, feeling her wetness on my sweats.

"Take them off," she whispered, wrapping her legs around my waist. Her gaze connected with mine, and I could see how much she wanted this with just one look. I pushed my hips up and moved one of my arms around so I could yank my sweats off. We were so close, only a sheet of paper could separate us, and as soon as the tip of my cock touched her skin, I nearly lost it.

"Baby Belle," I groaned out, my voice deeper and rougher than I'd ever heard it. "I need to feel you."

"Please," she begged with a tilt of her hips. That one move had the tip of my cock pushing against her wetness. Neither of us looked away as I wrapped my hand around the base and guided myself to her opening.

"Fuck." I tensed so much I was sure my teeth

would crack from the intensity. "You feel so fuckin' good." I was only an inch or so in, but it was all I needed to know nothing would be the same again. Not after kissing her. Not after touching her.

She wrapped her arms around my waist, and I pushed down on my knees and lifted her up. There was nothing I wanted more than to look down and watch as she pushed herself onto my cock, but I couldn't resist the lure of her eyes. They were pulling me in, holding me captive, and threatening not to let me go.

Her mouth opened, and a small gasp slipped out, and then I was fully inside her. She winced a little, but I knew it was just her adjusting to my size.

I gripped her at the waist, our chests connected, and then asked, "You ready, Baby Belle?"

She pressed her forehead to mine. "Always." That one word meant so much more than just *for now*, but I didn't want to think about it, not when she was attached to me in every way possible.

I lifted her slightly and then brought her back down, going slow, but she wasn't having any of it. She pulsed her own rhythm, and it was driving me crazy. Every inch of my body wanted to take control. Belle was testing my limits, but if there was anyone I could give in to, it would be her. But I couldn't do it right then, so I moved us back down to the bed and pistoned my hips faster and harder, loving the way her boobs bounced from the movement. My hand was connected with hers, our gazes locked, and it was right then I knew…

Nothing would ever be the same, not after this.

————

BELLE

I wasn't sure what to say. For hours my brain had been thinking of word combinations, but each time I opened my mouth, nothing would come out.

I'd slept with Ford.

I'd had sex with him.

I'd shown him a part of me I never thought I would.

And I didn't regret a single second of it.

But whether he did was another matter. We'd only had a couple of minutes in bed after the epicness that was our sex before his cell had rung. I wasn't sure if he knew I'd seen my dad's name flashing on the screen, but his slew of curse words as he jumped out of my bed and yanked his sweats on made me nervous.

And now we were alone again. His call had lasted a couple of hours, and I could hear the rest of the team as he switched to his laptop. I had no doubt he was on a video call, and after what had happened last night, I wasn't surprised they were talking for so long. But it didn't help my nerves.

Would he tell me it was a mistake, just like he had the day after he kissed me in my bedroom? Or would he stand by what he said? He'd been confronted with the reality of who I was only minutes after shattering my world with a mind-blowing orgasm. So what now? What happened from here? I had no idea, but what I did know was I wanted to do it again. The ball was in his court, and I hated how much he controlled it.

Ford walked beside me as we moved toward his car. He opened my door for me, just like he always did, but I noticed how he made sure not to touch me. My shoulders sagged. I'd laid myself bare for him, and he'd taken me without a second thought. And now...now I was the girl who had been taken for a fool and—

My cell ringing cut me off just as Ford closed the door. I pulled it out, not really looking at the screen as I pressed the answer call button and placed it next to my ear.

"Hello?"

"Belle?" Mom shouted down the line and nearly pierced my eardrum. "Thank god! Your dad just told me what happened last night. Are you okay? Do you need me to come down to you? Maybe you should come home and—"

I laughed at how fast she spoke. "I'm fine, Mom. I promise." I glanced at Ford as he started the engine, but his attention was focused ahead of him as he drove out of the lot.

"Are you sure? I can be down there in a few hours. I'm ready, all I have to do is—"

"Really, Mom. I'm okay." I swallowed and looked out of the passenger window, watching as other cars drove by us. "Ford is here and—"

"Ford." I heard Mom heave a sigh. Ford and Mom knew each other from way back. In fact, they'd known each other longer than Dad and Ford. "Thank fuck he was there."

"Mom!" My eyes widened. "Language."

"What?" she asked, and I could imagine her face was one of innocence. "I think if there is one situation where I can say 'fuck,' then this is it. Someone tried to break in and steal my baby. When I find out who it is, I'm gonna skin them alive. And I swear to god, they will not know what hit them. I'll chop their balls off and—"

"Okay, okay. Calm down, you psycho." I held my hand out in front of me even though she couldn't see it. Mom wasn't a violent kind of person. She'd told me about her past and the violence she'd had at the hands of someone who was meant to love her, but she still hated it as much as she did back then. Unless it was someone she loved. Then I could imagine she'd kill for them. Mom was protective, but that was nothing compared to Dad. And I couldn't help but think about what they'd do if they found out Ford and I had slept together. One of their friends, part of the family, and we'd crossed a line I wasn't sure we could ever come back from. I shook my head and tried to focus on the here and now, even though Ford was literally inches away from me.

"We all know what a badass you are, Mom." I closed my eyes and tried not to think about last night and how frightened I was. "I'm sure it won't happen again."

"But what if it does? I'm terrified, Belle." I could hear the shakiness in her voice, something I'd only heard a couple of times. "You shouldn't have to be worrying about this. All you should be thinking about are boys, studies, and parties."

I smirked as Ford pulled up in a parking spot outside the building my first class was in. "In that order?"

"Well, maybe studies, boys, and then parties."

I tilted my head to the side, glad we weren't talking about the events that had taken place last night and that my mind was overthinking what had happened after it. "So not parties, boys, and then studies?"

"Hmmm, it's a tough one, sweetie. I think you need parties before boys so you can meet boys at parties but—"

"The hell you talking about parties for?" Dad's booming voice came over the line, and I winced,

182

knowing there was no way I was going to get away without speaking to him.

"What? I'm not," Mom said, her voice high-pitched. "I'm—"

"Who are you talking to?" Dad asked, and he was even closer now.

"Belle." There was some shuffling and a grunt, and then Mom shouted, "Hey, give me that back!"

"Belle?" Dad asked, and I imagined he'd taken the cell off Mom.

"Hey, Dad." I looked at Ford, but he was staring out of the windshield, his hands gripping the steering wheel like it was his lifeline.

"You should come home," Dad ordered, brooking no room for an argument, but I wasn't going to bow down to him.

"We've been through this, Dad." My head dropped back, and I stared at the ceiling of the car. "There's only a couple of weeks until spring break. I'll be fine until then, at least." I didn't want to think about how slow the time from now until then would go. I wouldn't admit to any of them how scared I was because I knew the moment I did, there wouldn't be any turning back. They'd shoot down my need to stay at college and take over, but that wasn't what I needed. I needed to feel safe in my own home, and I wasn't sure if that would ever happen again.

"I don't like it, baby girl. You're out there with

only Ford and he can't—"

"He's doing his job, Dad." I closed my eyes, and the image of Ford on top of me was the first thing I saw. That wasn't his job, but damn if I didn't want to relive it all over again. "Look, I've got to go. My class starts in five."

His frustrated groan rang over the line, and I could imagine the muscle in his jaw ticking. "This conversation isn't over, Belle."

I opened my eyes and sat up straighter. "Okay."

"I'll call you later." There was a pause, and then he continued, "Here, let me put your mom back on. She's giving me a death stare."

"Damn straight, I am. You're using your height to best me." There was a grunt and then a groan, and Mom said, "Serves you right, Brody. Now, what was I saying?"

I chuckled and shook my head. I missed living at home sometimes. "To go to parties and meet lots of boys?" My gaze swerved over to Ford, but I couldn't look at his face, so concentrated on his knuckles as they turned white on the steering wheel.

"Ah, yes. That's it." Mom laughed. "Are you really okay, sweetie? I can come and stay with you; it's no trouble."

"Really, Mom, I'm good. Look, I gotta go to class. I'll call you later?"

"Okay, sweetie. I love you so much."

"Love you too, Mom." I waited a beat until I

ended the call, and then complete silence surrounded me.

I glanced up at the building my class was in, but not one part of me wanted to walk in there. Someone had tried to get me inside my own home, and I couldn't help think how much easier it would be in a busy college. Maybe Dad was right. Maybe I should go home. But no, I couldn't surrender. I just needed some time. I needed some space to think about what had happened and—

Ford started the engine, and I whipped my head around to face him. "What are you doing?"

He didn't answer me for several seconds, not until he was pulling out of the lot and back on the road. "I'm taking you somewhere," he gritted out, and I couldn't tell if he was angry or frustrated.

"But I've got class—"

"And there's no way you're going to be able to concentrate." He pulled up at a stoplight and looked at me. His hazel eyes were darker than usual, but it was the small smile he gave me that put me at ease. "Give yourself a day, sweetheart." He reached out and grasped my hand, and brought it onto his lap. "You need to give yourself time to think everything over." The light turned green, and he turned his attention back on the road, but he didn't let go of my hand. "Besides, I have a surprise for you."

"You do?" I asked, relaxing back in the seat and watching him. The farther we got from the college, the more he lowered into his seat and seemed to relax too.

"Yep." He lifted our joined hands and placed a kiss on top of my knuckles, and that was all I needed to know he didn't regret what happened this morning. He was showing me what he felt rather than telling me, and I was more than okay with that.

I grinned at him and closed my eyes, basking in the happiness surrounding me, even if it was only for a couple of minutes. At some stage, I must have fallen asleep, because Ford's palm whispering over my cheek and his murmured, "We're here, sweetheart," woke me up.

My eyes fluttered open, and it took several seconds for me to take in my surroundings. "The shelter?" One side of my lips lifted, and butterflies took flight in my stomach. He knew how much I loved the animals here, so he'd brought me to the one place that would make me feel better.

Ford didn't say anything as he pushed out of the car and checked around us, then opened up the passenger door. He took hold of my hand again and pulled me close to him, but bypassed the back entrance.

"What are you doing?" I asked, my brows furrowing. We never went in the front entrance.

"I have an appointment," he said so casually it was as if he was telling me the sky was blue. I opened my mouth to tell him I was confused, but he opened the door and led me inside. It was like I was in an alternate universe as I saw Courtney behind the main desk. Courtney was the manager of the shelter, and I'd only met her a handful of times.

"Special Agent Ford," Ford greeted her, holding his hand out, and my stomach dipped at the way he said his name and the deep tone he'd used. "I have an appointment."

"Ah, yes…" Courtney fumbled with some paperwork, her gaze moving to mine and flitting away again before she realized who I was. "Belle?" she asked.

"Hey." I wasn't sure what else to say because I had no idea what was going on here in the slightest. I was an innocent bystander along for the ride.

Courtney stared at me for a beat and then moved her attention back to Ford. "She's all ready for you. I wasn't expecting you until later, though. When you called this morning, I must have misheard you—"

"No, you didn't," Ford interrupted and widened his stance. "There was a change of plans. Is that okay?"

Courtney nodded, way too many times to look normal. "No, no, it's okay. I'll just …erm…" She shuffled some papers. "I need you to sign these, and then the adoption will be finalized. Of course, as a law enforcement agent, there are a few other forms you need to fill in too." She handed Ford the papers. "I'll go and get her and the feeding leaflet."

I stared at her as she moved into the back of the shelter and then looked over at Ford. He let my hand go and picked up the pen sitting on top of the papers and started to sign them without even looking.

"You should read those," I told him.

"Already did."

"Huh? When—"

"Last week." He glanced at me, a smirk on his face. "It gets boring watching you sit at a computer when you're on shift."

"Hey! I do more than just sit at the computer." I planted my hands on my hips. "I feed the dogs, I take them for walks, I play with them. I stroke the cats—"

"I know you do." Ford placed the pen back on the counter and pushed the forms forward. "Damn, Belle. You look so goddamn sexy when you're mad." He stepped toward me, and I wanted to melt into him when his arm wrapped around my waist. "Fuck. You've got me tied up in knots over here."

"Good." I narrowed my eyes at him. "Now, tell me what is going on."

"I'm adopting an animal," he said and dipped down so his face was level with mine. "That okay with you?"

"I…you can't have it at the apartment. I already told you, Justin is allergic—"

"Then Justin will just have to deal or not come around while I'm there." His eyes flashed. "Got it?"

I swallowed and pressed closer to him, my hand moving from my hip to his chest as I whispered, "Got it."

I lifted up on my tiptoes, our lips centimeters apart, but the sound of a bark had me stalling. My eyes widened as I dipped to the side and saw Lottie standing there next to Courtney. She didn't pull on her leash to get to us, but I could tell she wanted to by the way she was standing with her weight forward.

"You…I…Ford, what…"

Ford spun around so he was looking in the same direction as me, his arm latching on to my waist. "Belle, I want you to meet my new dog, Lottie."

Tears sprung to my eyes, and I couldn't help but kneel on the floor and hold my arms open for her. Courtney let her go, and Lottie lunged for me, her tongue coming out and licking my face in excitement.

"You were just in time, too," Courtney said as she moved back behind the counter. "There were only two weeks left until she'd have to be put—"

"I know," Ford growled, cutting her off. "Is the paperwork in order?" he asked her, and even though I wanted to see what they were doing, I was too engrossed with getting doggy cuddles from Lottie. She was excited, more excited than I'd ever seen her, and it was then I realized what Ford had done.

He knew Lottie would have to be put down, so he'd saved her. He'd saved her because he knew how much she meant to me. He may have adopted her, but I had no doubt she would be just as much my dog as she was his. And he'd read the paperwork a week ago. That was after he'd told me us kissing was a mistake. It was after he'd let me believe he didn't feel anything for me.

Ford always said actions spoke louder than words, and if this action was his way of saying sorry, he was forgiven entirely.

Chapter Ten

FORD

I stared at the screen of my laptop as I waited for the call from Brody. The footage from the cameras in the apartment was on my screen, and I couldn't stop looking at Belle. She sat on the sofa in the living room with Lottie curled up on her feet, not willing to move even an inch away from her. They'd been like that from the moment we'd brought Lottie home from the shelter a few days ago. She was her shadow, and I had no idea how she'd act when we had to leave for classes or for one of Belle's shifts.

So far, we'd stayed inside, only going out when Lottie needed walking. Belle said she was ready to go back to class, but I wasn't prepared to put her at risk. The near break-in last week had put me on high alert—even more so than I already was. Not to mention what had happened afterward.

I'd let myself go. I'd taken what I'd wanted, and I didn't have a single regret. Not that morning, or each morning after that as I woke up beside her, her body pressed against mine, and her coconut-scented hair in my face. We were living in a bubble, a bubble I knew wouldn't last forever, but I was enjoying it while we were there.

My cell rang, the tone piercing the silence in the air, and I spotted Lottie's ears perking up at the sound. Brody's name flashed on the screen, so I clicked "answer call" and spoke through the speaker part of my headphones.

"Brody," I greeted.

"Ford," his gruff voice replied. "I have all the guys with me." A chorus of greetings rang out, and I could imagine them all sitting in Brody's office. Kyle was almost always on the sofa in there, and Ryan would definitely be next to the window with Jord not far from him leaning against a wall. They were predictable, too predictable sometimes.

"You got an update?" I asked, keeping my gaze fixed to the screen of my laptop as Belle stood and moved into the kitchen. She disappeared from one frame and then appeared in another. I'd installed more cameras since last week. The ones that were already there were fine, but I needed to ensure there wasn't a single blind spot in or outside of the apartment.

"Trial started this morning," Brody grunted. "DA thinks it won't take more than two weeks."

I frowned, sure I'd heard him wrong. Trials like this always took longer than that, unless they plea bargained. There'd only been one case in my entire career where the court proceedings had lasted less than fourteen days. "Two weeks?"

"Yep." I heard some shuffling over the line. "We have a solid case, so it's just a waiting game now. As soon as he's sent down, Belle will be safe, and you can come home."

Home. I wasn't sure where home was anymore. When I was a teenager, home was with my mom. We may have lived on one of the roughest, poorest blocks in the neighborhood, but I never went without. Mom always said she was too good for the likes of the people around us, and she acted like that too. She'd stick her nose up in the air and ignore the people around her. It rubbed off on me in a way people didn't like, and that was how I'd learned to defend myself. When people had an impression of you they didn't like, they made it known any way possible, and for me, it was by older kids trying to bring me down a peg or two.

Right up until the day she died, I only fought back when I absolutely had to. And then the year I turned fifteen, she passed away suddenly, and from that point, I drifted from one place to another, becoming angrier and angrier by the day.

I wasn't sure anywhere would feel like home. I hadn't felt that for over twenty-five years. But as I watched Belle sit back on the sofa with a small smile on her face, I knew she gave me the sense of home. I felt at peace when she was near me, and my raging thoughts quieted when she touched me. She didn't look at me like the monster I was inside. She didn't see the invisible blood on my hands from the men I'd killed. She didn't see the scars on my knuckles from the fights I'd both won and lost. She didn't see any of that. She just saw Ford, the man who would protect her at any cost.

When I was away on jobs, Belle would be one of the first people I'd want to see afterward because she was the closest thing to family I had. But now… now I wasn't sure. Half of my mind was stuck on how I'd seen her for her entire life, but the other half couldn't stop thinking about the noises she made when we kissed, or the way her body felt pressed against mine.

I was at a crossroads, knowing I should have taken the left turn, but when it came to Belle, I would always take the right.

"Ford?" I shook my head at the sound of Brody's voice. Fuck. I'd been thinking about his daughter while I was on a call with him, and that was the crux of this situation. Belle had me all out of sorts, and I didn't know where I was landing. She made me forget where I was, and that wasn't good for anyone, not when people relied on me to be observant.

"Sorry," I murmured, and I had no doubt they were all surprised. I never apologized...for anything. "What did you say?"

The silence stretched between us, and then he said, "Spring break. The lake house." I closed my eyes as I thought about the plan for next week. The lake house was a tradition Brody and Lola had set up years ago, but I didn't think they'd be doing it this year, not with everything that was going on. But maybe that was a reason to do it. We needed to come together and remember why we did what we did. "Asher, Lola, and I are going up on Thursday evening."

I cleared my throat. "Belle has class Friday morning, but we'll come up afterward. Should be there late evening."

"Got it," Brody grunted. "The rest of the guys are coming up Sunday." Brody huffed over the line. "I need a break. I swear this case has aged me twenty years."

I heard a snort, and then Kyle quipped, "Don't blame that gray hair on the case, old man. It's just your genes."

"Fuck you, Ky," Brody barked back, but there

wasn't anything behind it. These guys had worked together for over thirty years, and I'd been working with them for twenty. We had a banter most people didn't understand. We had to find funny in situations that would destroy us otherwise. The job we did was shadowed in darkness, but we all needed light in our lives.

A grin spread on my face as I leaned back against the headboard of Belle's bed. I was aware that things were moving at lightning speed, but I couldn't help myself. I'd never given myself to anyone the way I did with Belle, and although that should have scared me, it didn't. She was the light to my darkness, and I needed the light more and more as time went on.

Something on my laptop screen moved as I listened to Ky and Brody fling insults back and forth, and I pushed closer to see what it was. The front door opened, and then Justin and Curtis waltzed in, and my nostrils flared.

"Motherfucker," I whispered, then gritted my teeth together.

"What?" Brody asked. "What was that?" I didn't answer him for several seconds. Instead, I watched Curtis as he wrapped his arms around Belle in greeting. I had nothing against the guy, I simply couldn't stand him. I'd sat and watched him feed Belle tequila weeks ago, and I knew if I hadn't been there, he would have taken advantage. I could see it in his eyes. He wanted her, but he couldn't have her. He'd never have her if it was up to me.

He lingered too long in the hug with her, so I stood. "I gotta go."

"Ford? Everything okay?" Brody asked.

"Yeah, yeah. My cell is about to die. I'll call you tomorrow." I ended the call and slammed the lid on my laptop closed, throwing it onto Belle's bed. There was no way I was going to sit in here and watch as Curtis got closer and closer to Belle, so I pulled her bedroom door open, pushed my shoulders back, and then exited the room, intent on showing the fuckface that she was mine, and only mine.

BELLE

A lot had changed in the last week, and I wasn't sure how to process it all. I went from not having a care in the world, to realizing just how dangerous this situation was in the blink of an eye. I understood why Mom and Dad kept wanting me to come home, but what happened the other night hadn't changed my mind. I wasn't going to let the cartel win and change my entire life. I wouldn't press pause just because of them.

And then there was Ford. I wasn't really sure

what was happening between us, all I knew was that I didn't want it to stop. From the moment he'd kissed me in the club, I hadn't been able to think about anything else, but now he was showing me how he felt, each and every night. There was a side to a person you saw when they gave in to their desires, and with Ford, it was the deepest part of him.

He's always kept himself so closed off, only giving everyone around him a cut-down version of himself, but when it was just him and me, he dropped the mask he wore, and his real face was so enthralling, I could barely look away. I'd thought I'd had a crush on Ford when I was a kid, but this was so much more compared to that. He'd told me I had him tied up in knots, but he had me under his spell, and I didn't want a cure. I wanted to stay exactly where he wanted me, by his side, his skin touching mine, and our lips connected.

I ran the sole of my foot along Lottie's back, and she looked up at me, her brown eyes full of content. Ford still hadn't told me the real reason he'd adopted Lottie, but deep down, I knew it was because she'd have been put down. Since he'd been staying here and following me everywhere, he'd gotten to know the animals in the shelter, but like me, he'd always drifted toward Lottie.

When we brought her home a few days ago, I

thought it would have taken her a little while to settle in, but within minutes of walking into the apartment, she'd found her spot next to the sofa and fell asleep. Just where she was right now. Her front paw covered my foot as I half lay, half sat on the sofa, watching something on the TV. I wasn't even sure what was on because I was concentrating on the noise coming from my bedroom.

Ford had gone in there thirty minutes ago, and I hadn't seen him since. Tonight we were meant to be ordering takeout and watching trash TV, but when the front door opened and Stella, Justin, and Curtis appeared, I knew it wasn't going to happen. We'd have company, which would mean we couldn't be too obvious. I hadn't seen Justin and Curtis since before the near break-in, but Stella said she'd told them I wasn't well. She knew we had to keep what was happening a secret, not just for my safety, but for hers too.

Lottie was on high alert as she sprung up into a standing position. Her lip curled back on her teeth in warning, but all it took was a stroke from me, and she calmed down, although she didn't go back to sleep. She just sat there and stared at them as they made their way into the living room.

I stood, and Curtis wrapped his arms around me in greeting. "You got a dog?" Curtis asked, holding his hand out for her. She sniffed it but didn't move forward. She stayed close to me, her tail not moving an inch and her side pressed against my thigh.

"Ford got a dog," I said, running my palm over her soft fur. She was technically his dog, but I knew she was partly mine too.

Justin sneezed and then groaned. "I told you I'm allergic."

"And I told Belle," a gruff voice said, and both Lottie and I turned to face Ford as he sauntered into the living room. His eyes were narrowed on Curtis, and then his gaze moved to Justin. "I don't give a shit."

Stella's lips quirked. She was a dog person, just like I was. Lottie had taken to Stella, and Stella had even taken her for walks. I had a feeling she enjoyed the fact Lottie was here now, even though it meant Justin would suffer.

"I thought we were friends, bro," Justin groaned and sneezed again.

Ford raised his brows and slid his gaze to mine, and I could tell exactly what he was thinking. Justin thought everyone was his friend, and he was oblivious to the things around him. He still hadn't noticed we had a new door or an alarm system. And I was positive if he weren't allergic to dogs, he wouldn't have even known Lottie was in the room with us.

Curtis moved closer to me and went to sit on the sofa, but with a growl from Lottie, he backed up into one of the chairs. "Okay, okay, jeez."

"Taught her well," Ford murmured, but only I could hear him. I turned my head to look at him, and as soon as I did, he winked. "I ordered pizza," he told me. I wanted nothing more than to step forward and wrap my arms around his waist, but with people here, I couldn't do that.

"Good, I'm starving," Stella announced, bouncing down next to me on the sofa. As soon as she was sitting, Lottie moved forward and rested her head on Stella's knees. "Hey there, Lottie. Have you had a busy day?" She rambled on and on as Justin sat on the other chair, leaving only one space for Ford, which was next to me.

"What are we watching?" Justin asked, and I knew then that they were here to stay.

I threw the remote to him and shrugged. "Don't know. You choose." Justin grinned at me and leaned forward as he started to flick through movies we could watch. My skin buzzed as the seat next to me dipped, and I stared down at Ford's thigh as it pressed against mine.

"That was your dad on the call," he whispered to me. I turned my head to look at him, but he kept his attention on the TV. "We were talking about the lake house. I told him we'd be there Friday night."

My eyes widened, and my stomach dipped. We hadn't really talked about what was happening between us. We were just going with the flow, but I knew we couldn't do anything in front of the family. They'd jump on it right away, and I didn't want it to end when it had barely begun.

"Okay," I murmured back, not sure what else to say. He finally looked at me, and I could see the questions in his eyes. Maybe he didn't think it was a good idea? Maybe he wanted us to stop doing what we were doing? Or maybe he—

A knock on the door brought me out of my own head, and Ford ambled over to it. He glanced down at his cell a second before he opened it, and I knew he was looking at the security footage. I didn't want to admit the number of times I'd checked the footage while I was in my bedroom. Ford had linked it up to my laptop, and I was becoming obsessed with watching it, just in case anything happened. I'd rather be prepared than ignorant, which was what I'd been. I hadn't taken it as seriously as I should have, but now that I was aware of just how dangerous things were, I was on high alert.

The smell of pizza wafted through the air, and I stared at Ford as he closed the door and moved into the kitchen.

"I'll get plates and glasses," I told the group, but I wasn't sure if any of them was listening. I was in a daze as I moved into the kitchen, and I knew Ford was aware of me as I pressed my back to the wall. I was covered where I stood, so no one in the living room could see me. It was a conscious choice I'd made, and as soon as Ford turned his head and his gaze met mine, he knew it too.

"So, you're coming to the lake house too?" I whispered, tilting my head to the side. "What happens now?"

He took two slow steps toward me and placed his palms on either side of my head. His breath flowed over my face, but not one part of his body touched mine. "What do you mean what happens now?"

"I…" I swallowed and swayed forward, not able to stop myself. "With my mom and dad? With us? I…I don't want to sound like one of those needy girls—"

Ford's low chuckle cut me off, and I narrowed my eyes at him. "Baby Belle." One of his hands moved to my face and down to my neck. "You'll never be one of those needy girls." He paused, his hazel eyes connecting with mine. "I don't know what's happening between us, but I do know I don't want to stop." He pressed closer to me, his body touching mine, and I exhaled in relief. "I don't think I could look at you and not want to kiss you." His thumb rubbed over my bottom lip. "But your dad—"

"Will kill you," I finished for him. I was half

joking and half serious. I had a feeling it would be my mom who killed him, but that was just semantics. "We can keep it a secret?" I asked, my voice low.

"I hate secrets," Ford growled and pressed his forehead to mine. "But for you, I'll do it."

Our lips were so close, all it would take was for me to move an inch and they'd be touching, but there was something about the wait for his lips that had me dying for more of him.

"Our secret," I whispered, and a thrill went through me. Keeping a secret was hard work, but when that secret was Ford, I somehow thought it would come easy. I pushed a little closer to him, and his eyes flared. "I hope you're ready for bikinis at the lake." I bit down on my bottom lip, fully aware of what I was doing, but loving every second of it.

"Don't test me, Baby Belle," he growled out, and goose bumps spread over my skin at the tone of his voice. He pressed his lips to mine in a firm, closed-mouth kiss, and then pulled back so he could say, "I won't hesitate to go caveman on you."

I laughed and dipped under his arm, keeping my gaze connected with his. "Don't make promises you can't keep." I snatched up some glasses, not really taking anything in because I could feel the burn of his eyes on me. He tried to reach for me, but I managed to skirt away from him.

"You're playing a dangerous game, Belle," he warned.

"I know." I wet my lips. "But I'd only play it with you." I spun around and headed back into the living room with a grin spread across my face.

Chapter Eleven

FORD

"You know we're only going to the lake house for a week, right?" I asked, trying to push the huge suitcase into the trunk of my car. I knew Belle didn't pack light, but Jesus Christ, this was ridiculous. Didn't she already have things at the lake house?

"Yep." Belle smiled at me, and no matter how much I tried, I couldn't be mad at her, not when she was standing next to me with Lottie beside her. The pair of them knew exactly what to do to get their own way. "I have many things." She shrugged and tried to act innocent, but I knew she was anything but that.

"Get in the damn car, woman," I demanded, but my tone wasn't the one I'd wanted to use. I couldn't help but be softer when it came to Belle. It had always been that way, but since I'd been staying with her for the last couple of months, it had gotten worse. If this was any other case, and any other person, I wouldn't have let them get away with half of the amount Belle did. But fuck, I couldn't help myself.

"Okay, okay. Jeez. You're so bossy."

I slammed my trunk shut and dived for her, wrapping my arms around her waist and lifting her off the ground. Her back was pressed to my front as she squealed and then laughed.

"I'm only bossy when it comes to you," I ground out in her ear, and I heard her breath hitch. There was no way I could deny the way her body reacted to mine. I'd tried to ignore it from the moment I'd walked back into her life and demanded to follow her every move. "Now get in the car. We have a long journey ahead of us." I slowly let her down, relishing in the way her body slid against mine. Seven days. We wouldn't be able to touch like this for seven days. We'd be surrounded by her whole family. Her dad— my boss. We had to keep a low profile, we both knew that, so I was going to take my fill while I could.

Belle didn't say anything as she opened up the door, and Lottie jumped into the back, but she did turn to face me a second before she slipped into the car, and with that one look, I knew this vacation wasn't going to be easy.

Torture was in my very near future, but it would be the best kind of torture a man could ask for. I was used to having to hide parts of me, so I knew I could put a front on with everyone. The question was whether Belle could. She was always so open and honest, and I feared she'd slip up.

I spun around and headed around to the driver's side of the car and yanked my door open, then took one last look at the apartment door. I'd given Stella access to the cameras while I was gone, but I also told her that while we were away, she should probably stay at Justin's place. Even though I didn't think anything would happen, it didn't hurt to take precautions. The cartel didn't care if you had nothing to do with the situation. If you had even the smallest connection with someone they wanted, they'd use you.

Shaking the thoughts from my head, I pushed into the car and turned the engine on. The trial had been going for a full week now, and the DA was hopeful that by this time next week, we'd have a verdict. I wasn't so sure, though. Trials could last for months, so even though we'd wanted a speedy trial, I couldn't help but wonder if that was a bad thing. What if he got off? What if the judge was replaced with someone else?

"Hey, you okay?" Belle asked, her hand landing on my arm. Goose bumps spread over my skin at her touch, and I pulled in what felt like my first breath for hours.

I glanced over at her face, soaking in the sweet smile she flashed at me. "Yeah, sweetheart, I'm good. Just thinking."

"Well, don't think too hard." She laughed and slipped her hand off my arm. "It may hurt you."

"You're lucky I'm driving," I warned her, and she bit down on her bottom lip. Belle was quick-witted, she always had been, but there was something else to it now. Some kind of connection that I'd never had with her before.

She twisted in her seat and opened the center console while I concentrated back on the road ahead of us. The six-hour drive to the lake house would take us past where Belle grew up and where I lived, but I had no intention of stopping. Brody was expecting us there by a specific time, and protocol always came first.

I glanced at the rearview mirror, and Lottie's gaze met mine. She lay on the back seat, her harness attached to a special dog belt. The first time I'd met her, I knew I couldn't let her be put down. This dog had been trained, but more than that, she had instincts. I could see that in the way she watched a room and the way she was aware of everything going on. But the most important thing was, Belle loved her.

"Oh my god!" Belle shouted, her voice so high-pitched it caused me to move the steering wheel to the left. I pulled back to the right and straightened the car, looking back and forth between the road and Belle.

"What?" I asked, not able to tell what she was looking at. "What's the matter?"

"Oh my god," Belle repeated, but this time, her voice was lower, and…was she laughing? "This can't be real."

"What? What do you have?" I gripped the steering wheel tighter, trying to remember what was in my center console. I didn't keep anything in there that could be used against me, but—

"Montgomery? Your first name is Montgomery?"

Ah fuck. "Belle," I warned, my voice low. "Put that back."

She laughed, the kind of laugh I wanted to listen to over and over again. "Nu-uh, Montgomery. Not until you tell me if this is your first name."

"Belle…"

"Is it?" She paused. "Why did I never think about your first name? Of course you have a first name. Oh my god, I slept with someone and didn't even know their name."

"Belle Easton," I ground out. "Put it back."

"Why Montgomery, though?" she asked, completely ignoring me. "Why would your mom name you that? I mean, isn't that a name for like, rich kids?"

I shook my head and ground my teeth together. I'd managed to go so many years without people knowing my first name. In fact, I wasn't even sure Lola knew what my name was. I'd always just gone by Ford. Ever since Mom had died, that had been my name. She was the only one who called me Montgomery, so to hear—

"Ford? You okay?"

"Only my mom called me that," I told her, my voice breaking. I shouldn't have been talking about this, not when I was three hours into a six-hour car ride. I saw a sign for a service station coming up, and decided we'd stop, even if it was only to let Lottie have a bathroom break.

"Sorry," Belle whispered as I pulled into a parking space. She placed my ID back into the center console, her movements slow. "I shouldn't have pried—"

"No." I turned the engine off and then grasped her chin with my thumb and finger. "I should be able to talk about this stuff." I wasn't used to opening up, especially about my past. There wasn't a thing I could do to change it, so what was the point? But as I stared into Belle's dark-blue eyes, I knew if there was someone I would talk to about it, it would be her. "Mom always said she was better than the place she lived." I chuckled as I heard her voice in my head. "She said we were surrounded by white trash, but that we'd get out of there as soon as we could."

I could see our small house clearly in my mind. It was the only one on our block which wasn't covered in trash or falling down. Mom didn't just say she was better than everyone else around her, she acted it. She was all I'd ever known, her and her sister, but her sister was the polar opposite to her. Where my mom was refined, my auntie was the white trash Mom hated.

"She passed away when I was fifteen."

"Oh, Ford. I'm so—"

"Don't say you're sorry," I gritted out. "You don't have to be sorry. It is what it is. Made me who I am today." I stared into Belle's eyes, trying to convey as much as I could silently. "I've done bad things in my life, Baby Belle, I never denied that. But you need to know that just because I have a badge, doesn't mean I'm innocent." I was going to a dark place, one I never wanted Belle to witness, but she was smack bang in the middle of it, so there was no use trying to hide it. "I've killed people, I've tortured them—for my job and before that." I paused, letting her soak that in. "But I'd never hurt you, Belle. Never."

She was silent for so long, I wondered if I'd done the right thing by telling her that. I hadn't meant to. I had no intention of speaking about even a second of my past, but I couldn't help it. I hadn't ever felt as comfortable as I did when I was around Belle, and although I knew people wouldn't like us doing what we were doing, I couldn't fathom the thought of not touching her in the way I craved. She was tying me up in knots, but I didn't want any of them to be undone.

"I know you wouldn't." She placed her hand on the side of my face, and I closed my eyes at her touch. "Montgomery."

My eyes flung open, but the smile on my face couldn't be denied. "You're not gonna stop calling me that, are you?" When she shook her head, I moved closer to her. "Only when we're alone," I told her. "Never in front of anyone else."

She bit down on her bottom lip and nodded. "It's a deal." She let out a breath, and I felt it against my lips. "Now, are you going to kiss me? Or are you going to make me wait?"

I raised a brow and stared her down. "I'm gonna make you wait." I pulled away and pushed open my door, letting Lottie out.

"What?" Belle shouted, but she didn't make to move out of the car as Lottie took care of her business. "That's not fair!"

I dipped my head down to look back in at her. "Neither is being named Montgomery, but we have to play the cards we're dealt."

She shook her head and crossed her arms over

her chest, and I grinned at her. I'd never had this level of banter with anyone else, and I was going to soak up every inch of it. I'd have to go home at some stage, and what we were doing right now would end. I knew that. I just didn't want to think about it.

Lottie trotted back over to me, and I stroked her head, then she jumped into the car. After a couple of minutes, we were back on the road, half of our journey complete. The silence stretched between us the farther down the road we got, and that was when I realized Belle had fallen asleep. I didn't bother waking her up, not until I was pulling into the long driveway that led to the lake house. And it was then I regretted not kissing her at the service station. That had been our last chance.

"Belle?" I stroked my palm over the side of her face as I pulled to a stop behind Brody's Mustang. "We're here." It was just after eleven now, and most of the lights in the house were off. "Belle?"

"I'm tired," she moaned, turning her head on the seat to face me. "I need my bed."

"Come on," I told her, pulling my keys out of the ignition. "It looks like they're all asleep anyway."

She turned to stare at the lake house, her lips lifting into the biggest smile. "Nah, Dad will still be up. In fact, I bet he's"—the outside light turned on, and Lottie perked up on her seat—"yep, there he is."

Brody's large figure appeared in the doorway to the lake house, and as soon as he spotted my car, he took three giant steps forward and flung open the passenger door. At the sight of the newcomer, Lottie growled and darted forward. The belt she was attached to snapped, and I widened my eyes. How the hell had she—

"It's okay, Lottie," Belle said, and I stared wide-eyed at a very still Brody. I'd forgotten to tell him about Lottie. "Hold your hand out to her, Dad," she said, keeping very still.

Brody reached his hand forward, and Lottie snarled again. A couple of seconds went by, and Lottie finally sniffed his hand, then licked it. She was a protective dog, but she was also a big softie.

"You didn't think this was something you should have told me about?" Brody gritted out, his gaze focused on me as he pulled his hand away from Lottie.

I swallowed as Belle jumped out of the car, followed by Lottie, and I stared at them as they embraced. Brody hadn't seen his daughter in three months, and the sight of them together made me realize what I was doing. I was sleeping with his baby girl, and I couldn't bring myself to regret it.

Lottie's side pushed against Belle's leg, trying to gain her attention, so she pulled back, then turned to face me. Her gaze met mine as she smiled, and that was all I needed to get through the next seven days.

————

BELLE

I hadn't woken up with the sun shining on me, and birds chirping around me, in so long, and I knew instantly where I was. There wasn't a single place as special as the lake house. It was full of memories of my childhood, but more importantly, it was a place where we all had fun and just spent time together. Mom insisted on no cells at the lake house, and the rule was mainly for one person—my dad. He'd work all day every day if he could. He loved his job, just like Ford did, but he never knew when to switch off.

I stretched and opened my eyes, but I couldn't deny I missed having Ford's heat pressed against my back. For the last few weeks, he'd slept beside me every night, but now, we had to have separate rooms. He dropped me off outside my bedroom last night, and I was sure if Dad hadn't been standing there, he'd have kissed me. But all he'd managed to say was a quick goodnight, and then he sauntered down the hall and to his bedroom.

"Belle Easton!" Mom shouted, her fist banging against my bedroom door. "You better get your ass out here right now and explain to me why there is a giant furball in my lake house."

A brash laugh escaped my throat, and I jumped out of my bed and dashed toward my bedroom door. I flung it open and didn't waste a second throwing my arms around Mom and hugging her as tight as I could. Her arms wrapped around me just as fiercely, and I basked in the safety of them. I hadn't spoken to her much, not since someone had tried to break in. And although I liked to put on a front that I was okay, the reality of the situation had sunk in, and I was scared. But right then, I didn't feel an ounce of fear. Not when my mom had her arms around me. There wasn't anything that compared to a mother's love and protectiveness.

"I missed you so much," she whispered, and I nodded, not able to voice a reply. I wasn't sure how long I stood there wrapped in her arms, but after a while, a second set came around us both.

"I missed you too," Dad's gruff voice said, and I tilted my head to look up at him. "Didn't get to say that last night, thanks to your guard dog."

At that, Mom pulled back and placed her hands on her hips. "Yeah, missy. Don't think I've forgotten about your furball that you didn't tell us about."

I laughed as I spun around to grab my fluffy robe. "She's not my dog," I told them as I pushed my arms through it and tied it around my waist, then walked past them both, feeling the wood floorboards against the soles of my feet. "Ford adopted her from the shelter."

"The shelter?" Dad repeated. "You mean, the shelter you didn't tell us you work at?"

I didn't turn to look at them as I walked down the stairs, but I could hear them following me. "I don't work there," I said, walking into the large kitchen. Dad had remodeled the lake house ten years ago, completely updating it. Now the kitchen had floor-to-ceiling sliding doors, which took you out onto a balcony and then led to the dock and lake. "I volunteer there."

I spotted Aria standing at the kitchen counter, her hands wrapped around a coffee cup as she stared out the doors and onto the lake. Her red hair was pulled in a messy bun on the top of her head, and her face had a small smile on it, which got bigger as she looked at me.

"Semantics," Dad growled. "You should have told us."

I pulled the refrigerator open and moved closer to Aria. "You would have made me quit." I didn't look up at Dad, because he knew it was true. I'd needed something just for me.

"And the coffee shop?" Mom asked. "You don't need to work, Belle. You—"

"I wanted to." I poured myself a glass of OJ and finally stared at them both. They were putting up a united front as they stood across the counter. "I don't want to talk about it. I don't even want to think about college and what is going on right now. I just want to spend time with you all and not look over my shoulder in case someone is trying to get me." I took a swig of the OJ and heard nails clacking on wood. A couple of seconds later, Lottie whizzed into the kitchen and straight to me.

I bent down and wrapped my hands around her, pushing my fingers through her fur as Ford and Cade followed her in.

"So it's your dog, Ford?" Dad asked, his voice low.

"Yeah," Ford replied, and just hearing his voice had my hairs standing on end and my stomach dipping. "I told you that last night."

"PB still asleep?" I heard Cade ask, and I grinned up at Aria and pressed my finger to my lips to tell her to keep quiet.

"She is," Aria replied to him, and then moved around the counter. I had very different relation-ships with both of my brothers. Cade was sixteen years older than me, which meant we hadn't grown up together, but we were really close. Whereas Asher and I had the kind of relationship where everything was a fight, but we protected each other fiercely. Although he may have been my little brother, he'd been taller than me since he'd turned twelve.

Conversation flowed as I stayed in my hiding

place, and then I slowly moved around the counter, spotting Cade's feet and then diving for them. He jumped in the air and squealed like a girl, and I laughed so hard I could barely breathe.

"I'm gonna get you for that," Cade warned, his blue-eyed-gaze meeting mine.

I jumped up and ran around the counter, trying to get away from him, but he had a foot of extra height on him, so one of his footsteps was equal to two of mine.

"No, Cade!" I weaved in and out of Mom and Dad and then spotted Ford. I grabbed him around the waist and spun us so he was between Cade and me. "Ha!" I looked over his shoulder at Cade. "You can't get me now."

Ford's hand touched my waist, and although to anyone else, it would have been innocent, when my gaze slid to his, I knew it was anything but. He hadn't kissed me since we left my apartment yesterday afternoon, and all I could think about was how his lips would feel against mine.

"You're always cheating," Cade groaned out and stepped back. "No fair."

He turned around, and my shoulders drooped, but at the last second, he darted for me and grabbed me around the waist and threw me over his shoulder. Lottie started to bark, and I thought Cade would put me down, but Ford commanded her to stop.

"Cade," I warned as he stepped toward the sliding doors. "Don't you dare."

He gripped me tighter and stepped out onto the balcony. "This is what happens when you scare me, PB. You do the crime, you gotta do the time."

My eyes widened as he walked onto the dock. "No, seriously. Stop. Cade. Don't you—" He let go of me with a push, and for a second, I was flying in the air, and then my back was hitting the cold water, sending shocks through my body and having my breath catch in my throat.

I spluttered as I came up to the surface and gripped on to the dock. I couldn't believe he'd actually done it. "I'll get my revenge," I ground out as I stared up at Cade, who had a shit-eating grin on his face. The fluffy robe was absorbing water like a sponge and trying to weigh me down.

He widened his stance and crossed his arms over his chest. "Shouldn't mess with the big boys, should ya, PB?" He chuckled, and I flicked my gaze to the right and tried my hardest to keep a straight face. Asher—who was now just as tall as Cade—tiptoed down the dock in his bare feet and sweatpants. It looked like he'd been up for hours, and it didn't surprise me. Out of all of us, he was the early bird. I couldn't remember a time where I'd woken up before him. Since he'd started training in martial arts as a kid, he was always up early practicing.

I dunked my head under the water and then

pushed my hands through my hair to get it off my face. "You're mighty cocky there, old man." Cade narrowed his eyes at me and let his hands drop from his chest. If there was one thing I knew Cade hated, it was being called an old man. He was only thirty-six, but it didn't hurt to come at him about his age, especially not when he used his height as an advantage.

"PB—"

Asher's hands collided with Cade's back, and Cade windmilled his arms, his eyes as wide as saucers, and then he fell, stomach first into the lake.

I threw my head back, my laugh echoing in the vast open space, and then held my hand up for a high five to Asher. He slapped it with a grin on his face. "Hey, big sis," he greeted at the same time Cade spluttered above the surface.

"Should have known you were around," he gritted out, but his tone was different from the look on his face.

"Make way!" Asher shouted as he backed up a couple of steps and then ran and jumped into the lake with us. I couldn't remember the last time we'd all been together like this. It had to be this time last year, and it made me sad to think about it. There was a time where our being together happened at least once a week, but as we got older, we all drifted apart. Asher was a teenager, about to take his last year at high school, and Cade had his own life to live.

I peddled my feet under the water, trying to keep my head above it, when Asher grabbed my legs. "Get on," he said, and he sounded so much like the little boy who used to jump from one sofa to another as we played pirates and argued about who was going to be the captain. I didn't hesitate to wrap my arms around his neck and attach myself to his back so he could keep me above water.

"So…" I pressed the side of my face to Asher's and looked directly at Cade. "How's things?"

Cade laughed and splashed water toward us. "Same old, same old," Cade replied, but his brows furrowed. "I think we should be asking you, PB. How are you?"

I shrugged, not really wanting to talk about me. I'd had enough time to overthink everything that had happened, and I still hadn't sorted through it in my mind. "I'm okay."

"Yeah?" Asher asked, and even though I couldn't see his face, I knew he'd have a look of concern etched onto his features. He may have been my little brother, but he acted like he was my older brother. So many times he said he'd have come to my rescue at school after witnessing me crying when I came home, but because he was four years younger, we never attended at the same time. "You should have seen Dad's face when he found out you'd been to a club."

I couldn't help but laugh because I could imagine it perfectly. "Yeah, well, I'm a party animal, what can I say?" I was anything but that, and they both knew it. I blew out a breath and held on to Asher tighter as he moved us back toward the dock. "I didn't know what the place was," I murmured. "I never would have gone if I had."

"We know, PB," Cade confirmed, placing his hand on my head and ruffling my wet hair. "Ford said he about shit a brick when he first saw you."

Asher snorted. "I bet he thought you were gonna blow his cover."

I grinned as I remembered the look on his face. He'd had the perfect mask in place, but his eyes were screaming at me to turn around and pretend I didn't know him. We'd never spoken about that night, not since he'd taken up bodyguard duties.

Asher boosted me higher, and I reached for the dock, then pulled myself up. I should have known Mom would have been there waiting with towels. She wrapped me up like a burrito, just like she did when I was seven years old, and the memory sent warmth through my body.

Cade and Asher followed me out, but they wouldn't let her do the same to them, so she flung her arm around my shoulders and walked with us back to the balcony and into the kitchen.

"It don't matter how old you get," Dad started as we walked back inside. "You'll always act like kids." His lips were pulled into a grin, causing his eyes to wrinkle at the corners.

He was right. It didn't matter how old we all got because when we were together, we'd always have the bond we'd built. Just like me with Ford. I turned to look at him, and his gaze was fully focused on me. The bond we had was unbreakable.

At least, I hoped it was.

Chapter Twelve

FORD

Brody's idea of a vacation at the lake house was to get up as the sun rose and pack the boats for a day out on the lake. I didn't mind getting up early because I was used to it, but I hadn't expected Asher to be out there before we were, running around the lake and doing pull-ups on a branch on the biggest tree surrounding the house.

"Hey, Uncle Ford," he greeted, jumping down and wiping his T-shirt over his sweaty face. I winced at his greeting, remembering a time when Belle had called me that, but it had stopped a long time ago.

"Asher," I grunted, leaning against the tree trunk. "What are you doing?"

"Training," he replied and downed some water. "I've got a tournament in a couple of weeks. Need to make sure I'm in the best shape I can be." Asher was an MMA fighter, and we all knew he wanted to be a pro. He'd been making headway since he was ten years old, but the last fight I'd been to had been at least three years ago.

"Sounds good," I said, at the same time Brody came out of the side of his house carrying a tackle box. "If I'm not on assignment, I'll come watch."

Asher grinned at me, and I couldn't help but compare him to Brody. He had his eyes and his jaw, but he had his mom's mannerisms and kindness. I didn't doubt that outside of the ring, he wouldn't hurt a fly, not unless they deserved it.

"Get the rods," Brody told Asher, and Asher nodded in reply and moved away from me. I'd watched how he was with his sister yesterday, and I could see the concern he had for her and the way she was acting. I wanted to voice it to Brody, but I wasn't sure how I'd be received. She'd gone into her shell since someone had tried to break into the apartment, and I didn't know how to make it better. I'd never thought about how someone was feeling after an incident. It was my job to put the bad guys away and then move on to the next case, but it was different when it was someone you cared about.

I pushed off the tree trunk and walked over to Brody, who was putting things in one of the two boats we were using today. We'd spoken briefly about the case since Belle and I had gotten here two days ago. Tomorrow the court would be back in session and we'd get more updates. It was a possibility that I'd have to testify, but the DA knew the importance of keeping my cover under wraps even though it had been blown. Testifying would put any future assignments at risk, and we had to do everything we could to protect that.

"Hey," I greeted Brody. "Need some help?"

He turned to look at me, his face a mask of worry. I had no idea how he was feeling about the situation, but I could understand he wanted to step in even though he couldn't. "I got everything for this boat. Asher is getting the rest." He widened his stance, placed his hands on his hips, and huffed out a breath. "I hope this shit is over soon."

I nodded, agreeing with him. When I'd first met Brody, I knew there was something off about him, and I'd been right. He was working undercover to take down my then boss Hut, and in the end, I'd helped. Lola had been the deciding factor—that and making sure my cousin Jenna could start over fresh somewhere. Between the two women in my life, I'd tried to do right by them, but since staying with Belle, I knew I'd go beyond anything I'd ever done for anyone else to protect her.

"Me too," I told him, crossing my arms over my chest. "What happens once the case is over?"

Brody scrubbed his hand over his face. "You come home." He paused. "And I want to try and get

Belle to come home too. I don't like her being so far away, not when this is happening." I read between the lines of what he was saying. Even when the court case was over, it didn't mean it was entirely over. There'd always be something hanging over her head.

"I don't think she will," I ventured, but what I really wanted to say was that she definitely wouldn't. Belle being stubborn was an understatement.

"Thought you'd say that," Brody huffed out. "She won't have a choice if he gets off. I won't let her be at risk and so far away." He paused as tires kicked up gravel, and a second later, voices we both recognized echoed around us. "Team is here," Brody confirmed.

I hadn't seen any of them since I'd gone under-cover nearly a year ago, but it wasn't unusual for us to go so long without seeing their faces. Them turning up made me bite my tongue and not say what I desperately wanted to. He couldn't order Belle around like she was a kid. She was a grown woman who could make her own decisions, and he was forgetting that.

Kyle was the first one to come leaping around the back with a case of beer tucked under his arm. He was followed by Jord, and then Ryan. "Well, look what the cat dragged in!" Ky shouted, making it to me on the dock in a few steps. He handed off the beer to Brody and then wrapped his arms around me. He was the fun-loving guy of the group, the womanizer. He was energetic and never afraid to say what he thought, though he never actually thought about what he was going to say before it came out of his mouth.

"Hey," I said, feeling him trying to crush me in his embrace, but it would be impossible because I was twice as strong as he was.

He pulled back with a huge grin on his face and slapped my back several times. "You look older," he commented, and I replied with a punch to his arm. The fucker.

Jord greeted me next with a handshake and hug combo. He was a man of fewer words than Ky, but it was nothing compared to the silent but contemplative Ryan. He was the serious, broody one of the group, even broodier than me.

We caught up, all standing on the dock in a weird kind of circle. The case would never be far from our minds, but today was about being together and having fun. That didn't mean I wouldn't be aware of our surroundings at all times. We were in the open and would be out on the lake, so it would be easy pickings for someone to try and get to us, which was why I'd be on high alert.

Footsteps pounded on the dock followed by a bark, and all the guys turned around in time to see Belle running toward us. One by one, their smiles grew, and even Ryan looked happy to see her, but it was Lottie trotting beside her with her tongue hanging out that had Kyle backing away.

"What the fuck is that?" His voice was high-pitched as he grasped on to the back of my shirt.

"That's his new dog," Brody grunted. "He adopted it from the shelter Belle works at."

Kyle snorted. "That girl has you so wrapped around her little finger—"

"Uncle Ky!" Belle shouted. He let go of my shirt and stepped toward her, wrapping her in his embrace and picking her up off the dock. He wasn't wrong in what he was saying, she did have me wrapped around her little finger, but she had every other male in this family wrapped, too. She wasn't the kind of person who used it to her advantage. In fact, I wasn't even sure she was aware of it.

Lottie halted in front of me and sat down, her dark-brown eyes focusing on mine. She'd been sleeping in Belle's room the last couple of nights, so she wouldn't see me until the morning. I wondered if she was confused about what was happening and why I wasn't in the room with her. She may have only been a dog, but she was a clever one.

"I missed all you guys." Belle's voice broke through my thoughts and stare-off with Lottie, and I turned to face her. She met my gaze briefly, her cheeks pinking, and then she glanced away.

"Wouldn't miss us if you came home," Jord commented.

Belle groaned. "Not you too, Uncle Jord."

"What?" he asked, trying to sound innocent, but it wasn't working for him at all.

"You know what." Belle raised her brows. "Don't think you'll persuade me to come home. I only have just over a month left of this year."

I hid the quirk of my lips behind my hand and stared at the dock as Lola walked toward us with Cade and Aria behind her. I'd lost count of the number of times Brody and Lola had tried to persuade Belle to come back home where it would be safer.

"We all ready?" Lola asked, her gaze swinging between all of us.

"Yeah, darlin'," Brody said, holding his arms out for her. "The kids can go on the other boat, and we can be on this one."

Lola nodded. It was what we normally did. Asher, Belle, Cade, and Aria would go on the smaller boat, and the rest of us would go on the bigger one. But I couldn't let Belle be out on the lake on her own. And as soon as Brody's gaze met mine, we both knew I'd be going on the boat with Belle.

We loaded up onto the boat, and Lottie was surprisingly eager to get onto it. I held my hand out for Belle to help her on, and as soon as our hands touched, a spark flew, and my breath caught. I hadn't been able to touch her for two days, not in the way I wanted to, and it was driving me insane. If this vacation was going to teach me anything, it would be how much I wanted Belle.

Her gaze met mine, and something swirled in the dark-blue depths, something I knew would be showcased in my eyes too. She moved her foot onto the side of the boat and pushed up, her body coming dangerously close to mine. For a second, I didn't move. I let there only be a few inches between us until I remembered who was around us and let go of her hand so fast she stumbled a little.

Belle's grimace mirrored mine. We'd been good the last couple of days, but the tension between us was building, and I wasn't sure how much longer I could be around her and not press my lips against hers or feel her body against mine.

I shook my head and spun around, trying to get out of my own head, and then headed toward the steering wheel. It was fully enclosed on three sides with an opening on the left to get in and out of. Cade was manning the steering wheel, and when I told him, "We're all set," he started the engine and then pulled out ahead of Brody's boat.

My shoulder leaned against the plastic frame of the enclosure, and I stared out the front of the boat. Belle and Aria were sitting in the seating area with Lottie next to them, staring at the lake and barking each time water splashed up the side of the boat. Asher lounged across from them, his shirt having evaporated into thin air. An open notebook was on his bent knees, and his pencil flew across the paper as he drew. Asher wasn't just about MMA fighting. He was also an incredible artist.

"So…" I cleared my throat and glanced at Cade, then back at Belle and Aria. "How's Tyson doing?" Cade snorted at the nickname I had for Aria. It had stuck over the years, and it was all because she'd knocked someone out with one punch. Aria wasn't a violent kind of person, but she was desperate at the time. Desperate to be seen, to be heard, to feel something. I felt a kindred spirit in her. I remembered being a teenager and having no home and no family who really gave a shit. I had to take on all the burdens and be strong for myself because there was no one else who would do it for me.

"She's great," Cade murmured. His gaze met mine, and I could still see shadows of pain in his eyes. They'd been through so much together, and I'd never forget the way his eyes died and his body had bowed in when he'd found Aria on the ground all those years ago, helpless to the demons which had captured her and taken over. "She's just changed one of her meds, and she seems to be doing better than ever."

"That's good," I said, and I really meant it. You'd never have guessed the dark and tumultuous past Aria had, but she was working through it each day, and I had a feeling it would always be something she had to work on.

"Better question should be, how's my sister?" Cade asked, his voice deeper now. "She seems okay, but god knows the women in this family like to hold shit in."

I couldn't have agreed more with him. I remembered a time where Lola put on a brave face, day in and day out, and she had everyone fooled. Everyone but me. I saw through the walls people tried to erect around them, just like I did with Belle.

"She's as okay as she can be." I moved off the frame and pushed my hands into my shorts pockets as Cade slowed down. We were far out on the lake now, so much so we couldn't see the house. "She wants to finish this year at college before she makes any decisions, but if all goes to plan, she'll be back to her normal life in a week or two."

Cade raised his brow as he turned the engine off and dropped the small anchor in the lake so the boat would stay where he placed it. "You really think he'll stop looking for her—or for you?"

I knew the honest answer deep down, but I couldn't voice that to Cade, so I nodded and stepped back. "Life will go back to the way it was," I told him, my voice now emotionless. It didn't matter how much I didn't want things to go back to the way they were before.

Before I'd kissed Belle.

Before I'd felt what it was like to have her body pressed against mine.

None of that mattered, because when it came down to it, I knew we couldn't be together, not how we were when we were alone and in the safety of her apartment, but I promised myself I'd cherish every moment until that time came.

———

BELLE

I wasn't sure how long I'd been lying in my bed and staring at the window, watching as the blind waved back and forth from the morning breeze. For the first time since I walked into that club a few months ago, my mind was empty, not a thought in sight. And it was bliss.

Until a couple of gentle knocks echoed through my room.

My gaze moved from the window to the door, and I looked at it for a couple of seconds, debating whether to get up or pretend to be asleep. I'd been at the lake house for four days now, which meant it was only three days until we went back to my apartment, and I hated to admit that I was dreading it.

I didn't want to go back, but I knew I had to. I refused to be weak, especially when I was surrounded by people who were constantly strong. I had to live up to their expectations, even if they were self-imposed.

"Belle?" a deep voice whispered through my door, a voice I craved. "I'm coming in."

I sprung up into a sitting position, and my eyes widened as the door opened, and Ford slipped into my room. His gaze met mine, and he didn't look away as he closed the door slowly behind him. His feet were bare, and a pair of shorts hung low on his hips. That was all he wore. He was trying to torture me, but I didn't mind it one bit.

"Ford?" I murmured, and my hands started to shake as he stepped closer to my bed. His abs tensed with each step he took, and my fingers twitched with the need to touch them—to touch him. I expected him to at least look around my room, but then, he already knew what it looked like. Not much had changed in the last ten years. It was still painted a dark purple, the closest to black Mom would let me have.

"Your dad and the guys are all out on the lake fishing," he told me, taking another step and coming to the end of my bed. He leaned down, his hands pushing into the comforter and gripping it. "Your mom and Aria have gone to the store for supplies." He ripped the comforter off of me and threw it down to the floor. "Which means…"

"We're alone?" I asked, my voice a breathy whisper. The breeze from the window drifted across my exposed legs, causing goose bumps to rise.

"Yeah, Baby Belle. We're alone." Ford placed both of his knees on the bed and crawled over me, his body hovering, and it was driving me insane. I needed to feel his skin against mine, and I needed it right then and there. Four days was too long to go without him. I'd never been so desperate to touch another person in my life, and I knew deep down that it wasn't normal to feel the way I was. It meant there was more there, but there had always been more with Ford. He made me forget who I was, and right then, it was exactly what I needed.

I placed my hand on his chest and let my fingers drift over his pecs and down to his abs. His smooth tan skin felt like velvet against my fingertips. "I missed you," I murmured, staring into his eyes so he could see how true the statement was. I had missed him. He may have been here with me, but he wasn't next to me when I wanted him most—in my bed.

"Fuck, sweetheart," he groaned, jerking as my fingers flowed over his abs and played with the waist of his shorts. "I missed you too."

His face was centimeters from mine, so little distance, and yet I couldn't bring myself to close it. The torment of waiting was one I enjoyed, and from the way Ford's hazel eyes darkened and swirled, I had a feeling he felt the same. His hand grasped my waist while his other one held the side of my face, and I wasn't sure how much longer I could wait for our lips to connect.

"I'm not sure I can go slow," he warned me, and I nodded because I didn't need slow. Not right then. I needed hard and fast. I needed Ford. I needed us.

"Fuck me, Ford." I wrapped my arms around his shoulders and my legs around his waist, and pulled him down onto me. "Fuck me like you've never fucked me before."

He growled, the only answer to my demand, and then his lips slammed down onto mine. He pushed his tongue into my mouth, and at the same time, he ripped my panties, the material falling off me in two pieces from the force.

His fingers trailed over my clit, rubbing against the spot I'd needed him. A gasp left me, and I tried to close my legs, but it was impossible with him between them. The pace he was going at was too much, and I wasn't sure I'd be able to last long. Not when I'd been watching his every move the last few days, imagining what it would be like when he finally touched me again.

It was all too much.

His fingers on my clit, his mouth moving down to my nipples and sucking on them. And then there was the fact I was in my bedroom at my parents' lake house. We were taking a risk doing this here, and that made me pant even more. In the back of my mind, I knew Ford wouldn't have come in here if he thought we'd get caught, but there was still the possibility, which was making me more eager for him to put his cock inside me.

"Yes," I groaned out. "Yes, Ford, right there."

I widened my legs, needing more of him, and he took the opportunity to yank his shorts down and thrust inside me with one fluid movement. He didn't give me any warning, and I bowed my back at the sensation.

"Look at me, Belle," he demanded, and I flung my eyes open, capturing his gaze in an instant. He thrust a second time, causing me to move up the bed, but his hand didn't stop rubbing against my clit, pushing me closer and closer to the place I wanted to be most.

"It's too much," I gasped out, feeling sensations I'd never experienced before. Was this what it was like all the time? Or was it just because it was Ford?

"Feel it," he ground out, slamming inside me again. "Feel all of me."

I clasped on to his biceps as his hand moved faster, pushing me off the cliff and making me tumble to an orgasm that overtook my entire body. Ford stilled inside me as I dug my nails into his skin, sure to leave marks, but I didn't care.

All I could feel was him and the burst of energy from the fireworks exploding inside of me. And then it was gone, but Ford was still there, staring down at me with awe in his eyes.

"You're so fuckin' beautiful, Baby Belle." I bit down on my bottom lip as he whispered his hand over my face. "I'm gonna fuck you real hard now, okay?"

"Okay," I murmured, swallowing as he leaned back from me.

His hands trailed down my legs to my ankles, and he maneuvered them so they were on his shoulders. "Hold tight," he warned, grasping my ass for leverage. And then he was pummeling me so hard, but it felt so goddamn good. He didn't move his gaze off mine as he lifted me higher and thrust harder.

"Fuck," he ground out.

My back bowed as he hit my G-spot, and my hands clutched the sheet underneath me. "Right there, Ford." I gasped a breath. "Fuck me just like that."

My words spurred him on, and he adjusted me so he could move one hand to my chest and play with my nipple. He twisted it as he kept hitting my G-spot, and I wasn't sure how much longer I could — "It's coming," I gritted out, feeling another orgasm brewing, but this one was different.

"Let go, Belle," Ford begged. "Let go just for me."

A breath left me in a whoosh, and he pinched my nipple one final time, and then I was flying high, feeling something I'd never felt before as he continued to thrust inside me.

"Fuck yeah, I can feel you pulsating around my cock."

I moaned and flung my head back, loving every second of my orgasm but being greedy and wanting more. And then Ford stilled, and I felt every jerk of his cock inside me as he came. He let his body fall onto mine, wrapping his arms around me, then rolled over so I was on top of him.

Our skin was sweaty, my room smelled like sex, but I was content. I was always content when it came to Ford. And for the first time in four days, I finally felt like I was home.

Chapter Thirteen

FORD

Sitting across the table from Belle felt easier as we all gathered out on the balcony for a cookout. I had a feeling it was because of what we'd done this morning. All my pent-up frustration had bubbled up, and as soon as I knew we were alone, I'd gone to her without a second thought. The sleeves on my T-shirt covered the nail marks she'd left me with, a wound I was proud of.

I stared at her as she spoke to Asher, the pair of them in animated conversation, and I wondered if she could feel my gaze on her. Could she tell when I was watching her? Did she like it when I didn't take my eyes off her?

"You're staring," a new voice whispered to me,

and I whipped my head around and came face to face with Aria.

"What?" I asked, acting as if I hadn't heard her loud and clear.

Her lips curved on one side, and she leaned back in her seat. "You heard me." She stared at me for several seconds and raised a brow. "Do anything fun this morning?" she asked, but she didn't give me a chance to answer as she continued, "I was meant to go to the store with Lola, but I wasn't feeling too good, so I stayed home."

I frowned, wondering what she was talking about and then—fuck. She was home this morning, which meant—

"Tyson, I—"

She held her hand up to stop me. "My lips are sealed, Ford." She grinned then, the type of grin I didn't see on her face often. "I expected dirty talk from you, but jeez, Belle has a mouth on her too."

"What?" Belle asked from across the table, obviously having heard her name. "Belle has a what?"

I didn't take my gaze off Tyson, knowing if I looked at Belle, I wouldn't be able to keep my mask in place. Tyson knew what we'd done, but I had no idea if she'd keep it to herself or tell the entire table. And if she did—no, she wouldn't. There was a time where she and Cade had been a secret, and I'd been one of the only people to know.

"I was just telling Ford how Lottie lay with me

while I didn't feel well this morning," Tyson told Belle, and I finally managed to look away.

"She's a cool dog," Asher said, joining in on the conversation which he had no idea about. "She watched me work out this morning, and was jumping in time with each of my pull-ups." He chuckled, and I smirked, imagining Lottie doing that. She'd fit right in with the family in seconds, and now I was sure they'd all miss her when we were gone.

"I didn't know you didn't feel well," Cade interrupted, obviously having been listening to us talk. His hand landed over Tyson's on the table, and I could see the concern in his eyes.

"It's just the new meds," Tyson told him. "I stayed at the house while Lola went to the store this morning and—"

Belle spluttered, and I glanced at her, meeting her gaze and having a silent conversation. She understood what Tyson was saying now, and one look at me, and she knew that Tyson knew. Her eyes widened, and I could see the panic worming its way up, so I pushed lower in my seat and wrapped my legs around her ankles, giving them a squeeze in reassurance. She didn't need to worry because I knew deep down Tyson would never out us. Not yet, anyway.

Brody's cell rang from the table, and he moved from the grill to see who it was. All of us stared at him, and when he looked up, his attention was solely on me. He answered the call and grunted, "Agent Easton." He listened to whoever it was and then said, "Two seconds," down the line, and flicked his head toward the sliding doors of the kitchen.

I moved my legs from around Belle's ankles and stood, followed by the rest of the guys on the team. Silence surrounded us because everyone around the table knew that for all of us to go inside, it was about a case, and right then, the only case we were all on, was Garza's.

We moved into the lake house and through the kitchen, into the hall, and then entered Brody's office. He waited until we were all inside with the door closed, then placed his cell on the table.

"You're on speaker," he told whoever was on the line. "I have my team with me."

"Oh, okay." A throat cleared, and then he said, "I'm calling to tell you the case is adjourned. The judge has listened to both sides and is making a decision." He paused, and I stared at Brody. "The judge said he'll hopefully have a decision by next Tuesday/Wednesday, but in the meantime, Eduardo Garza is still on bail."

We all knew that was what would happen, but it didn't make it any easier. While he was out on bail, it meant Belle was still at risk, and so was I.

"And how do you think the case went?" Brody asked.

"Obviously, I'm the prosecutor, so I think we won, but you can never be certain. It's a bench decision, which means it could go either way." We could all hear his deep breath over the line. "But I'll be honest, the state has tried to bring charges against him numerous times, and he's never actually been found guilty of them. He knows what he needs to do to get away with the crimes he commits, so you should keep that in mind going forward."

I heard him loud and clear. Just because he thought the court case went well, didn't mean he'd be found guilty. And the likelihood of Garza being sent down was slim, so we needed to start preparing for what would happen if he didn't go down. And the first person who came to mind was Belle.

"Thanks, Scott." Brody lifted his cell off his desk. "Keep me informed." He ended the call and blew out a breath in frustration. We could only do so much, and the parts we could do were over. Now we had to wait and see if the judicial system would work and put the piece of shit behind bars.

"What we gonna do if he don't get sent down?" Jord asked. It was a question we were all thinking.

"You're gonna have to keep a low profile for a while," Brody told me. "And Belle ...she's gonna have to move back home."

Ky snorted. "Good luck making that happen."

"She won't have a goddamn choice," Brody burst out and slammed his fist down on his desk.

"I'm not leaving her out there for him to be able to get to. He's already tried to break into her apartment once, and even that didn't scare her enough to get her to leave." I kept my lips sealed, not willing to tell him that it had scared her. I'd been there when she was terrified to go to sleep at night or do her shift at the shelter and coffee shop. It had affected her. She just hadn't shown him that.

"Let's just see what happens. We have until next week, and in the meantime, we do what we've already been doing." I paused and stared at each of them in turn. They could have an opinion all they wanted, but the fact of the matter was, it was me who had been undercover, and me who was watching over Belle. "We'll go home on Friday morning, and I'll take extra precautions until the verdict comes back."

"No." Brody crossed his arms over his chest. "You can come back home until the verdict is read. She's safe with all of us around."

I shrugged and stepped back. "I'll let you be the one to tell her, then."

Brody growled. "Fine." He let his head drop back as he stared at the ceiling. "You all go back to the office tomorrow, keep an eye on Garza's whereabouts, and we'll stay here and act like nothing has happened."

"Got it," Jord said, and Ky and Ryan repeated his sentiments.

"And Belle?" I asked.

"I'll tell her Friday morning." He stepped around his desk. "But right now, we're gonna act as if nothing has changed and go eat burgers."

He walked between us and pulled his office door open, and everyone filed out after him, me being last. I shook my head and clenched my fists in frustration. He should have known by now that telling Belle she had to do something never went well.

I kept a few steps behind them all as they made their way back outside, and as soon as they were seated, I spotted Belle staring at me, biting down on her bottom lip. She opened her mouth to say something, but I shook my head. I couldn't tell her what had happened, not when everyone was here with us. She'd find out soon enough, and I was sure she wouldn't go down without a fight.

"So, Asher," Ky said, distracting the table from the silence that had surrounded it. "I hear you have another tournament coming up."

"Yep." Asher reached for a burger as Brody placed them in the middle of the table, and I sat back in my seat, trying to keep my mask in place.

The temptation to walk around to Belle and tell her what was going on was too much. I wanted to tell her what had happened on the call. I wanted to confide in her about the court case and what her dad wanted her to do, but I couldn't. I was part of a team, and that had to come first. Not just because it was my job, but because it was keeping her safe.

"You getting us tickets?" Ky asked as Brody sat at the head of the table. I caught Brody's gaze and made sure he knew I wasn't happy with what he'd done in his office. He hadn't listened to me, he hadn't been willing to hear me out, and I couldn't stand it.

"If you want," Asher said, then turned to Belle. "Are you gonna come?"

Belle blinked at him, her soft voice asking, "When is it?"

"Two weeks."

She turned her head to look at me, but I couldn't give her anything. It didn't matter what I wanted to say. It mattered what I *could* say.

"I…I'm not sure. I'll let you know, okay?"

"Okay." Asher frowned at her, and I knew he could feel her unease too. She could sense things around her, and I had no doubt she could feel my frustration. I needed to push it all aside, but it was hard when I'd gotten close to her. So close, I wasn't sure where she ended and where I began.

I pushed my chair back, the scraping of the legs ringing out around us. I opened my mouth, not sure what I was going to say, but then I closed it. I didn't have control over how I was feeling, so instead of saying something, I stayed silent and walked back into the lake house with Lottie trotting behind me.

I refused to be part of a plan that didn't give Belle a voice. For now, I'd keep quiet, but Friday morning, I'd make sure to back Belle up.

———

BELLE

The house had been a flurry of activity since we woke up this morning. We were all leaving together, and I wasn't sure if it was a coincidence or a plan, but one thing I did know was that I couldn't wait to be alone with Ford again. Since the one time in my bedroom, we hadn't touched again. Not since we found out Aria had heard us.

My cheeks heated at the memory of what we did on this bed, and then they reddened even more at the thought of Aria hearing us. She hadn't said another word since Tuesday evening, and even though I wanted to go and talk to her about it, I feared someone would overhear. So I pretended she hadn't alluded to hearing us, and resolved to ask Ford what he thought once we were on the road and back to my apartment.

My bedroom door was open, which meant Asher waltzed right in with a grin on his face. "Hey, sis." He dived onto my bed, missing the suitcase I was packing by mere inches, and then star-fished.

His legs hung off the end, but he looked every bit like the little kid he used to be.

"'Sup, Asher."

He snorted at my greeting. "You're such a nerd." He stared at me for a beat, and his grin slowly turned into a frown. "I'm gonna miss you."

"Awwww." I zipped my suitcase and jumped onto the bed next to him. "Summer isn't long away. Then we can terrorize the neighborhood, just like old times."

He chuckled at my words as he sat up. "I'm already thinking of pranks we can play." He flung his arm around my shoulders. "It's not the same at home without you." I knew what he meant because my apartment wasn't the same without my annoying brother across the hall.

I opened my mouth, about to confess that to him, but footsteps moving toward my room stopped me. "Your dad wants to see you," Aria said, stopping in my doorway.

"Okay." I stared at her for several seconds, wondering if she'd bring up anything, but she just spun around and headed back down the stairs.

"That seemed—"

"Ominous," I finished for Asher. I raised my brows at him, wondering what was going on, and then stood. "Carry my suitcase down, Asher. Your muscles need working out."

I heard him heave from behind me, but didn't

turn back to look at him as I made my way out of my bedroom and then down the stairs. I could hear hushed voices coming from the kitchen, and as soon as I walked in, they stopped.

The silence stretched between everyone, and when Asher halted behind me, he asked, "What's going on?"

"Belle," Mom started. "Hear your dad out before you—"

"Before I what?" I frowned and turned to look at Ford, but his narrowed eyes were focused on my dad. What the hell?

"You're coming home with us," Dad said, his voice brooking no room for argument. He pushed his cell into his front pocket. "Let's go." He stepped forward, but no one moved after him. He was used to giving a command and people following it without questions, but this was his family, not his work.

"No," I ground out. "What the hell is going on?"

"You're coming home with us, that's what's going on," Dad demanded. "Ford can bring your suitcase, but you can come in our car."

"And if I refuse?"

Dad took two steps toward me, leaving only a few feet between us. "Then, I'll put you in my car myself."

I raised a brow and turned to face Mom. I

pointed at Dad, my anger starting to bubble up inside me, threatening to overflow. "Is he serious?"

Her nostrils flared, and I could see plain as day that she wasn't happy either. "Brody, why don't you—"

"No, Lola," he cut her off. "She's coming home where she's safe. At least until the verdict is back."

I stepped to the side and willed Ford to look at me. And when he finally glanced at me, I knew he wasn't happy with the way Dad was acting either. Mom and Dad started to whisper-argue, acting as if we all couldn't hear what they were saying, but I continued to drift closer to Ford, feeling his intense stare down to my very soul.

He tilted his head, a silent promise to back me up, so I spun around. "No." I looked at Mom and then Dad, driving my point home. "I'm not going home. I'm going back to college."

Dad moved toward me. "No, you're not—"

"Yes, I am." I paused and stared at him, letting him see the me who I was now and not the little girl he thought he had to protect from everything. "You can't tell me what to do or where to go. I'm safe where I am. I've been safe since Ford turned up."

"You're not safe!" Dad roared. "Jesus Christ, Belle. I'm trying to look out for you, and you're not letting me."

"No. You're trying to command me like you do with people at work, but you should know better." I glanced around the room, catching each of their gazes in turn. Mom looked furious with Dad, Cade looked torn, Aria was shying away in the corner, and Asher looked plain mad.

"Why the fuck do you think you can do this?" Asher asked, causing everyone to look at him. "You can't control everything, Dad. Fuck's sake. Do you seriously think we're all gonna stand by while you order Belle?"

"I'm protecting her!" Dad shouted, and I stepped back, a lump forming in my throat. I'd never heard him shout like that. Never in my entire life.

"She'll be safe with Ford, Brody," Mom whispered, placing her hand on his arm. He stared down at her, his shoulders dropping at her touch. "She'll be safe."

"But what if he comes for her?" Dad asked. "I won't allow her to get hurt. I took the chance with you all those years ago. I took my eye off the ball, and look what happened." I had no idea what he was talking about, but the atmosphere in the room became suddenly chilly.

"This isn't that, Dad," Cade said. "Belle isn't Lola. She has Ford there every minute of the day. Nothing will happen."

I had no idea what they were talking about, and even though part of me craved to know all the details, the other part of me didn't need to know because the emotions in the room were enough to tell me it wasn't anything good. Mom had talked to me about her past before, but I had a feeling she'd left things out that she didn't want me to know about.

"I'm taking her back to college," Ford finally said, and his deep voice had my back straightening.

Dad turned to face him, his gaze meeting Ford's and then mine. They stood there, not a word said between them for several minutes. They were battling silently, and I wasn't sure who was going to win. I didn't know what I expected to happen, but it wasn't Dad saying, "Okay." He moved toward me and then wrapped me up in a hug. "I just don't want you to get hurt, Belle."

I clutched on to him, trying to physically show him I was okay. "I'll be fine, Dad. And if I'm not, I'll come home. Okay?"

He squeezed me one last time and then pulled back, his brown eyes staring into my blue ones. "Promise that you'll come home and not try to brave it out?"

"I promise," I whispered, and I meant it. I'd been scared when someone had tried to break in, but the fact of the matter was, I was safe with Ford around, and the moment I didn't feel that, or Ford said we weren't, I'd listen to him without a second thought.

Dad nodded and then let me go, and the

atmosphere in the room changed. Gone was all the tenseness, and in its place something fragile we all were scared we'd break.

Mom flung her arms around me and squeezed me to death, whispering in my ear, "He's just being a caveman, sweetie."

"I know," I told her. Dad wanted to protect us all, but sometimes he went too far. And this was one of those times.

Asher walked past me with my suitcase with Lottie on his tail as Cade and Aria said their good-byes. "Come on," Cade said, throwing his arm around my shoulders. "I'll walk you out to the car." I wrapped my arm around his waist as he led me out onto the balcony, and down toward the lake, then around to the front of the house. The peacefulness in the air had an edge to it, but it was probably because of what had happened in the house with Dad.

Dad stood next to Ford's car, whispering something to him as Asher closed the trunk. Cade gave me one last hug, and then Asher came forward. I didn't wait for him to hug me because I flung myself at him. "I'll try to get back for the tournament."

"Okay," he said, but his voice broke. "Look after yourself, okay?"

"I will." I pulled back and placed each of my hands on his face. "Try to stop growing while I'm gone, yeah? I'm sick and tired of all you men being giants."

He grinned, the kind of grin I had no doubt sent the girls in his school crazy. "Can't promise that one, sis."

I rolled my eyes, but the smile on my face couldn't be replaced. I missed all of my family, and sometimes I wondered if I made the right decision going to college five hours away, but I wasn't one at looking back. All I cared about was what was right in front of me and the future ahead. And as I glanced over Asher's shoulder, my gaze caught Ford's, and I knew what would be in my immediate future.

Ford pulled the passenger door open, and with one last wave to everyone, I stepped toward him and into the car. We were seconds away from being alone, and I could hardly wait. Lottie's head was smashed against the back window as Ford got in and turned the engine on. He didn't look at me as he started to drive away from the lake house, and I waved out the window.

It wasn't until we were thirty minutes away that he pulled over and finally looked at me. "I've been wanting to do this since I walked out of your bedroom days ago." His hand cupped the side of my neck, and I met him halfway as he pushed closer to me, and finally, his lips were pressed against mine.

My stomach dipped at the contact, thousands of

butterflies taking flight, and I clutched at him harder, promising to never let go. I didn't want the kiss to end. I wanted to stay glued to him for as long as possible, but I knew it couldn't be forever.

"I missed your lips," I murmured as we pulled away. He leaned his forehead against mine, his breath flowing over my face.

"Me too." Neither of us moved for several minutes, just soaking each other in. "We should get on the road," Ford whispered.

"Okay." I paused. "Just one more kiss before we do."

"One more kiss," he confirmed, and then pressed his lips against mine.

Chapter Fourteen

FORD

I'd been driving for nearly six hours straight without a break, eagerness to get Belle back to her apartment and alone again pushing me forward. Belle had fallen asleep about an hour ago, and Lottie had joined her, the dog snores mixing in with the low music playing on the radio.

My gut churned as I got closer to her college, an indication something wasn't right, but I was on high alert. We hadn't been followed. In fact, the roads seemed emptier than usual. It was Friday evening, which meant most students would be going out for the night, but I had every intention of staying indoors, in Belle's room, with just her as company.

I pulled into the apartment block lot, parked my car in my usual spot, and then turned my engine off.

I didn't move for several seconds, waiting and watching, making sure it was safe to get out. When I didn't see anything, and Lottie had also stared around the lot and not alerted me to anything, I placed my hand on Belle's leg.

"Belle?" I pressed harder as she groaned. "We're home."

She moved her head on the seat to face me and slowly opened her eyes. "Hey," she murmured, her voice groggy.

"Hey yourself." I pressed my palm to the side of her face and pushed some of her hair behind her ear. "You ready to go inside?"

She moved her head off the headrest and placed her hand over mine. "Yeah."

I was tempted to kiss her, just like I had earlier, but I refrained. We were exposed sitting here, and I wanted to get her to safety. Brody hadn't been right in his approach to try and keep Belle home, but he wasn't wrong about the danger. Garza was still out on the streets, and with only a few days until his verdict would be read, it meant he was on edge. We had no idea what he'd do or how he'd react.

Belle waited as I got out first, and then I walked around to her side of the car and opened the door. Lottie followed Belle out, and then we headed up the stairs in what had become our usual formation. I was in front with Belle behind and Lottie next to her.

"What about our bags?" Belle asked as we made it to her floor.

"I'll get them in the morning," I told her, pulling my keys out and then opening up the front door. The alarm system beeped, and I flicked the light on to put the passcode in as Belle closed the door behind me.

Lottie trotted around the apartment, smelling everything, and then headed down the hallway toward Stella's room. I needed a shower after all of that driving, so I started to walk toward Belle's room as I heard her say, "What's the matter, Lottie?"

I placed my hand on Belle's bedroom door handle and turned to look at them. Lottie sat in front of Stella's door, her ears up and her one paw forward as Belle stared down at her. She lifted her hand to knock on the door and called, "Stella? You in there?"

Lottie barked at the door, and that gut feeling I had earlier came back tenfold. Something wasn't right, but logically, I knew it couldn't be anything. The alarm had been on, which meant Stella was either asleep, or she wasn't here.

Belle reached for the door handle and pushed down on it, and I saw the light coming from Stella's bedroom as she pushed it open. There were two seconds of silence, and then Belle's piercing scream.

My body knew what was happening before my brain had time to catch up, and I sprinted across the apartment and toward Belle and Lottie, where they stood in the hallway, staring into Stella's bedroom in horror.

"Belle, Belle!" I grasped her shoulders and turned her to face me, not taking anything in but her face. "Calm down."

"I... Oh my god." She hiccupped a sob. "What... I..." She wailed, the kind of wail that was filled with so much pain and anguish, I could feel it down to my very soul.

I wrapped my arms around her, pulling her head to my chest as I stared into the room. I wished I hadn't. I wished I'd moved us away so I never had the image in my head, but it was too late.

Stella and Justin were lying on Stella's bed, fully clothed, and above the covers. Red pooled around them, some wet, some dry, and as I gazed at them from head to toe, I realized their throats had been slit, but that wasn't what had me pulling Belle away from Stella's room. It was the hands nailed to their chests, a symbol of the Garza cartel, that had me pushing Belle against the wall so she could listen to me.

"Belle." She wouldn't look at me, so I gripped her head in my hands and tilted it back so she could stare at me directly in the eyes. "I need you to concentrate on what I'm saying." I waited a second, and when she nodded, I continued, "When I say go, you're going to take my keys, and we're going to run out of the apartment and straight to the car. Don't stop. Don't look back. Get there as fast as you can. I'll be right behind you."

She swallowed and stared at me, her eyes glazing over, but her whispered, "Okay," let me know she'd heard what I'd said.

I reached into my pocket for my keys, handed them to her, and then shouted, "Go!"

She didn't hesitate as I let her go. She sprinted for the front door and flung it open, and with one last look at the gruesome scene in front of me, I followed her and Lottie out. I was only a few feet behind them as I slammed the door closed, and then we were running for my car, trying to get to it as fast as we could. I had no idea if someone was watching us, but I knew as soon as we were in the car, we would be safe.

The lights beeped as we made it down all the flights of stairs, and Lottie was beside Belle, protecting her, understanding something bad was happening. Belle flung the passenger door open, and Lottie jumped in with Belle right behind her. I wasn't sure what was going on around me as I pulled my door open and then got inside.

I locked the doors so no one could get in, and took a breath, wishing I could close my eyes but knowing all I'd see was the scene in Stella's bedroom. I yanked my cell out as Belle handed me the keys, but I had no intention of moving, not until

I knew there was someone here to look at the crime scene.

I called the local PD, giving them a rundown of what had happened and what we saw, and telling them who I was. As soon as I ended the call, I clicked on the app to view the security footage from the apartment, but there was nothing there. Several blank screens greeted me, and I gritted my teeth. I needed to find out if they'd been wiped all together, because at least then it would give us a timeframe.

Within minutes of calling, sirens were sounding, and several cop cars were in the lot. Once they'd gotten into the apartment, I turned the engine on and backed out of the space. There was only one place I'd be taking Belle, and that was the safe house. I handed Belle my cell and demanded, "Call your dad and put it on speaker."

She did as I said, and even though I could see her fingers shaking, I couldn't concentrate on that. I had to make sure she was safe first. Brody had been right. He was never wrong when it came to his gut. I couldn't help but wonder if Lottie hadn't been with us, would we have even known what had happened to Stella and Justin until the morning? By then, it could have been too late.

Had someone come in, expecting to get Belle, but instead come across Stella and Justin? I hadn't been keeping an eye on surveillance while we were gone because I didn't think I had to.

"Ford?" Brody's voice rang out in the car.

"We're on our way to the safe house," I rushed out.

"What? What happened?"

"Belle's roommate and her boyfriend have been murdered." I cringed at the sentence, wishing what I said wasn't the truth, but it was, and at my words, Belle hiccupped a sob. She'd opened the door to the scene. She'd witnessed her best friend in the worst way possible, and I wished I could scrub the memory from her brain.

"Belle?" Brody asked. "You there?"

"Yeah, Dad," she whispered, her voice broken. "It was...oh god." She placed her hand over her mouth, but there was nothing I could do to comfort her because I was driving. The nearest safe house was an hour away, but I intended to get us there in half the time. "There was blood everywhere, Dad. And her hand..."

"Her hand?" Brody asked, and I could tell by his tone he had a feeling he knew what she was going to say. We all knew the trademarks when it came to the cartel.

"It was..."

"Nailed to her chest," I finished for Belle.

"Fuck!" Brody shouted. "I goddamn knew something was gonna happen."

The silence stretched between us as I took a

corner fast. "I'll call when we're at the safe house," I told him.

"I'm tracking you," Brody told me, and I knew what his unspoken words were. Anything could happen between now and then, and although I wasn't being followed, I had no idea if someone had been watching us back at the apartment. Maybe they only wanted to scare us, or perhaps it was a warning. We wouldn't know until someone was down at the crime scene.

Brody dropped the call, and I had no idea what to say to Belle. I wanted nothing more than to tell her it was going to be okay, but I wouldn't make promises I couldn't keep. I'd do anything to protect her. I'd go to lengths I never thought possible so she wouldn't get hurt. And not just because she was Brody's daughter, but because she was Belle.

My Belle.

———

BELLE

They never portrayed in the movies how tired you felt after witnessing a dead body—a murder scene. They'd make it look like the person was in shock, scared of what had happened, but they never told the story of the tiredness that hit you.

It was an effort to keep my eyes open, but every

time they'd close, all I could see was Stella and Justin lying on the bed, blood pouring from their necks. Their faces though...they looked peaceful, a complete contrast to what they must have felt in the last moments of their lives.

My brain was trying to shut down and protect me, but I couldn't let it. I had to stay alert. I had to make sure I was prepared to run at any stage because I didn't know what was coming next. I kept my gaze fixated on the windshield as Ford sped down roads I'd never seen before. He hadn't spoken since we'd called my dad, and I wasn't sure if it was because he was thinking or was letting me process.

This was all my fault. If I hadn't gone to the club in the first place, then I wouldn't have seen Ford, and everything that happened after that would have never transpired.

Stella was dead. Justin was dead.

Ford slammed the breaks as he pulled up outside a house in the suburbs. It looked the same as the rest of the houses on the street, but as he opened his door and came around to my side, I realized this was the safe house. Hiding in plain sight. It was clever but risky.

I pushed out of the car, Lottie following me, and together, we kept two paces behind Ford as he walked up the path separated by grass. In the darkness, I could see some flowers, but I couldn't tell what kind they were.

There were three steps that led onto a small porch. Ford bent down and lifted one of the pots full of flowers to reveal a keypad. He input a code, and a second later, a click rang out, and he opened the door.

He ushered me inside with his hand on the small of my back, but even his touch wasn't working. I wanted to be alone. I needed to work through everything and try to figure it all out.

Ford pulled his gun from his holster. "Stay here." I glued my feet to the floor and waited as he checked the whole house and returned a couple of minutes later. "All clear." He halted a couple of feet in front of me, and I stared up into his eyes, but there was nothing there. Gone was the Ford I'd gotten to know, and in its place was the Ford he portrayed to everyone else around him. "I need to make some calls," he said, his voice monotone, and all I could do was nod. "The bedrooms are upstairs. Why don't you go and lie down?"

My mouth wouldn't work to answer him, so instead, I walked past him. Lottie followed me. I didn't take any details of the house in as I made my way up the stairs and into the first bedroom I spotted.

Tiredness took over, and I lay down on top of the sheets and stared at the wall. I curled my legs up to my chest and held them there, trying to go over every minute since we'd left the lake house. The last week had been so good, and all I'd been able to think about was getting home so that Ford and I could touch each other.

I'd been selfish.

I hadn't thought about Stella. I couldn't even remember the last time I'd spoken to her. At that thought, I sprung up into a sitting position and pulled my cell out of my pocket. I immediately went to my messages, searching them, and finally finding Stella's name.

Stella: Tell Lottie I miss her. :(

Belle: Just told her, she barked in response lol. We'll be home Friday night. Netflix and chill on Saturday?

Stella: You betcha!

Belle: My dad is a nightmare. I swear he's such a caveman.

Stella: Why? What happened?

Belle: Just my dad being my dad. You know how he is. We're finally on our way home. See you tonight!

Stella: Later, gator!

A tear streamed down my cheek as I read the messages, and I realized she'd been alive today. Her heart had been beating, and air had filled her lungs. *And then…*

My cell buzzed in my hand with a new message.

Curtis: Hey! Stella said you're back today. We should all go out tomorrow night. Free drinks from the barman. ;)

I hiccupped a sob and slapped my hand over my mouth so I didn't draw attention to myself. I could hear Ford talking downstairs, and even though I wanted to listen to what he was saying, I was scared to find out what had really happened.

My shaking hands clicked the top of the message from Curtis as I tried to get myself under control, and I pressed the call button. I hadn't spoken to Curtis often on the phone. Normally we texted, but I couldn't tell him what had happened over a message.

The ringing tone echoed over the line as I pressed my cell to my ear, and my other hand reached for Lottie, where she had her head on the bed. She stared up at me, her dark-brown eyes full of sadness.

"Well, hello there, stranger," Curtis' deep voice said. He seemed happy. Obliviously happy.

"Hey, Curtis," I managed to croak out.

"Belle?" he asked, and gone was the easygoing attitude he'd had seconds ago. "You okay?"

"I…" I stared down at the comforter on the bed. "No, I…I…"

"Hold on, I'm on break, let me go outside." He was at work. He was on a shift, and I was about to tell him that his best friend was dead. I was about to reveal to him that things wouldn't ever be the same again. Not at college. Not in his apartment. "I'm back." I heard his breath over the line. "What's going on?"

"I…I don't know how to say it." I pulled in a breath and held it for five seconds, then let it go again. Silent tears streamed down my cheeks, but I didn't move to wipe them away. "Stella and Justin… they…I…we…"

"What about them?" Curtis asked. "Belle, what's going on? You're scaring me."

"They're…they're dead." The whispered words felt like they'd been shouted, and the silence that followed told me he was in shock, just like I was. "I…I came home, and they were…there was blood and…"

"Wait." Curtis' voice was different now. There was a crack in his tone. "Blood? Why was there blood? How did they die? I don't understand. I saw him a few hours ago, and he was fine."

"There's been some things going on, and…I

can't tell you everything, but they're dead…
someone killed them in my apartment."

"What the fuck," he whispered, and then the
silence stretched between us. I wasn't sure what else
I could say. I wasn't sure there was anything I could
say. "Are you okay? Where are you?"

"I'm—" My cell was ripped out of my hands,
and I gasped and whipped my head up to face a
very angry-looking Ford. He ended the call and
dismantled my cell. "What are you doing?" I asked,
raising my voice.

"What am I doing?" he asked, his voice low and
threatening. "What the hell do you think you're
doing? We're in a fuckin' safe house, Belle. You can't
call people."

"I…I was just talking to Curtis. He needed to
know what happened." My shoulders drooped, and
my body sagged against the headboard. "Justin is his
—was—his best friend. He has a right to know."

Ford's nostrils flared, and his hands clenched at
his sides. His chest moved on each inhale, and I just
stared at him, wondering what he was going to say
and do. I'd never seen this side of Ford before, and
even though on the outside looking in, I knew it was
scary, I also knew he'd never hurt me.

"It takes seconds for someone to trace you from
a call, Belle. Seconds. They're sending you a warning. They're sending me a warning." He widened

his stance. "I'm trying to keep you safe. I'm trying to keep you alive."

"I…I know that," I whispered. "I'm sorry. I wasn't thinking."

Ford scraped his hand up and down his face and then through his hair. "I know, Baby Belle." His voice was softer now, more like the Ford I'd gotten to know these last couple of months. "You can't use your cell. Not until we know it's safe."

I blinked at him. "And when will that be?"

"Verdict comes in on Tuesday. Until then, we stay here. Your dad is sending some of the guys to guard outside." His body seemed to droop the longer he spoke, and finally, he sat on the edge of the bed. "How are you doing?"

I swallowed and stared at his hand as it landed over my knee. I wasn't really sure what I was feeling right then, but I knew with Ford here, I'd be okay. "I'm sad," I told him. "And angry. You have to find who did this, Ford. You have to."

"We will," he promised. "We'll make sure they don't get away with it." My eyes felt like sandpaper as I stared at him, and the tiredness I'd been fighting was coming back full force. "You're tired. Get some sleep."

He rubbed his hand over my leg and then stood, but I reached out to him, holding him as tight as I could. "Stay with me," I begged. "I don't want to be alone." I tried to convey to him how I was feeling with my eyes.

"Okay," he murmured and shuffled onto the bed. His arms wrapped around me, cocooning me in his safeness. I closed my eyes, and for the first time tonight, I didn't see Stella and Justin on the bed covered in blood.

Instead, it was Ford and me.

Chapter Fifteen

FORD

Four nights.

Four long nights of barely any sleep and trying to make Belle feel as safe as she possibly could. She hadn't come out of the bedroom for two days and only ventured out after that to ask if we'd found out who killed her best friend and her best friend's boyfriend. Each time I told her we were working on it.

I wasn't lying. We were working on finding out who had done it. But I didn't give her the details. Like how all the footage for the entire day had been wiped. Or how every camera for three blocks had been shut down four hours before we got back into town. Someone had been planning something, I just wasn't sure whether Stella and Justin had been the targets, or whether it was meant to be Belle and me.

She didn't need to know those things. All she needed to know was that we'd find the killer, no matter how long it took.

Now it was Tuesday, and the judge had made a decision, which meant all we had to do was wait to find out what was going to happen. I was trying to explain it all to Belle as she sat across the table from me while eating her lunch.

"So, if he gets sent down, that means I can go back to college?"

"Yeah." I drummed my hands on the table. "If you want to."

She bit down on her bottom lip and played with some crumbs on her plate. "I only have a few weeks left." I nodded because I knew that. "Even if I just go back for those few weeks, then I can decide what to do about my last year over the summer."

"You can do that."

Her gaze met mine, sorrow shining in the depths. "But what about you? And the apartment?" She shook her head. "I can't go back to my apartment, Ford. I…I just can't."

I reached forward and clasped her hand in mine, trying to reassure her. Brody and I had already put a plan in place if Garza got sent down, but we'd also put a plan in place if he didn't.

"We've got you a room in the dorms. It's ready

and waiting with some of your things in it." I paused, debating whether to tell her the rest. I didn't want to keep secrets from her. She'd been sheltered her entire life, but now wasn't the time to leave anything out. "But if he doesn't get sent down"—I swallowed—"you'll have to go into witness protection."

"Witness protection?" She gasped and held my hand tighter. "As in...I won't see any of my family ever again?"

"Only until he's dealt with. It won't be long."

She let her head drop and placed her hand over her face. "I can't believe this. All because I came to the club that night. It's all my fault—"

"No." I let go of her hand and pushed off my chair. "It's not your fault, Belle." I crouched down beside her and held her face in my hands. "Listen to me, sweetheart." Her gaze met mine, and a tear slipped down her cheek. "This is not your fault. You didn't ask for any of this to happen."

"But—"

"No buts," I interrupted. "You didn't know what was going to happen. I had no idea the danger Stella and Justin were also in. If I had..." I paused and closed my eyes. Hindsight was a thing of beauty. You could see all the mistakes you made, but the horror of it was that you couldn't change a single thing. "All that matters is what happens now. We have a plan in place. All we need to do is wait."

She bit down on her bottom lip, and I knew she was trying to keep her emotions at bay. She'd cried every night since we'd found Stella and Justin, and I'd held her tight, promising not to let go. But the reality was that after today, I'd have to let go completely. It didn't matter whether Garza was sent down or not, because I couldn't be by her side. I was making things worse. I was creating a bigger target on her back, and I refused to see her suffer because of it.

Every part of me wanted to tell her that, but as I stared at the agony on her face, I couldn't. I couldn't bring myself to cause any more pain, so I pulled her to me and held her.

"It'll be okay, Baby Belle. I promise. It'll be okay."

I wasn't sure how long we were in that position at the kitchen table, both of us full of words neither could voice. The only sounds in the house were the ticking of a clock and Lottie as she trotted in and out of each room. But we stayed deathly still, afraid to move and break the bubble we were in.

The ringing of my cell blasted through the house like a bomb had exploded, and I yanked away from Belle and pulled it out of my pocket. Brody's name flashed on the screen, so I turned it around so Belle could see it too.

"This is it?" she asked.

"This is it," I confirmed. I pulled in a breath

and hit the answer call button, then placed it next to my ear. "Brody," I greeted.

"Fifty-five years with chance for parole after thirty," Brody grunted, not skirting around the issue. Fifty-five years seemed like a long time, and Garza would probably be dead by then, but if he got parole, he'd be an old man by the time he got out. A really old man. I stared at Belle, and she stared right back with hope in her eyes.

"Has Belle decided what she'd going to do?" he asked.

"Yeah." I stepped toward Belle. "She's going back to college to finish the year out."

Brody groaned. "I thought she would." A beat of silence consumed us, and then he continued, "Take her there. Stay the night to make sure she's okay, and then come home tomorrow. We need to debrief and work out our next move." I wanted to tell him I didn't want to come home, but I couldn't. It had been over a year since I'd last slept in my own bed.

"Okay." I lingered on the line, not sure what else to say. "I'll speak to you later." I ended the call and stared at Belle. "He got fifty-five years."

Her eyes glazed over. "So, I can go back to campus?" She sounded sad that she had to go back, and I wanted to tell her she didn't have to, but I knew deep down she just wanted to finish this year and get it done with.

"You can go back."

She blew out a big breath and then stood. "Now?"

"We can wait a little—"

"No." She shook her head. "We need to go now, or I'll never want to go back."

"Okay." I stepped toward her as she stood, hesitating. Did she want me to comfort her? Or did she want to be left alone to try and work through everything? I wasn't sure which step to take, so instead, I just watched her as she spun around and headed up the stairs.

I was still in the same position when she came back down with a small bag of her things. "Let's go," she demanded.

I opened my mouth to say... I had no idea what to say. She was pushing everything aside and barreling forward. Whether that was a good thing or not remained to be seen, but at least she wasn't curled up on the bed any longer.

She waited at the front door with Lottie beside her, an old habit she'd gotten into. But I didn't tell her that or point it out. Instead, I opened the door, checked outside, and then gave her the signal.

———

BELLE

The drive to the dorms was slow. I wasn't sure if it was because I couldn't really remember the journey to the safe house, or whether it was because I was dreading being back in the same place. Ford had supplied me with a burner cell until my dad could get a new one delivered, but I hadn't even opened it to the messages that had come through.

I saw my mom's name flash on the screen, along with my dad's, Asher's, and Cade's, but I couldn't bring myself to answer. If I wanted to be able to do the last few weeks of this year at college, I had to push it all down, as far down as it could get. I could deal with it all later. I could go over and over it in my head when I had the capacity to work through it.

And right now, I didn't have the energy to think about it.

The last five months had been a whirlwind. So much had happened, and not just between Ford and me. I turned to look at him as he pulled up into one of the lots outside the dorm buildings, and I wondered what he thought. Did he think I should have gone home? Did he think I was making a mistake?

I wasn't sure because he'd pulled his mask on, and so had I.

A car pulled up beside us, and I whipped my

head around to face it. "What the…" Uncle Ky lifted his hand in a wave, and Uncle Ryan nodded at me. "What are they doing here?"

"They were at the house," Ford said, and I glanced at him. "I told you that." Maybe he had, but I couldn't remember it. I could barely remember the last five days. "They're gonna take Lottie home."

"What? Why?"

"She can't stay in the dorms with you, Belle." I knew what he was saying made sense, but if Lottie wasn't staying, did that mean he was going too? He must have been able to read my features because he said, "I'm staying. You'll have to sneak me in after curfew."

A breath whooshed out of me at his words, and my shoulders curved in. I was trying to hold myself together the best I could, but my stomach was churning, and nausea was making its way around my body at lightning speed.

"I'm gonna be sick," I managed to croak out a second before I swung the door open and puked. I heard slamming of doors as I brought up the lunch I'd eaten, and then someone was holding my hair and stroking my back.

"You're okay." Ford's voice made its way through the pounding in my ears. "Go get some water," he barked at someone else, and a second later, a bottle was pushed toward my face. "Take a drink," he said, his tone softer as he spoke to me.

I lifted my head and kept my eyes squeezed shut as I took a pull of the water and then spat it back out again.

"You sure this is a good idea?" I heard Uncle Ky ask. "Maybe she should just—"

"I'm not going home," I ground out, and opened my eyes. "I'm gonna finish these last few weeks, and then I can put all this behind me."

I pushed out of the car and walked around the back where Lottie was waiting with Uncle Ryan. "Sweet girl," I murmured, and crouched down so I could wrap my arms around her. She came to me willingly, almost as if she knew she wouldn't be seeing me for a while. Tears threatened to fall, but I managed to keep them at bay. I'd cried so much in the last week that I wasn't sure if my body could handle losing any more tears. "I'm going to miss you." I pulled back and stared into her eyes. "But I'll see you really soon, okay?" Lottie licked my face in reply, and then I stood, needing to get this over with and settled into my room. I had classes tomorrow and a shift at the coffee shop. I'd already missed one shift and couldn't afford to not turn up again.

"Let's go," I said, but I wasn't sure who I was talking to as I walked into the building and to the front desk. A security guard was manning it, and I gave him my name.

His eyes widened as he looked behind me, and I knew from the way my skin buzzed that Ford had followed me in. "Erm…yes, I have a package for you here."

The security guard handed me a manila envelope, and I opened it. Inside was a key, a pamphlet with rules on it, and also a map of campus. "Thanks," I told him, staring at the key and the fob which had Room 6F written on it.

I spun and came face to chest with Ford. I held the key up for him to see the room number and then walked over to the elevators on the back wall. I hit the up button and waited for the doors to open.

"Curfew is ten. So I'll have to sneak back in after that," Ford told me, keeping his voice low. I didn't answer him because there was nothing to say. My entire life had imploded, and now I was running on empty. I was cruising, trying hard not to hit the brake pedal.

The elevator opened, and we moved inside and then waited as it took us up to the sixth floor. Girls were moving from room to room on the floor as the doors opened, but I didn't take any notice of them. I was on a mission to get into my room, and finally take a breath again.

I recognized people's faces, and when they saw me, whispers started to surround the hallway. They knew what had happened to Stella and Justin—they had to know—and now they were looking at me with suspicion. I wanted to scream at them and tell them it wasn't my fault, but I didn't really believe that.

Ford took the key from my shaky hands and gripped on to my elbow to halt me. He unlocked the door marked 6F, and walked us inside. The door closed behind us, blocking me away from the rest of the world.

"It'll die down after a while," Ford told me, but his hazel eyes said something different. I nodded anyway, acting as if I believed him, but the truth was I didn't. I didn't think it would die down, and even when it had, the image of them would still be stamped into my brain.

I spun around in a slow circle, taking in the small room. A single bed was pushed against one wall with enough space between a closet and a set of drawers to walk between. A door on the left gained my attention, so I moved toward it and opened it up. A tiny bathroom comprising of a sink, a toilet, and a mini shower cubicle filled the space, and I was relieved I didn't have to use the communal bathroom. The toothbrush in the holder called my attention, and I couldn't resist picking it up and brushing my teeth. Once I was done, I placed it back in its holder and stepped back into the main part of the dorm room.

The door clicked closed as Ford asked, "You hungry?" I shook my head and pressed my hand to my stomach. The nausea had eased up a little, but I wasn't sure I could keep anything down. "Tired?"

"I…" I flicked my gaze to the bed and saw several of my things scattered about. Someone had set my room up. They'd been through my things and decided what I'd needed to make the place feel like home. "I could sleep," I told Ford and slipped my tennis shoes off.

"Want me to sit with you?"

I pulled the covers back and slipped beneath them but held them open for him. It was a small bed, but I couldn't imagine sleeping without him next to me. We hadn't so much as kissed since Friday morning, and just the thought of his lips pressed against mine sent a thrill through me.

It wasn't right that I was thinking about him naked after what had happened, but maybe my brain was trying to protect me from the evil that had surrounded me.

"Belle…"

"Get into bed with me," I demanded, my voice coming out breathy, and at my words, his eyes flashed. He knew what I wanted. He knew what I needed. The question was whether he was going to give it to me or not.

Ford stared down at me, his nostrils flaring, an obvious war waging through him. But eventually, he shucked his boots off, flicked the lock on the door, and slid into bed with me. His hand gripped my waist as he maneuvered me half on top of him and half on the bed.

"Make me forget," I whispered, so close to his lips, all it would take was a tiny movement to touch them.

"Sweetheart—"

"I don't need to talk," I told him, reaching for his jeans and undoing the button and zipper. "I just need this. You. I need you to show me how you feel."

He groaned as I slipped my hand beneath his jeans and boxer briefs, and one touch of his cock was all he needed to slam his lips down onto mine and roll me over so he was on top. He took control of the kiss. He dominated the position of my body. And within seconds, we were both naked, and he was pushing inside me, making me forget everything that had happened and promising to make it all better again.

Only he couldn't.

He couldn't bring them back.

He couldn't change the past.

But he could make the future better. And I clung on to that thought in the same way I clung on to Ford as he surrounded every inch of me and reminded me exactly why it would always be him.

Chapter Sixteen

FORD

Her breath fanned across my face as she slept. The morning sunlight streamed through the window, showcasing the dust floating in the air. She seemed peaceful as she slept, but I knew it wouldn't last. As soon as she opened her eyes, she'd remember what had happened, and she'd slip into the darkness of her mind.

I cataloged each one of her features and committed them to memory. I relished in the way her body felt against mine and tried to store the feeling away. I watched her. I stared at her. I tried to make an excuse as to why I had to stay. But there wasn't one.

Belle was safe now—at least, as safe as she could be. And I had to go home. I had to go back to my life and try and forget what had happened between us.

I'd spent one last night with her. One night where I showed her exactly what she meant to me, but in the grand scheme of things, it was nothing. It didn't matter that I'd kissed her for hours. It didn't matter that I was tender in the way I touched her. None of it mattered because I was leaving.

I was leaving her.

I was leaving us.

I closed my eyes and inhaled a breath, trying to prepare myself for what I was about to do. If I could slip out quietly, she'd never know, but I couldn't do that to her. I couldn't leave without saying goodbye.

Belle stirred in my arms, and I used that as motivation to push up out of the bed and get dressed. I wasn't looking at her, but I could feel the burn of her eyes on my skin. Her silence spoke volumes, but I had a feeling she had no idea what was about to happen.

I swallowed and pushed my shoulders back, then spun around to face her. Her dark-blue eyes focused on my face, and her smile told me she was still in the happy bubble we'd created.

"Morning," she whispered.

I needed to say something back. I needed to ease her into it, but what came out of my mouth was, "I have to go."

She frowned. "Go? Go where?"

I pushed my hand through my hair and gripped on to it. "Home."

She blinked several times, and then finally her face dropped as she understood what I was saying. Belle sat up and reached for her T-shirt on the floor. "You're leaving?" she asked, her voice sounding so different from how it normally sounded.

"I..." I dipped my head back and groaned. "I have to. Your dad wants me back at the office."

"But..." She paused and glanced around the room. "What about...what about us?"

I wasn't sure how to word it. I didn't know how to tell her that there couldn't be an us. She was the last person in this world that I wanted to hurt, but we couldn't be together. There were too many barriers in our way. My boss was her dad. She was twenty-two years younger than me. And she'd always be in danger. You couldn't have a weakness when you worked undercover, and that was what Belle was. She was the weakness people would target, and I wouldn't allow that to happen.

"There is no us," I ground out, trying to put on a front, and from the way she grabbed her stomach, I knew she felt it in her gut. "There can never be an us, Belle. Look at what's happened. Look at what we caused."

"But that wasn't our fault. We didn't—"

"No." I stepped toward her door. "We're better

off ending it now before it gets too complicated." My back was to her as I placed my palm on the door handle, and the breath whooshed out of me as she slammed her body against mine and wrapped her arms around me.

"Please don't, Ford." Her voice cracked on each word. "Please don't leave me."

A lump formed in my throat, one I wasn't sure would ever disappear. She was causing cracks in the mask I'd slipped on. "Let go, Belle."

"No." She held on tighter. "This isn't how this ends. It can't be, not after everything."

I placed my hand over hers, giving myself one second to remember the way her skin felt against my palm, and then I pried her hands off me. I turned around and stepped her back a couple of feet. "It is," I told her. "This is the end for us." Her beautiful face contorted into something I couldn't look at. I wouldn't stand here while she broke apart, because I didn't have the energy to walk away when all I wanted to do was fix her.

"It's for the best."

I pulled open the door, intent on walking out, but paused as she shouted, "I love you!" My body jerked, my entire being floating outside of my skin. "I love you, Ford. I love you. I love you. Please don't leave. Not yet. Please."

I turned my head to look at her and gave her a

sad smile. "I have to leave now, Baby Belle. Because if I don't, I never will."

"Please," she begged, and I almost gave in. I almost spun back around and reached for her.

But I couldn't.

I was protecting her. She wouldn't understand that right now, but she would eventually. She'd soon realize that with me around, she'd never be safe. She'd always be in danger. I stared at her for another second, then walked out of her room and shut the door behind me.

I leaned my back against the flimsy wood, hearing her cries coming from the other side, and whispered, "I love you, too."

———

BELLE

It was said that if you acted normal, eventually you'd become it. That if you pretended you were fine, you'd feel it after a while. But it had been three days, and I still felt just as broken as I had when Ford walked out of my door.

Logically, I knew he couldn't stay. He had a job to do, and he hadn't been home for over a year. But he wasn't just going home. He was leaving me. The moment I'd stared into his eyes, I knew there was no going back to how we'd been. I knew that. But it didn't mean I had to accept it.

I'd spent the entire day curled up on my bed, thinking about the losses I'd had in such a short amount of time. I was trying to process it all. I was trying to be an adult and not let it all get to me.

But it was getting to me.

I hadn't been able to keep anything down. I was sick several times a day, and I was so tired, yet I couldn't sleep. My body was refusing to work because my brain was broken. But nothing compared to the way my heart was bleeding out. It had been torn apart, ripped to shreds. And I had no idea how to fix it.

So I did what every other student on my floor did. I went to class. I did my work. I came home. I ordered takeout. I ate. I threw up. I lay on my bed. And then I repeated it. For three days, I'd been doing the same thing, walking around campus like a zombie and not talking to a single person.

My cell rang off the hook with calls from my mom and dad, but I didn't answer a single one of them. I ignored everyone and anyone, simply because I didn't have the energy to take anything else.

I walked with the fray of students down the hallway after my last class of the day. As soon as I was outside, I halted, taking in the sun as it beamed down on me. Spring was turning into summer, and usually, I'd have been excited to go to the pool with Stella or sit on the grass in the quad as we waited between classes.

But it was all gone now. Every good memory I had was destroyed with the image of that night.

Someone knocked into me, and I stumbled to the left. They turned and threw an apology over their shoulder, but I didn't take any notice of it. I needed to get back into my dorm room and wait until I had to come outside again.

I wrapped my hands around the straps of my backpack and held my head up high, intent on putting up a front as I made the five-minute walk to the dorm building. I was halfway there when someone called my name, but I didn't turn around. I had to keep my eye on the prize, and my attention focused on the task at hand.

"Belle!" The voice was closer now, and it was breaking through the wall I'd built. "Belle." A hand touched my shoulder, and I gasped at the contact. "Belle? You okay?" The person moved in front of me, blocking my way, and I stared up at him.

"I…"

"I've been trying to call you," he said, and I remembered the last time I'd spoken to him. I'd told him about Stella and Justin.

"I'm sorry, Curtis." I wasn't sure what I was apologizing for. "I…I have to go."

I moved to the left and walked past him, gripping my bag tighter and clenching my jaw. I couldn't look at him and not see Stella and Justin. The four of us came as a package, but now there were only two left. Two people didn't sit at a table of four. Two people didn't fill a small booth.

"Wait up!" he called, and I heard his footsteps behind me, so I walked faster. I couldn't face him. Not today. Not while I was still trying to process everything.

I didn't stop at the road outside the dorm building. I just ran right across it, not caring if any cars were coming.

"Belle!" he shouted, but I continued to ignore him and ran into my building and to the elevator. The numbers above the doors told me it was on the third floor, and I looked behind me, spotting Curtis jogging into the building. A look of concern was etched onto his features, and sadness shadowed his eyes. I couldn't bear seeing it, not when I was sure my own face looked the same.

The doors whooshed open as his gaze connected with mine, and I stepped in, pressing the button to close the doors and urging them to go faster as he ran toward me. He was only a few steps away when they closed, and I let my body sag against the back wall. My heart raced out of my chest, my pulse thrumming, but I had no regret. He probably wanted answers. Answers I didn't and couldn't give him.

The doors opened, and I shuffled down the hallway, taking no notice of the girls roaming to each other's rooms or the open doors. All I needed was to get into my own room and not come back out until tomorrow.

I unlocked my door just as my stomach gurgled, and then slammed it behind me and rushed to my bathroom. My knees clashed with the tiled floor, and I made it just in time to puke what little I'd eaten down the toilet.

Tears streamed down my face at the force of my heaves, and I didn't move for several minutes. Not until my cell vibrated against my hip from inside my jeans pocket. I didn't look at who it was, because it didn't matter. Not in the grand scheme of things. So I pushed up, rinsed my mouth out, and then slumped back into my room and curled up in my bed.

Another vibration reverberated against me, so I pulled my cell out, seeing a notification for a voicemail. My thumb hovered over it, debating whether I should play it or not. I knew it would be from Mom or Dad. I hadn't spoken to either of them for over a week.

This time last week, Stella had been alive with only hours left to live.

My thumb slipped over the screen of my cell, and the voicemail started to play: "Belle? Answer your phone!" There was a pause, and I stared at the screen. "I need to talk to you. It's important. Call me back, okay?"

The message stopped abruptly, leaving me in complete silence. I closed my eyes, wondering if this was what the rest of my life would entail. Would I always be thinking about Stella and Justin? Would I always wonder if Ford and I could have been together?

Would I always be this sad?

———

FORD

Brody had given me the rest of the weekend to adjust to being back home. He said I needed a break because once Monday came, we were going full force on our next case.

So that was what I'd done. I'd spent time at my house, Lottie and me. The place was too big for just the two of us, but because no one had been staying here for over a year, I had plenty to do to freshen it up. When I wasn't deep cleaning my house, I was working in the yard with Lottie running rings around the edge of the fence. And when I wasn't doing that, I'd remember.

Remember the way Belle looked at me.

Remember the way her smile made me feel.

Remember the way her lips felt against mine.

And if the way Lottie looked at me was anything to go by, she was missing Belle too.

I'd taken her into the offices yesterday so one of our dog handlers could tell me what he thought of her. He'd put her through her paces and confirmed she was a trained dog veteran. He'd offered to take her under his wing, but I'd declined. She wasn't there to be used for the task force. She was here to be a normal pet. Belle wouldn't want her being put to work.

But now we were here, on a Friday evening, with nothing to do. This time last week, I'd been driving us back to her apartment and then...then we'd walked in to find Stella and Justin. My fingers itched to pick up my cell and call Belle, but I knew I couldn't. I couldn't give her false hope, not when I'd most likely be undercover again soon.

It was the way my life was. I was away more than I was at home. She knew that. We all knew that. But it didn't make this any easier.

Lottie groaned and put her head on my knees, staring at me with those glossy brown eyes. "I know, girl," I murmured, running my hand between her ears and pushing my fingers through her short fur. She'd successfully malted over my dark-brown sofa and left her mark in every corner of the yard. "I miss her too." Lottie whined, a reply to what I'd said, but I didn't know what I could do. I wasn't sure there was anything I could do.

My cell rang from the arm of the sofa, and I stared down at the screen, seeing Brody's name flash. I groaned, wondering what had happened now. He'd said he'd only call if it was an emergency which meant—fuck, had something happened with Belle?

I slammed my thumb on the answer call button and pressed the cell next to my ear. "Brody?"

"Need you to come to the office," he grunted out.

I stood, already reaching for my keys on the coffee table. "Why? What's happened?"

"I'll tell you when you get here." He paused. "Better bring your dog."

My stomach sank, but part of me hoped he was sending me back to watch Belle. Garza was behind bars, and the immediate threat was gone, but that didn't mean she wasn't still in some kind of danger.

"I'm on my way." I ended the call and whistled for Lottie, but she was already next to me, her ears low as if she knew we were about to go into some kind of battle.

I exited my house and locked it behind me, then ran to my car, letting Lottie jump into the passenger seat first, and then I was speeding out of there, ready to get my mind working and not wallowing in everything that had happened over the last twelve months.

Chapter Seventeen

BELLE

I'd survived the weekend without leaving my dorm room, but now it was Monday, and not only did I have class, but I also needed to get some supplies from the store. So as I made my way out of the building, I resolved that I'd try harder today.

I'd try to smile.

I'd try not to drag my feet.

I'd try to be more like the Belle I used to be.

But as soon as I walked out of the main doors and saw Curtis' face as he leaned against the wall, I doubted whether I could do it. Too many questions were still floating around in my own head, so I was certain I didn't have time or space for his questions.

"Belle," he greeted as I walked past him.

"Hey," I replied, doing my utmost to sound normal.

We walked side by side down the sidewalk and toward the main part of town, silence separating us. I kept flicking my gaze to him, wondering if he was going to say something or not, and finally, once we were walking into the store, he said, "So you ran away from me on Friday."

I dipped down to get a handbasket and murmured, "I did."

Curtis chuckled, the sound so easygoing that it made me smile. He held his hand out. "I'll hold that for you."

I swallowed and passed him the handbasket. "I'm sorry, Curtis." A lump built in my throat, but I managed to push it down. "I just couldn't face anyone."

He smiled sadly at me. "I get it." He tilted his head. "What have we come in here for?"

"Supplies." I walked beside him as we moved up and down the aisles. It was different living in the dorm, so I just got the essentials: peanut butter, jelly, and bread. And some chocolate in case I had a craving for it.

"So no bodyguard today?" Curtis asked, and I whipped my head up to face him.

"What?" I spluttered. "I don't know what you—"

"Hey, hey." He placed his hand on my shoulder

and halted me. "I was only joking. I was talking about Ford. He's usually a couple of steps behind you."

"Oh. Well…" I wasn't sure what to say to him. I definitely couldn't tell him that Ford had been my bodyguard while he was here, but now he was gone, just like Stella. "He…erm, he went home."

Curtis nodded and bent his knees so his face was level with mine. I wasn't sure why that reminded me so much of Ford, but the way he grasped my chin with his thumb and finger was so similar it almost knocked me off-kilter. "You doing okay, Belle?"

I opened my mouth, about to tell him I was fine, but my head shaking answered for me. I wasn't okay. I knew that. The problem was, I wasn't the kind of person who could put a front on. At least, not for long anyway.

"I just…Stella and Justin." I hiccupped a sob and regretted coming out of my dorm. I should have stayed inside where I didn't look like I was losing my mind. "They were…they…"

Curtis wrapped his arm around me and pulled me to his chest, rocking us back and forth. He was trying to comfort me, but there was only one person's arms I wanted around me, and I couldn't have them.

"It'll be okay," Curtis whispered. "They'll find who did this. The police came and talked to me yesterday and said they're close."

"They are?" I asked. I hadn't spoken to anyone to know any updates, but maybe that was why Dad had been calling me what felt like nonstop since Saturday morning.

Curtis pulled back a little and swiped his palm over my cheek to dry my face of the tears. "Yeah. And Justin's mom called to tell me they're arranging a funeral as soon as his body has been released." He whispered his hand over my shoulder and down my arm. "Have you talked to Stella's dad?"

I shook my head. I hadn't. I hadn't thought about any of that. It hadn't even crossed my mind.

"I should call him."

"You should," he replied. "Now, what's say we get loads of junk food, go back to your dorm, and watch a movie? Forget about everything that's been going on?"

I inhaled a breath, and it was on the tip of my tongue to tell him no, but what came out of my mouth was, "Okay."

Curtis grinned, the kind of grin I hadn't seen in what felt like weeks. "You get the candy, I'll get the chips and popcorn. Meet back at the cash register?"

I nodded and stared at him as he spun around, wondering if I was doing the right thing. But, no, I couldn't keep wallowing. I couldn't keep going over and over everything and trying to find something I could have done differently so they'd still be alive.

More importantly, I couldn't keep thinking Ford

was just going to turn up, apologize, and tell me he loved me too.

I had to put it all behind me, and this was the first step to that. So I found the candy aisle, filled my arms up with packets of the stuff, and then ambled toward the cash register. Curtis held his hand up to me from where he was already in the line, waiting to be served, but something out of the corner of my eye caught my attention.

Shampoo and conditioner bottles covered the shelves, but it was what was opposite them that had me halting and staring at it with wide eyes. And then everything clicked into place. Everything made sense. The way I'd been feeling. The way I'd been acting.

I rushed over to Curtis and handed him the candy. "I need to get something else. Meet you outside?" I didn't wait for him to answer as I darted back to the aisle and stared at all the boxes.

My life had changed so much over the last six months, but this…

This could annihilate everything.

BELLE

I stared at the lone word.

One word. Eight letters.

That was all it took to change my perspective on everything. I'd expected the walls in my tiny bathroom to close in on me, but instead, I felt free.

I'd been on a roller coaster of emotions as I walked back from the store to the dorm yesterday, and it had taken until Curtis left last night for me to pluck up the courage and take it.

And now I couldn't stop smiling. For the first time in nearly two weeks, I wanted to call someone. For the first time, I wanted to cry happy tears and not sad.

This changed things. It changed everything.

My stomach dipped as I walked into my room and reached for my cell, and I placed my hand on my stomach.

Pregnant.

I was pregnant with Ford's baby.

I was growing a tiny human inside of me.

My hands shook as I found his number, and I took a breath as I pressed the call button. I held it to my ear and willed him to answer as it rang out. It clicked over to voicemail, but I didn't give in. He needed to know. He had to know.

After five times and he hadn't answered, I started to pace the room. I was still in my pj's with fluffy socks on my feet to keep my toes warm because the air conditioner was constantly on in the dorm. I kept the test clutched in my hand as I continued to try and dial him, but still, there was no answer.

Maybe he thought I was calling him to beg him to come back to me? Maybe he thought I was in the same frame of mind as I had been when he'd left a week ago. But so much had changed since then. So much.

Hours passed, and still no answer. I was on the verge of calling my mom to see if she could get ahold of him, when someone knocked on my door. I rushed over to it, not sure what I was expecting, but when I opened it, and Curtis' face appeared, my shoulders slumped.

"Hey," I greeted and spun around so he could come inside. I clicked the call button again, probably my hundredth attempt as I paced back and forth.

"You okay?" Curtis asked, and I held my finger up as the dial tone rang out and then clicked to voicemail again.

"Yeah." I bit down on my bottom lip, debating whether to tell him or not. This was something I would have spoken to Stella about, but she wasn't here anymore. And Curtis was my only friend now. "I'm…" I held the test in front of me. "I'm pregnant."

Curtis' brows flew high on his forehead as he stared at the test, and his wide-eyed gaze met mine, shock being the only emotion to pass over his features. "Holy shit." He blinked several times. "Whose is it? I mean, what are you going to do? I mean"—he shook his head—"how do you feel about it?"

"I feel…" I smiled and stared at the wall behind his head. I'd stared at that exact spot when Ford had left, but what I felt now was the polar opposite to then. "I'm happy." I sighed. "And it's Ford's baby." I paused, not knowing what my next step was. "He won't answer his cell." I held my cell up as if that would back me up. "But I have to tell him. He needs to know."

Curtis stared at me for what felt like forever. "I…erm, can't you just go to him?"

I shook my head and let my hands flap at my sides. "He lives back home. Five hours away."

Neither of us said anything for several minutes, and I tried calling him again. Maybe he'd answer now? Or maybe he was in a meeting and couldn't get to his cell? But I knew he always had it on him.

"I could take you?" Curtis asked.

My head whipped up to face him. "What?"

He shrugged. "I could take you to him so you can tell him."

"You'd do that?"

"Sure." He pulled his keys out of his front pocket. "I'd need directions, though."

Butterflies took flight in my stomach at the prospect of seeing Ford. I didn't know how he'd react, but I knew I wanted to keep this baby. I was already so in love with it.

"Okay," I whispered, and then repeated, "Okay."

Curtis laughed. "Get dressed and meet me outside." He spun around and walked out of my dorm, and I got my ass into gear. I rushed around to get ready and grabbed a bag of overnight clothes, just in case. There was no way I'd be back here tonight, not with how long it would take to get there, and if Ford was happy, then maybe I'd stay over his place. And Lottie. I'd get to see Lottie.

I hooked my bag over my shoulder and tried Ford one last time, but when he didn't answer again, I pulled my door open and resolved to tell him face to face.

It felt like I was floating on air as I made my way out of the building and to Curtis' car. I pushed inside the black Camaro and grinned over at him. "Thanks for doing this."

"No worries. It gets me out of today's classes." He chuckled and pointed at the navigation system. "Put the address in, and we can get going."

I leaned forward and put in my home address because I could direct him to Ford's from there, and then we were off on the five-hour-long journey. I was in my own head for so long, playing over all the outcomes in my head, that I didn't realize we were so close until we drove past the school my mom worked at.

I pointed it out to Curtis, and he said, "It feels like I've known you for three years, and yet I haven't known you too." I knew what he meant because I'd kept my home life separate from college, but I didn't think too much about that as I directed him to Ford's house.

Curtis pulled up outside, but Ford's car wasn't parked on the drive. "I don't think he's here. Let me go and knock, but if he isn't, he'll probably be at my mom's house."

Curtis nodded and idled the engine as I jumped out and ran up the drive. I pounded my fist on the door and spun back to face Curtis as I waited. After a minute and knocking a second time, there wasn't an answer, so I ran back to the car.

"He's not there," I told Curtis. "Go back the way we came, and I'll tell you when to turn."

He did as I said and glanced around at all of the houses. "So, this is where you grew up?"

"Yep." I stared at my cell, seeing it was just after 2 p.m. "Take this left." Curtis turned into my road, and I frowned at all of the cars lining the street. Each side was full of vehicles, and the closer to my mom and dad's house we got, the busier it became.

"Looks like someone is having a party."

I hummed in agreement and pointed outside the house. "Pull over here. I'll see if he's there."

"Want me to wait here or find a space to park?"

I opened the car door and looked up at the house. I recognized my dad's car and Uncle Jord's, but the others I had no idea who they were. "Wait here. I'll come back out if he's here, and then we can ask Dad to move his car over so you can get on the drive."

"Okay," Curtis replied, and I pushed out of the car.

Each step I took closer to the house I'd grown up in made me more nervous. Even if Ford wasn't here, I knew Dad was, and he'd want to know what was going on and why I was here and not at college. But I couldn't tell him, not until I'd spoken to Ford.

The front door opened as I got closer, and two people who I didn't recognize walked out and past me. And that was when I realized all these cars were from people who were inside the house. I could hear the quiet chatter from out here, and as I stepped inside, I scanned the living room. The house was full of people standing in little groups and talking. What the hell was going on?

I managed to push past everyone and make it into the kitchen. I turned left and right, trying to spot someone I knew when I heard, "I'm so sorry for your loss," from behind me. I spun around, trying to see who had said it, but I couldn't put a voice to the face. The woman was talking to me, but I had no idea who she was.

"My loss?" I asked, utterly confused.

She patted my arm and flashed me a small smile, then walked past me. What the hell was she talking about?

"Belle? What are you doing here?" I blinked and stared at Aria. She'd come out of nowhere.

"What's going on?" I asked, not willing to answer her question.

Her mouth pulled down into a frown, and she wrapped her hand around my arm. "We've all been trying to call you for days." She pulled on my arm to move me. "Let's go somewhere private." I let her lead me through the living room and toward the bottom of the stairs, and that was when I saw it—the sign that the front door had covered up as I walked inside.

My feet stopped working, my brain fizzled in and out, and I felt like I was going to throw up.

"Belle?" Aria called, but her voice was far away as I stared at the sign and read it over and over again. *In Loving Memory of "Ford." May you rest in peace.*

"Rest in peace?" I whispered. I couldn't stop staring at the picture of Ford, and over and over again I read the words, not believing what they said.

"Shit," Aria cursed, and her grip tightened. "Come upstairs, and I can tell you what happened."

"Where's Ford?" I asked her, ripping my arm away from her and stumbling into the wall. My body knew what was happening, but my brain needed conformation. Her mouth was opening and closing, but no words were coming out, so I repeated, "Where is he, Aria?"

"He's..." She paused, hesitating, and then finally whispered, "He's gone." She glanced to the side, and I followed her gaze to Cade, who was barreling through the crowd toward us.

She had to be wrong. He couldn't be gone. Not now. Not after what I'd found out.

My hand moved to my stomach, protecting the baby we'd created together from the sadness surrounding us.

The front door opened, and someone else walked in. Cade was getting closer to us. But I couldn't stay here. I couldn't be here. Was this why they'd been calling me nonstop? Were they trying to tell me what had happened to Ford? I should have answered my calls, I should have—

My eyes widened as Cade got even closer, so I twirled around and darted out of the house, spotting Curtis still idling in the middle of the road.

"Belle!" Cade shouted.

I ignored him as I pulled open the passenger door and demanded, "Drive!"

"What?" Curtis asked, frowning at Cade as he sprinted toward us.

"Drive, Curtis!" I slapped my hand on the dash, and the sound caused him to slam his foot down on the gas and speed away from the house I'd grown up in.

"Where are we going?"

"Anywhere but here," I whispered.

"Back to college?"

"No." I shook my head and cradled my stomach. "I can't go back there. I can't...I need to leave."

"Leave?" he asked. "Leave to where?"

"I don't know. I just..." I squeezed my eyes shut. "I can't be here. I can't be at college. I need to go somewhere new. Somewhere no one knows me."

The silence stretched between us, and when I opened my eyes, Curtis said, "I know a place we can go for a while." He pulled up to a stoplight and reached across to place his hand over mine. "What happened?"

I stared at him, trying to deny it to myself, but I couldn't. If I hadn't seen it with my own two eyes, I never would have believed it.

"He's gone," I croaked out. "Ford is dead."

The story continues in Tied Bond!

Acknowledgments

I'm not sure where to start with these acknowledgments because so much happened while I was writing this story.

My first *huge* thank you needs to go to Paige. You're the most awesomest Alpha Reader and PA. Thank you for loving my stories as much as I do, and generally just being you! But most of all, thank you for reading these on a time constraint. I'm not sure what I'd do without you!

Thank you to my husband and two awesome daughters who never fail to make me smile and continue to support the crazy road that is being an author. I love you all lots and lots like jelly tots!

My next thank you has to go to Jenn, my editor. I swear you saved my life and I appreciate so much you understanding everything that has been going on and *still* fitting me in. You're the best Canadian a girl could ask for!

Linda. I swear I'd be lost without you! Thank you soooo much for everything you do. You're always there no matter what, and I'm not sure what I'd do without you! You push me when I need to be pushed, and tell me to slow down when I need to stop. You save my ass more times than I can count, and I love you!

I'd liked to say a huge thank you to my BETAs readers: Nikki & Yvonne. You ladies are amazeballs and I couldn't do this without your continued support.

My second thank you needs to go to my husband and daughters. This book became such a huge part of my life, and I can't thank you enough for putting up with my weird ways.

To my ARC team. You ladies are simply amazing and I love for each and every one of your messages! Thank you for taking the time to ready my stories, I appreciate so much.

To the bloggers who help share EVERY-THING. I love you so much, and I can't put into words how grateful I am! You are a special bunch of people who continue to put a smile on my face.

My proofreader, Judy. Thank you for putting up with me! I continue to use commas in the wrong places and you continue to correct me. Never leave me, because I'd be lost without you!

To all the authors in the community. You continue to support me and I can't thank you enough for that. I love our little slice of heaven, and wouldn't want to be anywhere else!

Lastly, I want to say thank you, to you. Thank you for taking a chance on this book. Thank you for reading. And thank you for being awesome!

MAC Security Series (Alpha Security/Military)

Book 1: Fractured Lies

Book 2: Exposed

Book 2.5: Flying Free (Standalone Spin-off)

Book 3: The Distance Between Us

Book 4: ReBoot

Book 5: Catching Teardrops

Six Book Boxset

The Easton Family

Fallen Duet (Forbidden Angst)

Book 1: Free Fall

Book 2: Down Fall

Fated Duet (Student/Teacher Angst)

Book 1: Defy Fate

Book 2: Obey Fate

Bonded Duet (Age gap/Forbidden Angst)

Book 1: Torn Bond

Book 2: Tied Bond

Burned Duet (Age Gap/Forbidden Angst

Book 1: Fast Burn

Book 2: Deep Burn

————

Confessions Series (Romantic Comedies)

Book 1: Confessions Of A Klutz

Book 2: Confessions Of A Chatterbox

Book 3: Confessions Of A Fratgirl

————

A. A. DAVIES (Darker, alter ego)

Verboten (Extreme Taboo. Inferno World Novella)

————

Broken Tracks Series,

(co-authored with Danielle Dickson)

Book 1: Etching Our Way

Book 2: Fighting Our Way

————

Destroyed Series,

(co-authored with L. Grubb)

Destroying the Game

Destroying the Soul

About the Author

Abigail Davies grew up with a passion for words, storytelling, maths, and anything pink. Dreaming up characters—quite literally—and talking to them out loud is a daily occurrence for her. She finds it fascinating how a whole world can be built with words alone, and how everyone reads and interprets a story differently.

Now following her dreams of writing, Abigail has found the passion that she always knew was there. When she's not writing: she's a mother to two daughters who she encourages to use their imagination as she believes that it's a magical thing, or getting lost in a good book.

If she's doing neither of those things, you can be sure she's surfing the web buying new makeup, clothes, or binge watching another show as she becomes one with her sofa.

Connect with Abigail

Reader group—Abi's Aces
Newsletter

www.abigaildaviesauthor.com

- facebook.com/abigaildaviesauthor
- twitter.com/abigailadavies
- instagram.com/abigaildaviesauthor
- goodreads.com/abigaildavies
- bookbub.com/authors/abigail-davies
- amazon.com/author/abigaildavies
- pinterest.com/abigaildaviesauthor

Printed in Great Britain
by Amazon